THE CROW MOON

CROW INVESTIGATIONS BOOK TEN

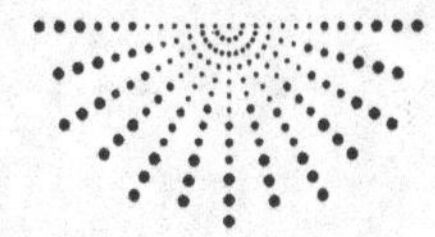

SARAH PAINTER

Siskin Press

In The Light of What We See

Beneath The Water

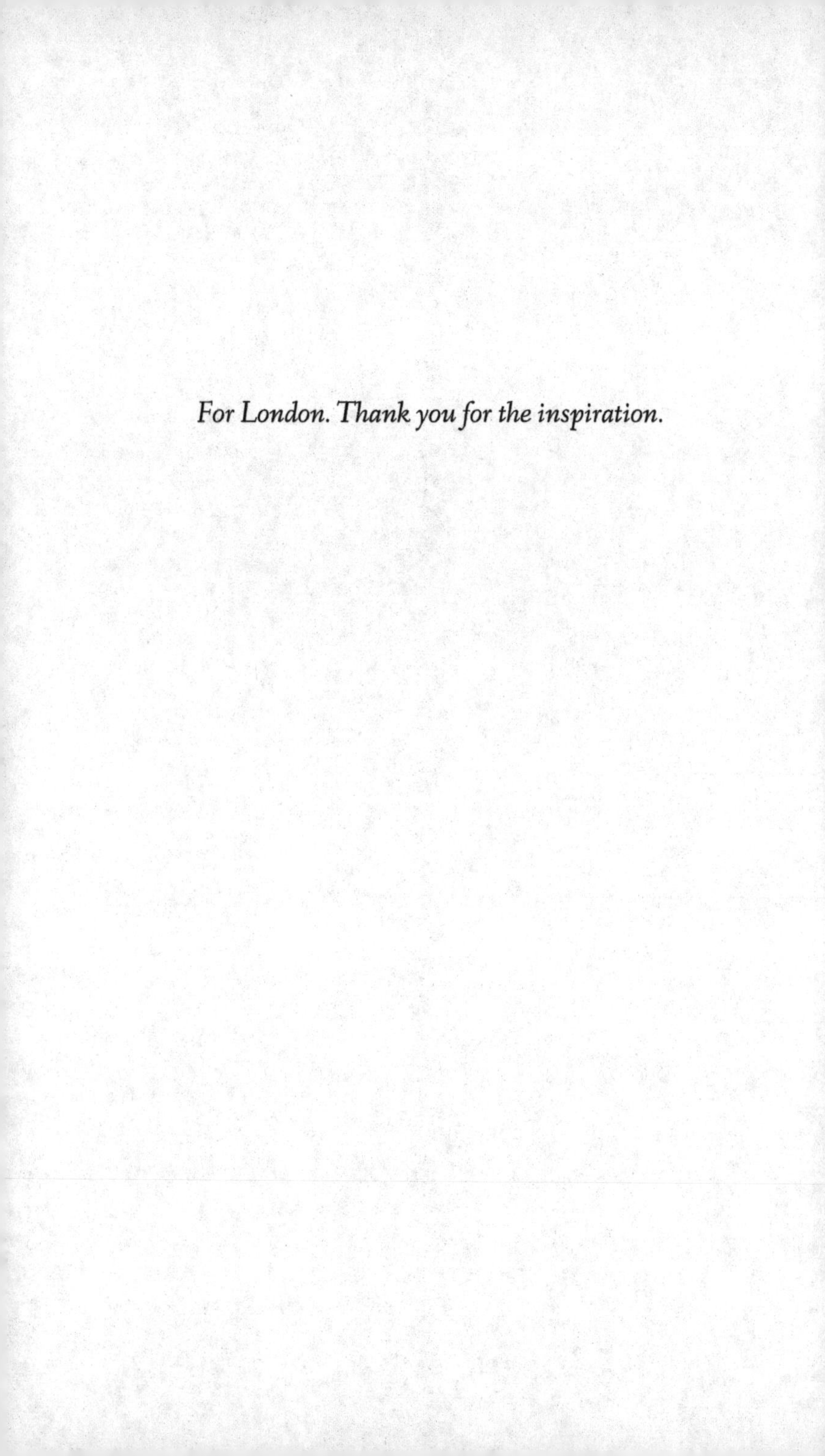

For London. Thank you for the inspiration.

CHAPTER ONE

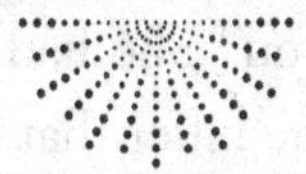

The sun was blazing in a blameless blue sky, and Lydia was down to a black vest top with her habitual jeans and DM boots. The Thames still looked grey despite the dazzling light, but the skyline, with the wheel of the London Eye and the jutting pinnacle of the Shard, was exciting enough to make several people stop and hold up their phones.

She was on a bench near Temple Pier. This meant she was dangerously close to being in Silver territory and could feel a bright tingling sensation on the back of her neck, telling her so. The Inns of Court and legal offices dotted behind her, up past Chancery Lane where the Silver firm squatted, seemed to press upon her skin. 'I know,' she muttered, glad to be alone on the bench. She might be on the border of Silver territory, but nobody owned the river. So as long as she stayed on the embankment she wasn't technically breaking any rules. Besides, she was the head of the Crow Family and the rules didn't apply. That wasn't true, of course, but it had sounded good in her mind. Gave her a boost of false confidence and one she needed.

It had been three days since the message from the @NaughtyJack social media account. The words had run on a loop in Lydia's mind with nothing new to replace them. 'I've finished playing with sweet Mary, but I ain't finished with you.' She had been high on closing the case, on finding the killer that had targeted the men responsible for a woman called Cherish's death five years previously, when the message had popped up across social media, bursting her bubble. Lydia might have caught Mary, the ghostly murderer, and successfully released her from this life, but she had clearly missed something. Wherever Mary had moved onto, Lydia hoped she was at peace, because Lydia sure as hell wasn't.

Jason was monitoring the hashtags #ActuallyRipper, #RipperReturns and #FromHell, but things were quietening down. With no new murder, the public's attention was draining away. The great sea of curiosity was already flowing toward other targets and, with the internet and twenty-four-seven rolling news, there was no shortage. She supposed the Met would be pleased. DCI Moss, Fleet's nemesis, was spearheading the investigation into the murders, and Lydia took grim satisfaction that he wouldn't be able to make his career based on solving it.

Cold comfort when she hadn't solved it either. Not really.

And that wasn't her only problem. Paul Fox had announced that he was marrying the new head of the

Pearl Family, something that could potentially destabilise the truce between the four Families. And, after Auntie had pronounced Ember 'theirs', she had announced that she couldn't look after him on a permanent basis. He had been allowed to stay with her for a couple of days, and Lydia could picture him in Auntie's cluttered living room, his backpack looking heartbreakingly big on his thin frame. He hadn't spoken to her at all or responded to her assurances that she wasn't going to call the social. 'We'll work things out,' she said quietly to him before she left, knowing that it lacked the adult conviction and certainty he needed. She was out of her depth and was pretty sure the kid knew it.

Now, time was running out, and she was going to have to pick the kid up later. She hadn't come up with a better solution, so Ember was going to have to stay with her for the time being. A thought that terrified her. She wasn't his mother. And she had absolutely no idea how to look after a child.

Her contact arrived, bang on time, and took a seat next to Lydia on the bench. He smelled of fried onions and had a roll-up sticking out of the corner of his mouth. He needed a shave, and his greasy hair was swept back from his high forehead, but his blue eyes were bright and attractively creased, as if he smiled a great deal. Casper worked on one of the party boats that plied the river, presumably somewhere below deck and away from paying customers. Lydia had a few contacts on this side of the river, people she paid to keep their eyes and ears open, and Casper seemed to know everybody in the catering trade along this stretch.

'Any news?'

'Nothing.' Casper shrugged. He had been in London for years, but still held onto his Danish accent. His English was, of course, impeccable. 'People aren't talking about the NewRipper anymore. Memories are so short these days.'

Lydia didn't want to dwell on that. 'Nothing being cancelled? No weird parties.' Once she had broken a case because Casper had told her about a private party that had included a media mogul, a cabinet minister, and a reality TV star. She liked to keep in touch with her sources, as she never knew when some titbit of information would become useful. It was something that had fallen away with the demands on her time as the head of the Crows.

'Just the usual.' He winked.

AIDEN WAS WAITING AT THE HOUSE IN DENMARK Hill when she got back. Lydia had made a resolution to embrace her new life and was trying to stop calling it 'Charlie's house' in her mind. She was mostly failing.

'Boss,' he tipped his chin at her. There were sweat patches on his grey T-shirt, and he was wearing a baseball cap rather than his usual beanie.

'Anything to report?' She had told Aiden to spread the word, and every Crow and resident looking to curry favour with the Family was keeping a lookout for Pearl activity. Scarlett appearing as the head of the Family and then making a move on Paul Fox so quickly was highly suspect. Lydia felt a sharp concern that was entirely business-related and nothing whatsoever to do with her feelings for the Fox. He was more than capable of looking after himself.

Aiden shook his head and wedged his cap back onto his head. 'Nobody's heard of Scarlett. Which I guess is a bit weird. It's hard to know where to focus with the Pearls, though. They're everywhere and nowhere.'

She knew what he meant.

'This was on the mat.' Aiden held out a flyer. At first glance, it looked like a standard advert for gardening services, but the business name was 'S. Clare' and it said 'Urgent. Corvids Don't Delay' before the mobile number. Another less-than-subtle overture from Sinclair. The secret service had been trying to make contact for the last couple of weeks. Lydia assumed she was after information on the #RipperReturns case, which remained officially unsolved. But since Lydia didn't need anything from the shadowy department that sat somewhere between MI5 and MI6, and she trusted the woman that had taken over from Gale, after he had tried to kill her, about as much as she trusted Maria Silver, playing nicely with the spook wasn't high up her list of priorities.

Lydia stuffed the paper into her jeans pocket. Sinclair would have to wait. Probably until hell froze over.

Lydia found Jason in the kitchen. He was standing in front of the open refrigerator. Even though she could see his body clearly, the light was spilling out of his back. He turned when she walked in and she saw the worry creasing his features.

'Are we out of eggs?'

'Yeah.' He shut the door. And moved to the cupboards, flinging them open. 'I don't know what to do.'

'I'm not hungry,' Lydia lied.

'Not about food.' Jason wasn't looking at her, he pulled out a bowl and a box of cereal. 'And you must be.' He located a spoon and poured out a bowl of crunchy nut, filling it almost to the brim.

Lydia sat obediently at the kitchen island.

'We got it wrong,' Jason said, still not looking in her direction.

It was nice that he didn't say 'you got it wrong'. The sun was cascading through the glass doors, and the green of the garden was filled with black-winged corvids. It was a beautiful day to revisit her failures.

'We let her down.' Jason paused, the box of cereal still mid-air. 'We have to make it right.'

'She's at peace,' Lydia said, hoping that was true.

Jason put the bowl and spoon in front of her and went back to the fridge for milk. He didn't speak while he poured milk until the bowl was almost overflowing.

'Mary did it,' Lydia said, referring to the murders of the four men. 'We were right about that.' The idea that she might have been wrong was unbearable.

'It was her,' Jason agreed, and Lydia felt her chest loosen. 'But someone was playing her,' he continued. 'Playing with her. He as good as admitted it with that post.'

Lydia thought there was a world of difference

between saying you were playing with someone and actually being able to control their actions. 'You think she was being used?'

'Controlled,' Jason insisted. 'You said yourself that it seemed like she went into another state when she was close to Brad Carter. Like a switch had been flipped.'

Jason had been on a spy film kick in recent weeks. They had clearly affected his thinking. 'You think she was a sleeper agent?' She teased. 'Set off with a code word?'

'Why not?' He put the milk away and then turned to look directly at Lydia. 'You got another suggestion?'

'She might not have needed to be programmed like that. She was an angry spirit. Full of vengeance. Maybe whoever this @NaughtyJack is just fed her the information. Gave her the list of names and where to find them.'

Jason was already shaking his head. 'You didn't know her like I did. She wasn't violent. She wasn't herself when she hurt those men.' His body began to vibrate around the edges, a sure sign he was distressed.

'All right. I believe you.'

'You do?'

'You are a good judge of character and you're right, you spoke to her much more than I did.'

Jason looked at her, still vibrating. After a pause, his form settled. 'Thank you.'

'So, we're looking for someone who knows that ghosts are real and can communicate with them.'

'Can control them,' Jason corrected.

None of this was new ground, their conversations had run in similar circles for the last couple of days.

Jason had been out and about, speaking to the spirits he knew, hoping that one of them had heard of something like this happening, that someone had a ghostly friend who had started acting strangely. Anything. Unfortunately, most of the spirits Jason had met were echoes. They weren't sentient in the true sense and just followed a particular pattern from when they were alive, a single conversation or action or routine, which they were doomed to repeat for eternity. Or until whatever force was animating them ebbed away. Lydia didn't know if that process would be the same as crossing over or even what crossing over meant. All of it made her head hurt. She had enough to worry about in the land of the living.

CHAPTER TWO

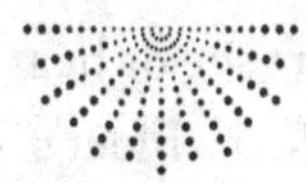

Later that day, Lydia was resisting the inevitable. 'Can't Auntie have him for one more night?'

'Nope,' Fleet said. 'She's done her time with little kids. Paid her dues. It's her time to knit and watch her shows in peace.'

'That a direct quote?'

He gave her a long look. 'What do you think?'

'Right then.' Lydia rolled her shoulders to try to ease the tension she was carrying. 'We'll have him here then. For now, at least.'

'That's fine with me,' Fleet said calmly.

'Yeah, well. You can always stay at your place,' Lydia said, feeling resentful about that.

Fleet put a hand on her arm. 'I told you I would move in.'

'That's not what I was getting at—'

'Wasn't it?'

Lydia paused. She didn't want to pick a fight with Fleet, so she sorted through her thoughts before opening her mouth again. 'I know you're all in. I'm just feeling jumpy at the thought of Ember staying here. It's a big responsibility.'

'I know. I feel it too. What does Jason say?'

Lydia reached up and kissed Fleet. She appreciated that he thought of Jason as a fully rounded human being, even though he couldn't see or hear him.

'What was that for?' Fleet's gaze was warm and getting more intense. His fingers flexed on her waist, and Lydia wondered if they had time for a swift—

'Boss?' Aiden knocked and walked into the room at the same time.

Lydia would have stepped back, but Fleet had tightened his grip. She turned in his arms and leaned back against his solid body. 'Yes?'

'Sorry,' Aiden said to them both.

'It's okay,' Lydia said. 'What's up?'

'I just had an approach. Guy said he worked for someone you know. Asked me to pass on a message to you.'

Lydia tensed and felt Fleet's hands tighten on her waist, keeping her anchored. 'Okay.'

'He said you need to stop avoiding Sinclair.'

LYDIA DIDN'T HAVE TIME TO WORRY ABOUT Sinclair and the secret service. Whatever the spooks wanted with her could wait. Fleet had to go in for a late shift, so she drove to Auntie's flat alone, and tried not to feel resentful at being left alone on kid-duty. Auntie had a resident's parking spot that her family used, and it was mercifully free, so she parked up and gave herself a talking to in the flip-down mirror of the sun visor. *You can do this. You are the head of the Crow Family. You can look after a ten-year-old for three hours before Fleet gets home.*

Lydia still felt tense as she walked into the flat and wasn't sure she would be able to hide it from someone as perceptive as Fleet's aunt. Thankfully, Auntie wasn't one for small talk, and they got down to business five minutes after Lydia arrived. Ember had already been sent to pack his belongings, and they were alone in the immaculately clean, but cramped living room.

'What did you mean when you said he is one of ours?' Lydia asked quietly. 'What did you see?'

'You know the answer to that.' Auntie leaned forward, fixing Lydia with a piercing stare. 'You must see it.'

'There is something about him,' Lydia allowed. 'A gleam. It's like Fleet's.'

Auntie's lips thinned. 'That man fathered children all over the world.' Auntie never referred to Fleet's father by name. Only 'that man'. 'Those children went on to have babies and grandbabies.'

'You think Ember's great-grandparent is the River Man?'

Auntie closed her eyes at the name, as if it was a physical blow.

'Sorry,' Lydia said quickly.

'I don't think,' Auntie said after a beat. 'I saw it in the bones.'

Ember walked into the small room, his bulky backpack hanging low off his narrow shoulders. 'I'm ready,' he said, and his tone was as blank as his expression. He stared at a spot on the carpet and didn't even glance in Lydia's direction.

Lydia didn't know if the kid was traumatised or just being grumpy. She wanted to tell him that she wasn't all that thrilled, either, but she knew it wasn't likely to improve matters. 'You've got everything?'

No response.

'You can stay with us for as long as you like, but I've put out feelers for a family. You'll get to meet them and decide for yourself. I'm not going to force you to live anywhere you're not happy.'

'You're going to call the social,' Ember said in a matter-of-fact voice. He kept his gaze on the floor.

'I'm not,' Lydia said, standing up. 'I'm head of the Crow Family and we are going to look after you. We're not big on the authorities, either.'

He brightened a little at that. Well, he looked at her at least.

'You come back and visit me young man, you hear?' Auntie said.

She didn't get up from her chair and Lydia realised that the older woman was exhausted.

'I could just stay.' Ember shot a shy look at Auntie. 'I could stay here. I'll do the dishes every night.'

Lydia had the impression that Auntie was as surprised as her.

'You can visit whenever you want,' Auntie said gently.

Ember hunched in on himself and he stomped to the door.

'Thank you for having him,' Lydia said. 'Sorry about—'

'No need,' Auntie said, waving the apology away. 'Poor child doesn't know who to trust.'

The drive back to the house in Denmark Hill was short and silent. Ember had got into the backseat of the car and stared out of the window. He hadn't responded to Lydia's first couple of questions, so she gave up on conversation.

Once he was in the spare room, ostensibly unpacking, Lydia headed to the kitchen and called Emma. 'What do ten-year-olds eat?'

Emma, thankfully, had picked up almost immediately. 'Fish fingers, pizza, maybe pasta. You know mine aren't that old yet?'

'I know, but it's mum knowledge.'

'Okay,' Emma said, not sounding convinced. 'Is this a test? What did your mum say?'

'I haven't asked yet. Don't really want to have the whole conversation about why I'm feeding a child.'

'I won't ask then,' Emma said. 'But I'm dying to know.'

'You can ask.' Lydia looked at the doorway, expecting Ember to appear at any moment. 'I have temporary custody of a kid. His name is Ember, and we saved his life. Me and Fleet. At least, I think we did. We definitely saved him from something. And he's on his own.'

Emma, to her credit, didn't ask about Ember's parents. She knew Lydia wouldn't be stepping in if it wasn't absolutely necessary. 'Ten isn't a baby. You can just ask him what he likes to eat, you know.'

'I have. He either doesn't answer or he looks like someone is about to kick him. I hate it. I just want to... I don't know. Put the right thing in front of him and have him eat it. And then get some sleep, 'cause he looks knackered. I don't know. Is that right? Should I be making him talk to me? Should I make him an appointment with a therapist or something?'

'Trust your instincts,' Emma said after a pause. 'And you're right to focus on his basic needs right now. Food. Shelter. Rest. Maybe a shower if he wants one.'

Shower. That was a point. When had Ember last washed? She had no idea. Was that something she needed to prompt? To offer? On the other hand, Emma had said it last, so that meant it probably wasn't very important.

'Is he okay?' Emma asked. 'Physically?'

'I think so,' Lydia said. She felt sick herself. 'But I don't know. What if he isn't?'

'If you're worried, you should take him to the doctor. Better safe than sorry.'

'Right. You're right.'

After Lydia had thanked Emma and said goodbye, along with her usual promise to keep in better touch, she called a number from Charlie's ancient paper filing system. The one he kept on index cards in a shoebox, shoved into the locked bottom drawer of his desk. It wasn't secure, of course, but Charlie had probably felt untouchable.

The Crow's family doctor was the person they called when someone needed patching up and they couldn't risk a trip to the hospital. It was the first place cops would look in the event of an incident. Dr Walker was used to patching up knife wounds and, occasionally, digging out bullets. She was evidently not used to checking over a taciturn ten-year-old under the watchful eye of the head of the Family.

Dr Walker looked from Lydia to Ember and back again. 'He's not injured?'

The bruises around Ember's neck from when an older kid had strangled him had faded, and he was slouched in the chair, regarding the doctor with a sullen expression.

Lydia explained what Fleet had seen back when they had first encountered Ember. Ember taking a drug and then collapsing. As she spoke, she sensed Ember listening intently, even though he was pretending other-wise. 'I'm just worried he has some hidden condition. A weak heart or something. And he's been on his own for a while. I don't know if he's been eating or taking vitamins or... I don't know.'

'You want a health check? That, I can do. For a detailed look at his heart, we'll need an echocardiogram and a session with a CT scanner, minimum.' She tapped her lip, thinking. 'I have contacts at King's. They can get us what we need, but it'll cost. And I need a couple of days to set it up.'

'Do it,' Lydia said.

Dr Walker turned to Ember, her whole demeanour shifting. 'I would like to listen to your heart, take your blood pressure and a blood sample, and have a look at your neck and stomach. Is that all right?'

A blankness rolled over Ember's face, something that Lydia was beginning to recognise as his expression of fear. But he nodded tightly.

Dr Walker might have been more used to digging bullets out of gang enforcers and sewing up knife wounds, but she clearly had range. Her voice softened as she worked, and Lydia could see she was being gentle as she felt around the boy's neck and jaw.

Ember was stoic for the blood draw, but he looked away from the needle in a deliberate way, and the tension in his face eased after it was over.

'Is it all right to lift your T-shirt?'

'Yeah,' Ember lifted it for her. Lydia could see him relaxing very slightly with each question, each demonstration of respect. She made a mental note to tip the doc heavily for this visit.

After she had used the blood pressure cuff and stethoscope, had him lie back on the sofa and palpitated his stomach, she told him to put his T-shirt back on. 'Thank you, Ember.' Then she asked a series of questions about feeling faint or breathless, whether he had asthma, or got regular headaches.

'So?' Lydia asked. The sight of Ember's thin frame,

his ribcage clearly visible, and the old bruises around his side and back, was imprinted on her retinas.

With a quick smile to Ember, Dr Walker said: 'Abdomen feels normal, no swelling or enlargement of liver, lungs sound healthy, and no heart murmur or abnormal rhythm. As I said, without further investigation I can't be a hundred per cent certain, but there was nothing to indicate a cardiac problem.'

'Told you,' Ember said.

'Arrange for the scans,' Lydia said.

'Why?' Ember looked properly mystified. 'You know I can't pay for that.' A look of pure fear crossed his face. 'It's so I owe you, right?'

'This is on the house, gratis,' Lydia said, trying to sound reassuring and not grumpy. This was the downside of cultivating a reputation as someone to be feared. It made it bloody tricky not to terrify a kid you were trying to reassure. 'You don't owe me or the Crow Family anything. Not a penny. Not a favour. Nothing.'

If Dr Walker was surprised by this exchange, she didn't show it.

'So, he's healthy? Nothing to worry about?'

'He could do with putting on some weight, but it could just be his natural size. Hard to know without his measurements over time. Blood tests will check for iron and B12. Eyes, nose and throat all clear. And whoever throttled him didn't break his trachea. That's it.'

Lydia thanked the doc. She had been packing away her equipment as she spoke and now she nodded to Ember. 'I hope I don't have to stitch you up anytime soon.'

CHAPTER THREE

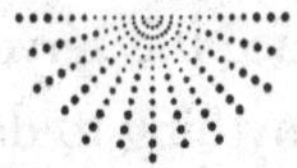

Jason was monitoring the online activity for the accounts that had used the Ripper hashtags, so Lydia sat up, wide awake, when he appeared in her bedroom the next morning carrying his laptop and with a serious expression.

'There's a new message.'

'Show me.'

Rubbing sleep from her eyes, she focused on the screen as he plonked the computer onto the duvet. Fleet had already gone to work, so Jason folded himself next to her on the bed.

The message was short. It was posted with the same account name as before, but didn't use any of the known Ripper hashtags. It said 'Want to play a game?'

'I've had a program running to trace the account, but it's not going to help.' Jason looked gutted, as if this was a personal failing.

'That's okay,' Lydia said. 'You don't exactly have the resources—'

'It worked,' Jason interrupted. 'It just doesn't do us much good. They're using multiple VPNs, and the connection gets bounced between servers.'

'What does that mean?' Lydia scrubbed a hand over her face, trying to wake up. 'I'm guessing that's a false result?'

'It means I can trace the servers used by the VPN, but they don't have anything to do with the location of the user.'

'Do VPNs not track their users?'

'Nope. That way they can't give information even if it's demanded by the authorities. They even use it in their sales copy.'

'Thank you for trying,' Lydia said. 'Fleet said that Moss wasn't looking at the social media messages as a significant lead. Apparently, he thinks they are unrelated.'

'Someone jumping on the Ripper idea and messing about?'

'Essentially,' Lydia said.

'How has that guy been given Fleet's job?' Jason asked in disgust.

Lydia shrugged and didn't voice the truth. His association with her had derailed his career.

ONCE LYDIA HAD SHOWERED AND GOT DRESSED, HAD two large coffees and stared at the list of messages she had to return for Family business, and the empty list of tasks for her investigation into the identity of the Ripper emulator who appeared to be alive and kicking, she went to the spare room to check on Ember.

Ember was up and dressed, sitting on the bed with his hands folded in his lap. He spoke as soon as she opened the door. 'I want to go out.'

'You're not a prisoner,' Lydia said. She heard Emma's voice in her head. 'But you are ten years old. So, I'd need to know where you're going and when you're going to be back. For safety.'

The boy's bottom lip stuck out. 'I've been living on my own for, like, a year.'

'I know,' Lydia said. She leaned against the doorframe, not quite entering the room. 'And I'm sorry about your gran.'

His shoulders curved inward, and he bowed his head. His next words were mumbled into his chest. 'You're not her. You're not...'

Lydia waited to see if he was going to finish the sentence. When he didn't, she said: 'I know I'm not your mother or your gran. I'm not pretending to be.'

'You can't tell me what to do.' He stared at the ground.

'You're my responsibility,' Lydia said. She took a step into the room. 'I've never done this before, so you're going to have to help me out.'

He glanced up at her then.

'Like, I have no idea whether children are supposed to have ice cream every day after dinner, or just on the weekend.'

'Every day,' he said quickly.

Lydia nodded. 'Makes sense. Ice cream is so good.'

Ember smiled. A quick flash of sunshine that was over before Lydia could enjoy it.

'See?' she said lightly. 'You can help me and I'll help you, and together we can work stuff out.'

It took Ember less than ten hours to worry Lydia into a state of panic. She did not enjoy it. 'How do you do this?' She demanded.

Emma's face, visible on the video call, was sympathetic. 'You need to contact the police.'

'Fleet is out looking for him,' Lydia said. He was police, even if he was searching unofficially. 'And it's been less than twenty-four hours.'

'He's a child, they'll help now.'

Lydia didn't know if that was true, but she paced the downstairs rooms and waited to hear back from Fleet. She made a bargain with herself: she wouldn't call the police until she had heard from Fleet. They could discuss it together. Like co-parents. Which is what they were in this moment, she supposed.

When the front door opened less than an hour later, Fleet ushered in a sullen Ember, and Lydia was too strung out to relax at the sight. She felt all the worry of the day morph instantly into anger and had an acute understanding of why her own parents had seemed so annoyed when she had come home late as a teen. She pushed it down. Ember wasn't her child, and he was used to surviving on his own.

She moved into the kitchen more quickly than necessary, trying to expel some of her energy so that she didn't explode at Ember. 'Hungry? We were going to have pasta.' Lydia opened the freezer and dug out two tubs of Angel's tomato and basil sauce. Jason usually cooked this meal for her, but she was capable of boiling some pasta shapes and microwaving the sauce. And she needed something other than Ember's unhappy face to focus on.

While she waited for the water to heat, Lydia tapped a quick message to Emma to let her know that Ember was home. She got an instant reply, with lots of emojis, and felt the tight knots in her stomach uncoil.

'You need to let us know where you are,' Fleet was saying. His voice was very calm. 'I know you're used to doing your own thing, but we're responsible now—'

'Don't see why.'

'Because you're living here,' Fleet said, his voice still gentle.

'I don't get it.'

'We're looking after you and that means—'

Thin shoulders raised in a quick shrug. Ember stared at the floor and mumbled. 'I don't get why I'm here.'

He had a point. There were plenty of kids in London, even in Camberwell, who could do with a new home environment. Lydia wondered how much Ember knew about his own heritage.

'Auntie said you belong to us. Do you know what she meant by that?'

Ember shook his head, his head still lowered.

'She thinks you are related to me,' Fleet said. 'We might have the same dad.'

Ember looked at him as if he had lost his mind. Which, given their age difference, was fair.

'I know it's a lot to take in. Did you ever meet your dad?'

A headshake.

'If we're right, that's a good thing,' Lydia said. 'Best if he doesn't know about you.'

'But you're safe,' Fleet said quickly.

Ember was watching them carefully. Lydia wasn't sure if they were freaking him out. How honest were you supposed to be with a kid? Another question to ask Emma.

After a long pause, he said: 'If I had a phone, I could call you. Tell you if I'm going to be late or whatever.'

The kid wasn't daft. Lydia had the distinct impression she was being played. 'You want a mobile?'

'iPhone,' Ember said promptly. 'I could nick one, but you said I shouldn't...' His eyes flicked between them. There was a light in them now, as if he was starting to relax, starting to realise that nothing terrible was about to happen.

Fleet glanced at Lydia, clearly trying to suppress a smile.

'Tell you what, you don't do a Houdini for a month and we'll talk about an iPhone.'

He perked up.

Lydia held up a finger. 'That means you tell us when you're going out. You tell us where you're going, when you'll be back, and you stick to it. No more vanishing acts.'

Ember pulled his bottom lip over his top and scrunched his eyes. 'A week.'

'Two weeks,' Lydia said. She was folding too quickly. It was a sloppy negotiation style that she wouldn't have been caught dead using with anyone else, but the little spark of humour in Ember's eyes was addictive. She wanted to keep it there.

Sinclair worked for the secret service. The four magical Families of London had been Gale's pet project and, as far as Lydia understood it, Sinclair had taken over after his demise. The department had always been pretty insistent on getting in touch with Lydia, whether she liked it or not, so it wasn't entirely surprising to find her sitting on a bench in Burgess Park, when she went for an early morning run.

Lydia stopped at the bench and began stretching her calf muscles, waiting to find out what had brought Sinclair all the way to Camberwell.

'You haven't responded to my requests for a meeting,' Sinclair said.

'And that should have been a hint.' Lydia turned her attention to her shoulders, crossing one arm over her chest and pulling it tight. 'For an intelligence service, you really ought to—'

'We've lost contact with an agent in the field.'

Lydia shut up. Dead operatives, much like dead police, were not a joking matter.

'They were working undercover but have dropped out of communication. I imagine I will find their body at some point.' Sinclair paused, staring at Lydia with unnerving intensity. 'And we have a serial killer loose.'

It took Lydia a beat to realise what Sinclair was referring to. Mary. 'Scotland Yard has that in hand, I have no doubt.'

'I know DCI Fleet was taken off the case,' Sinclair said.

'Then you should direct your enquiries to DCI Moss.'

'I would prefer to speak to you.'

'Why are you interested?'

She raised an eyebrow. 'There is a serial killer. In London.'

'Not your department.'

Her lips thinned. 'I find myself continuing the work of Gale, and it appears there is a supernatural element to these murders.'

'What do you mean?'

Sinclair gazed at her for a long beat. 'Do we really have to play these tiresome games?'

Lydia pretended to think. Then she nodded. 'On balance, yes.'

'Oh for goodness—'

Whether Sinclair was actually losing her cool, or pretending to in order to lower Lydia's guard, was uncertain, but it was still enjoyable.

'Looking at the crime scene at Cerberus, the killer just disappeared into thin air. Connor Bright was killed in a busy area with plenty of CCTV but nothing was caught on camera. Charlie doesn't show up on CCTV, as you are well aware.'

'He's dead,' Lydia said. Then it occurred to her in a rush. Mary was dead. Mary had been the killer. Death was not necessarily a barrier to Charlie. Keeping her face still to hide these thoughts, she went on the offensive: 'Are you formally accusing the Crow Family of these murders?'

A small smile. 'Of course not. I'm here to make a proposal, nothing more.'

'Let's hear it then.'

'An exchange of information.'

Of course. It was always information with Sinclair's kind. 'What do you want to know?'

'There hasn't been a murder in ten days. Are you expecting there to be any more?'

Lydia decided to be honest. 'Not by the hand of that killer. No.'

She nodded, digesting this. 'Thank you.'

Lydia put one foot up on the bench, next to Sinclair, and leaned into the stretch. Hoping that Sinclair would take the hint and leave.

Sinclair stood, but she wasn't finished. 'Do you know what MI6 calls MI5?' She didn't wait for a reply. '"The children" or "the fuckwits" or, if they're feeling kind, "the special squad". They don't mean it nicely—'

'Yeah, got it,' Lydia interrupted. 'So?'

'You can imagine what they call Gale's little pet project.'

'Not my circus—'

'Oh, but it very much is. Your family has been under investigation by Gale's department for a good many years, but you're of interest to the organised crime people too, and that means MI5 and MI6 keep a weather eye.'

'My,' Lydia flapped a hand at her face, 'you're making me blush.'

Sinclair sighed. 'Do listen for once. Five might not ever have officially recognised the rumours about the four Families and their unusual characteristics, but did Gale ever tell you that there was a designation for his department within the service? One that has never been made public, naturally enough.' She didn't wait for Lydia to answer. 'MI13. Which ought to tip you off that the service has been paying attention after all.'

'Fine. The grown-ups are watching, I get it. Why are you telling me?'

'Do you know what we do when we want more information on a group or organisation? When we want to influence certain events, exert invisible pressure?'

Lydia stilled. 'You get inside.'

'Infiltration, correct.' Sinclair smiled like an indulgent teacher.

'You're telling me there's an agent in my family?' Her whole body had gone cold.

'Not one of mine,' Sinclair said. 'But I can't vouch for my siblings. Five and six haven't been in a sharing mood recently.'

'So, what? What is this,' Lydia waved a hand, 'all about? Just another fishing trip?'

'MI13 was formed after the war. The four Families might have signed a truce, promised to play nicely, but the service wasn't about to take that on trust. And there were still plenty of other oddities to keep Gale busy. A discretionary fund from the treasury meant that he could run a few agents, build a small network of assets and generally follow his obsession. The budget was small enough that any results he brought were considered a bonus.'

Gale's department had been around for longer than Lydia realised. She supposed that he must have used his healing abilities on himself, or that ageing slowly was a side-benefit of them. The man must have been in his eighties when he died, but he hadn't looked a day over thirty-five. She tried to focus on Sinclair's words. 'He brought results?'

'Hardly any, as far as I'm aware. Thirteen certainly wasn't a respected part of the machine. Still isn't, which is why I'm not overly keen to be here.'

Lydia wasn't sure if she just meant her job or Burgess Park in particular.

'Have there been any changes recently?'

'There are always changes. You'll have to be more specific.'

'New people. Any random relatives popping up? Maybe within the Pearls?'

Lydia kept her face neutral. Scarlett. 'Why would I know anything about the Pearl Family?'

'I would hope you know about all the Families,' Sinclair said. 'Or you're not very good at your job.'

'The Pearls haven't been a threat for a long time. Rafferty Hill is the new head of the Family,' Lydia said. She was throwing out-of-date information, pretending to play ball.

Sinclair wasn't taken in. She gave Lydia one of her

rare real-looking smiles. 'That's not what my source tells me. Rafferty Hill is in the land of the free, soaking up movie money and stepping out with underfed starlets.'

Lydia widened her eyes theatrically. 'News to me.'

Sinclair leaned back on the bench. 'You're truly not concerned?'

'About the Pearls? No. I'm busy enough with the Silvers and the Foxes.'

'At least you're not battling your own anymore. You're welcome, by the way.'

'For what?'

'Releasing Charlie Crow into your tender loving care.'

'He escaped,' Lydia said flatly.

'People don't escape from our facilities.'

Lydia paused to absorb that. It was possible that they had let him go deliberately. Which had been no act of kindness. 'If you're after a favour in return, you should have set the terms. Sloppy.'

Sinclair raised her hands. 'Who said anything about a favour? I am just demonstrating what a good friend I can be.'

Lydia let her talons show. 'Why are you here? Really?'

'Enough small talk? Very well. I wish you to consult. On one matter.'

'I am not looking to work for the secret service.'

'One tiny consultation. That's it.'

'It's never one thing. And I doubt it's small. I'll pass.'

'It concerns the fifth Family.'

Lydia kept her face neutral. There was no fifth

Family. Fleet had a gleam, inherited from his supernatural father, The River Man, and Sinclair might be referencing that. But then she would say so. 'There is no fifth Family.'

Sinclair stood up, looking down at Lydia with a searching gaze that Lydia felt all the way to her toes. 'I have reason to believe otherwise.'

Lydia wanted to ask for Sinclair's reasons, but she knew how this worked. Information exchange, favours back and forth. And it would be a waste of time. She hadn't been lying to Sinclair: there was no fifth Family.

'I would rather work with you than against you,' Sinclair said as her parting shot.

'And I would rather jump in the Thames,' Lydia said, pleasantly enough, she thought.

CHAPTER FOUR

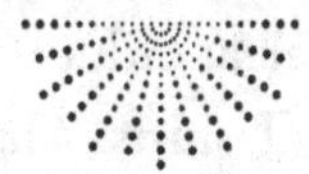

L ydia flipped her coin across the back of her knuckles. Her joy at having it returned was undiminished from that first flush, and she found herself mesmerised by the flashing disc's movement, as if she was a recalcitrant interviewee being given a bit of Crow whammy.

She was working in her office, but the pile of demands from Family members was as enticing as months-old carrion. She wanted to stretch her wings and fly, which wasn't a good feeling to have while in her roost.

New attitude, she coached herself. Embrace your role. Embrace the house. She picked up the first task. A neon pink sticky note from Aiden, which detailed a conversation with a reasonably important member of the wider Crow Family. They weren't happy about Scarlett taking over the Pearl Family and wanted a sit-down with Lydia to air their concerns and to hear her plans for surveilling the new leader.

Her phone rang, and she answered it gratefully. Fleet was with Ember at the outlet shopping centre by the river. Auntie had told them that his trainers were at least a size too small and that the few clothes that he owned were 'shameful'. Lydia wasn't sure whether Auntie meant their condition, style, or something else, but they had received clear orders.

'Jeans, joggers, T-shirts, hoodie and trainers acquired. We'll get school shoes at the end of the summer in case he grows again before then.'

'Good work,' Lydia said, smiling at the pride in Fleet's voice.

'We're grabbing food now and were thinking of going to the cinema.'

'Have fun.'

'He's just looking at the food options,' Fleet said, lowering his voice slightly. 'I think it's going well, though. He's even spoken in complete sentences a couple of times.'

'That's brilliant,' Lydia said. 'Emma said it's going to take time for him to trust us.'

'Yeah,' Fleet sounded distracted. 'I think he's chosen. Burgers. Right. Gotta go.'

Lydia stared into space for a moment after hanging up. Fleet might have mixed feelings about acquiring a dependent, but he seemed to be slipping into the parental role very well. That was good, obviously, but she had the strangest feeling of something unspooling very quickly. Things were moving fast, and she felt like she needed to catch up.

. . .

Jason was in the kitchen, whisking butter and sugar with an electric mixer. 'I was going to bake something,' he said. 'How do you feel about sponge cake?'

'I feel good,' Lydia said. Happy to see him doing something other than hunching over his laptop, chasing down IP addresses and trawling the corners of the internet for Ripper chatter. The thought raised a question. 'You know you said our guy was using VPNs and other stuff?'

'Yeah,' Jason replied, his eyes on his cake mix.

'Doesn't that mean it's unlikely to be a ghost?'

'How do you mean?'

'Unless it's a recently deceased tech bro, how would they know how to use a VPN and the internet and all...' She trailed off, realising who she was speaking to. Jason had been alive when personal computers were brand new. They had chunky keys and disk drives, and hardly anybody owned one, but that hadn't stopped him from becoming a hacker in his afterlife. He didn't need to sleep and had a voracious appetite for learning. He had learned everything there was to know about mathematics and computing and was using that knowledge for good. What if there was a version of Jason that was bent on using his powers for evil?

Jason was still mixing. She wasn't sure he had heard her over the whirring, but then he stopped and glanced at her. 'They could have learned. Like me.'

'Yeah,' Lydia said. 'But how likely is that? Really? I mean, you're pretty special.'

'Are you taking the piss?' He looked genuinely annoyed, which was unusual, popping out the beaters from the mixer and tapping them on the mixing bowl with some force.

Sometimes Lydia forgot that Jason was from another time. 'Special' had probably been an insult in the eighties. 'Special, like amazing. Unusual. Unique,' she said quickly.

'Right.' Jason still looked unsure. Like there was a punchline coming.

'And why would a ghost enlist Mary?' Lydia continued, keen to move past the awkwardness.

'Same reason anyone would,' Jason replied promptly. 'Revenge. Or to do their dirty work.'

'So we are looking for someone, dead or alive, who wanted those men punished? Someone connected to Cherish's death?'

'I don't know.' Jason shook his head. 'Maybe it wasn't that deliberate.'

'How so?'

'It's not the easiest way to kill someone. If someone wanted those men dead, why not stab them themselves? Or hire a professional? It seems convoluted to get a ghost involved. Mary wasn't a killer. She didn't know what she was doing, not really.'

Jason remained a steadfast defender of Mary. Having seen her confusion first-hand, Lydia had sympathy for the point of view. But she had also nearly been sliced up by the enraged spirit, which made her feelings more complicated. 'It's a good point. How could they be sure she would kill anyone? Let alone the right person?'

'Someone knows that we exist,' Jason said. 'And they

were pulling Mary's strings. Using her somehow. That's who we need to find.'

It was the same thoughts they'd had before. Lydia knew she was spinning in circles.

'We do know one person who fits the bill,' Jason said. He didn't look at her as he spoke.

'Do we?'

'We know you power me up. Mary got active once you moved in here.'

'Feathers,' Lydia said, as the implication sank in. Had she powered up Mary? Was she responsible for those deaths? And, a much quieter voice. *Shouldn't she feel bad about it?*

THE LAST TIME LYDIA HAD SEEN THE PRIVATE dining room in the Mayfair restaurant that had been the site of the restatement of the truce between the Families, it had been covered in broken glass and feathers. And her Uncle Charlie had been lying dead on the floor with a crossbow bolt through his eye.

Now, it was back to luxurious perfection; the glass had been replaced in the elegant arched windows, the table was covered in a crisp white cloth, candles, fresh flowers and sparkling silver and glassware, and the unblemished wooden floor shone with polished lustre. There wasn't a trace of the violence, and it made Lydia wonder how many places had hidden bloody pasts, effectively erased by the judicious application of both time and money.

It was five o'clock and the next booking wasn't until

six. A crisp fifty folded into the maître d's hand ensured their privacy. Since Sinclair had raised the spectre of Uncle Charlie, it had been in the back of Lydia's mind to check whether he was, well, a spectre. His had been a violent death, after all, and if anyone would have the willpower to cling to this mortal plane, it would be her shark of an uncle.

Jason was motionless in the middle of the room, his head tilted as if listening.

'Anything?' Lydia realised that her arms were crossed protectively and she unfolded them.

He took a step toward the front of the room. 'There's a voice.'

Her heart seized in her chest. 'Charlie?'

'No, female. Sounds quite old.' A beat. 'My apologies.'

His last words were clearly directed at the voice. Lydia could only hear the faintest scratching sound, too quiet to make out words, and she could see a vague shimmer in the air next to Jason. The ghost was barely there as far as Lydia's senses could detect, but Jason didn't seem to have any difficulty in communicating with her. He apologised a lot, so she got the impression that the ghost was not best pleased.

After a few minutes, Jason said a final 'sorry' and turned to Lydia. 'I think I've got as much as I'm going to. We should leave Mrs Fitzroy in peace.' The shimmer moved, and Jason winced, as if someone had shouted at him. 'Apologies, Duchess.'

Lydia asked Jason who he had been speaking to, but

he shushed her and wouldn't say another word until they were out on the pavement.

In the sunshine he looked even more transparent than he had in the glimmering light of the dining room, but his expression of relief was unmistakable. 'He's not there,' he said.

They walked to Grosvenor Square and found an empty bench. The grand Georgian buildings filled the four sides with their rows of mullioned windows, well-kept red brick and black railings. Imposing doorways, with flights of white stone steps, were all freshly painted, and one was even surrounded by an impressive arch of wisteria in full bloom. Everything was refined and tasteful and screamed old money. She expected to be accosted by police or a security guard at any moment and asked to move on. They were certainly making the place look scruffy. Or, she was, at any rate. Especially since she was sitting on a bench speaking to thin air.

'What did the Duchess have to say?'

Jason sighed heavily. 'So. Much.'

The hotel was founded in the 1850s and had been plying the titled and entitled with champagne and fine food ever since. The Duchess had shared a great deal of gossip, including the tale of a society lady who had met an unfortunate end at the hands of her wildly jealous husband. 'She was having an affair?' Lydia guessed.

'Unclear,' Jason said. 'She was very close friends with a Lady Somerset, but told me very forcefully that there was nothing untoward going on. Either way, he got it into his head that she didn't love him and never would.'

'I thought they were all loveless matches with their sort.' Lydia meant the upper classes in a period of history that was filed in her brain as 'uncomfortable dresses, repression and colonial atrocities'.

'She was just unlucky, I guess,' Jason said sardonically. 'She's extremely annoyed about it.'

'I heard you ask about other ghosts.'

'Yeah, that was a dead end.'

'Pun intended,' Lydia said, earning a quick smile.

'Nobody else there. Or nobody else she would admit to hearing, anyway. I get the impression if she thought they were beneath her socially, she wouldn't want to sully her good name by conversing with them.'

'What was she doing speaking to you then?' Lydia nudged him and received a literal cold shoulder for her trouble.

Jason held up a middle finger. 'Rude.'

CHAPTER FIVE

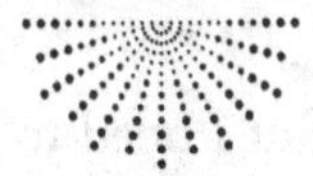

Lydia looked around the living room. She had made it into her office, hauling a desk, lamp, and chair into the centre and keeping the white shutters mostly closed. She wanted to tear it all down, to rip out the fixtures and the furniture and make it hers, but despite vowing to finally do it, she didn't know where to start. And there were more pressing matters. Besides, what if she replaced every item in the entire house and it still felt like Charlie's?

Echoing her fears, Aiden knocked on the door and walked in. He tipped his head. 'Boss.'

'I don't have time for Family business today,' Lydia said, trying to forestall him.

Aiden winced. 'There are a few things—'

'Can you deal with them?'

'People like to see you,' Aiden said. 'But I can handle them. Yeah.'

'Brilliant,' Lydia said. The smile she gave Aiden was completely genuine. 'Thank you.'

'I'll be back later, then,' he said. 'To give you a full report. And if I'm not sure about something, I'll check with you first.'

'It's fine. I trust you.' Her mind was already yearning to be back on the Ripper problem.

'There have been a few questions about the new Pearl. People are a bit...'

'I know, I know. But I need to find the NewRipper.' Whoever had powered up Mary and pointed her at her victims was taunting her. He might not have killed in the last two weeks, but Lydia had the feeling he was far from finished. And she knew she shouldn't jump to the conclusion that the NewRipper was a 'he' but it was hard not to. Statistical probability for starters.

'I know,' Aiden was saying. 'But a new Pearl? And this thing with the Foxes... People are antsy, and if they don't think you're handling it...'

'You're right,' Lydia said. 'I'm on it.'

Frustrated at her attention being divided, and that she was doing something that Sinclair would approve of, Lydia nonetheless called Paul Fox and set up a meeting. She had to be able to look her Family members in the eyes and tell them that she was paying attention to the new Pearl that had showed up. In her mind, it made sense to speak to Paul first. There was protocol, for starters, and, for second, she would prefer to speak to him than to the new Pearl.

Paul was waiting for her at the Potters Fields park, next to the Thames. The place was buzzing with an

Uzbek food festival, and the warm air was fragranced with cooking lamb and spices. Paul had said he was there with his siblings, so Lydia was wary, even if it was neutral territory and currently packed with what felt like a thousand culture-seekers.

He was wearing a black T-shirt that clung to his chest and jeans, and his hair was its usual close-crop. 'I've got something for you,' he said as she approached.

She had braced for the Fox magic, so she managed to keep her heart rate under control and her mind out of the gutter. Just about.

He pulled a small rectangle from his pocket. It was slightly larger than a standard business card and made of heavyweight card stock. Embossed gold lettering spelled out a date. The end of the month. 'I said email would be fine, but Scarlett insisted on proper invitations.'

Lydia stared at the card. When Paul had announced his engagement, she had imagined it as happening sometime in the distant future. 'You're not really marrying a Pearl.' Lydia didn't intend to ask a question, but her voice carried less conviction than she liked and she knew it had sounded like one.

'What makes you say that?' His gaze roved over the festival attendees, flicked to the sky to follow the contrail of a flight, and, finally, at Lydia.

'What would your father say?'

'He's not here.'

'Your family, though. What will they say?'

'They know,' Paul said, the edges of his mouth twitching.

Lydia didn't believe him.

He saw it in her eyes and gave her a wide smile. 'Trust me. They're just relieved it's not you.'

'I need to see your betrothed.'

'Is that a fact?'

'To say thank you for this lovely invitation and to formally RSVP.'

'Very convincing. You want to grill her about her intentions.' Paul grinned. 'Don't pretend you're not looking out for me, Little Bird.'

She looked at the card again. 'Hampstead Heath? Not Whitechapel?'

Paul's brows lowered.

Lydia pressed on. 'How much do you know about Scarlett?'

'You're worried about me,' Paul continued to tease. 'Or you're jealous.'

'I'm worried about us all. I think she might be a spy.'

His laughter was sharp and loud. 'A spy.'

'Yes. She could have been recruited by MI13. They've tried to recruit me.'

Paul's expression turned serious. 'Are you saying this because you don't want me to marry Scarlett?'

'I'm saying this because it's true. My concern is genuine.'

His eyes softened. 'Little Bird.'

'My concern is that she is working for the secret service, infiltrating the Families,' Lydia clarified.

'Sure.' Paul shook his head. It was a tiny movement, but she saw the disbelief in the line of his mouth. 'And this has nothing to do with us.'

'There is no "us". We have to work together, for the

truce, but beyond that...' Lydia waved a hand. There was
no way to encompass her feelings on this topic. She
didn't want to lie to Paul and say there was nothing, but
she didn't want to give him ideas, either. Ideas, like the
one he was clearly having right now. Lydia could feel
warm fur brushing the skin of her arms. She could smell
damp earth and greenery and the iron bite of fresh
blood. 'This isn't what you think.'

He tilted his head, smiling dangerously. 'You in my
head now, Little Bird?'

'I'm not jealous.' The words were wrong. Too stark.
Lydia wanted to snatch them back, but it was too late,
and the air between them thickened. 'I do care about
you,' she said, feeling as if the words were being dragged
out of her. 'But this is about the truce. About all of us.'

Scarlett was staying in a hotel between
Regent's Park and Hyde Park. Lydia had expected something nice, it was an upmarket area after all, but wasn't
prepared for the scale of the hotel. It had a central dining
space with an eight-storey glass atrium, filled with palm
trees and other foliage. Scarlett was on the top floor of
the building, in what turned out to be a suite. It had a
fireplace in the living area, along with a large velvet sofa
and chairs.

'They just want me to stay,' Scarlett explained, with
some satisfaction. 'They've been so kind. Philippe said I
can have it for as long as I like. He's the manager and is a
real darling.'

Lydia looked around at the luxurious suite. It had to

have cost more than two grand a night, and Philippe had given it to Scarlett for free. Indefinitely.

To be fair, if Lydia had owned a hotel, she might have let Scarlett kip down gratis, too. Put Scarlett in the bar for a couple of hours and she would double the punter spend. People would fall over themselves to buy her a drink, to have another round in order to stay close.

Scarlett had braids to the middle of her back and the smoothest, glowiest skin that Lydia had ever seen. She wanted to run her fingers over it, to lick it like a cat with a bowl of cream. She knew it was the Pearl blood doing a number on her senses, but that knowledge didn't help. Lydia knew she was leaning too close to the other woman, but she couldn't stop herself. Scarlett smelled like vanilla and joy, flowers and fresh air, spice and sex. Never mind that combination was impossible and ought to create a disgusting soup of fragrance. Anything that Lydia had ever found pleasant and attractive was flowing from Scarlett in an undeniable siren song. No wonder Paul had fallen.

'You are wondering about me.' Scarlett's lips curved in an inviting smile.

'You're the new head of the Pearl Family,' Lydia said, by way of an answer. This was a recce. Something to placate the Crows, who were unhappy at her recent appointment to the Pearl Family leadership.

Scarlett inclined her head, showing a stretch of neck that begged to be nuzzled. Nuzzled. Lydia produced her coin and gripped it tightly in her fist. The fog of desire receded enough for her to gather her wits and take a couple of steps back. If Scarlett noticed, she didn't react.

'Last year. I woke up one morning, and I felt different.' She gave a tiny shrug, the bangles on her arm clinking delicately. 'I can't put it into words.'

When Lydia had killed the Pearl King, the whole court of original Pearl Family members had crumbled into dust. Whatever power had been animating their unnaturally long lives hadn't died with them, it had escaped above ground. Lydia's theory was that it had sought the nearest people with enough Pearl blood in their veins to be recognised as heirs to that power. Which made it sound like it was sentient in some way, but Lydia didn't believe that. She imagined it more as a laws of physics type deal. The power had rushed into the nearest appropriate vessel, like air into a vacuum. If that was even right. Lydia had spent most of her science lessons at school writing on her arms with black pen and setting discreet fires when her restlessness hit critical levels. 'What did you do?'

'At first, nothing. But I quickly realised that I wasn't imagining it. People were treating me differently. Wanting to be close to me.'

'And that was new?'

'Not exactly.' An alluring smile. 'I have always enjoyed plenty of attention.'

'Beautiful people do attract admiration.' There was no point in denying Scarlett's natural attributes.

A nod. 'But after that day,' she snapped her fingers, 'it was adoration.'

Adoration didn't sound so bad on the face of it, but Lydia was well aware of the double-edged nature of power. 'That must have been confusing. Maybe a bit scary?'

Scarlett's lips parted. Her tongue darted out to wet the plump cushion of her lower lip, and Lydia realised she was staring, dragging her gaze up to Scarlett's amused expression. 'Are you trying to bond with me, Crow?'

Scarlett may have been newly minted to the ranks of the Pearl Family, but she had the attitude down. 'Better we bond than fight.' Lydia flipped her coin into the air between them and slowed the spin so that it hung for a few moments before slapping back into her hand. 'Pearl.'

Scarlett's smile was a little lop-sided and Lydia felt as if it was her first true reaction. Then she licked her lips, and Lydia was forced to squeeze her coin to keep the waves of Pearl-induced desire in check. Scarlett and Paul together were going to be a formidable duo.

As if reading her mind, Scarlett said: 'You've known Paul a long time.'

'Yes.'

'You and he used to...' Scarlett left the sentence hanging.

Lydia didn't pick it up. She waited, keeping her expression open and neutral.

'Well, it's good that you're all friends now. Good for business, I imagine.'

'Why are you here?'

Scarlett feigned confusion. 'It's a very nice hotel.'

'No. Why do you want to involve yourself with the Families? The Pearls are weak. Your bloodline is diluted beyond recognition. Whatever you think you can achieve by joining with the Foxes—'

'What would I want to achieve?' A line appeared between her perfect brows. 'Beyond marital bliss, naturally.'

A stab of white-hot jealousy pierced Lydia's chest. Bliss. Marital. She pushed the feeling to the back of her mind. Into a box that she then locked with a key. She had no business having any kind of emotion about Paul Fox's life choices. 'That's what I'm asking.' She was glad that her voice was even.

'You don't think marrying Paul Fox is enough of a prize?'

The question was posed earnestly, but it had an undercurrent of menace. Scarlett appeared to be baiting Lydia into insulting her betrothed. Or maybe trying to plant more images of what marrying Paul would mean. Just the current girlfriend needling the ex, establishing her sexual territory. 'Love should always be celebrated,' Lydia said, and gave Scarlett the widest, falsest smile of her life.

CHAPTER SIX

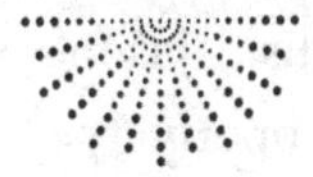

The next day, Lydia sat at her desk, alternating cans of Coke with coffee. She wanted a nip of whisky or, preferably, an entire bottle, but she resisted. Her supernatural-ability to handle alcohol still seemed to be in place, but she wasn't taking any risks. She had to be sharper than sharp.

Ember hadn't come home.

The words hammered her mind over and over. She had been out and about during the day, and Fleet had been at work. He was back at six and had let Lydia know that Ember wasn't in his room. Lydia had gone home via Ember's old flat, just in case he was hanging out there and wanted a lift.

By midnight, they had both been properly worried.

Now, at ten the following morning, she was wondering whether she ought to call the police and report him as missing.

Jason floated into the room. His feet weren't touching the carpet, which was generally a bad sign. 'I've been asking around,' Jason said. 'No one has heard of anything like what happened with Mary.'

Lydia was still thinking about Ember, and she felt a little bit of hope deflate.

'Oh, right. Yes. Thank you for trying,' Lydia said, distracted by images of Ember hit by a car or worse.

'It's high up my list.' Jason's voice was sharp, and Lydia looked at him properly.

'Sorry, yes. Of course.'

Jason frowned. 'What's wrong?'

'Ember didn't come back last night. I don't know where he is.'

Jason digested this for a moment. 'You're worried?'

'He's ten years old,' Lydia said. She waved a hand. 'I'm pretty sure he shouldn't be on his own.'

'You didn't know where he was a month ago, either,' Jason said. 'He was fine then.'

'He was living in his flat,' Lydia countered. 'And I didn't know about him. It's different now he's here. I feel responsible.'

'Okay.' Jason folded himself into a cross-legged position on the sofa and opened his laptop. 'I'll start looking.'

Lydia didn't know what computer-wizardry Jason was going to use to find a wayward ten-year-old, but she was truly grateful. 'Thank you.'

A moment later, Jason's body jerked. He looked at her, wide-eyed, and then disappeared. The laptop dropped onto the cushions.

Before Lydia had time to react, he reappeared, almost translucent, and then rapidly coalesced into his usual solidly physical presence.

'Shit.' Jason looked around and down at his laptop. 'Did I break it?'

'I'm sure it's fine,' Lydia said. 'That still happens, then?'

Jason had been disappearing without his own control for as long as she had known him. It was something that had seemed to get a lot better as he had become more powerful, more physically fixed in the world, and it was upsetting to see that it was still an issue. He didn't know where he went or what it meant, only that it frightened him.

'That felt weird,' he said. 'Different.'

'Different good?' He had only been gone for a few seconds. Maybe that was a sign he was more securely anchored to the living world.

Jason picked up his laptop and folded into a cross-legged position on the sofa. He looked up at Lydia, distress clear on his face. 'It felt violent.'

FLEET HAD GONE INTO WORK EARLY. HE HAD promised to ask the colleagues he trusted to keep an unofficial lookout, but when he got home that afternoon, he didn't have any positive news. 'He'll be okay,' Fleet said. 'He's been looking after himself for a long time.'

'What if he hasn't run away? What if he has been taken?' It was an awful thought, but the NewRipper had been taunting Lydia with a 'game'. What if Ember had been taken as part of that?

Fleet frowned. 'There would be a ransom demand.'

'Already?'

'It's been twenty hours and he is a minor. Yes, you would expect to have heard from the kidnappers by now if it was that kind of operation.'

'That's not set in stone. There must be variation—'

'I don't think he's been taken,' Fleet said. 'The only reason to do so is because of his connection to you, and nobody knows he's here.'

'People watch me,' Lydia said. 'Someone knew about Mary. Powered her up.'

'That's possible. Or it might have been a coincidence.'

'You believe that?'

Fleet paused, then shook his head. 'No. Okay. Fair point.'

Lydia was thinking fast. 'I haven't caught any surveillance. Aiden's on alert, too.'

'I think you're getting a little paranoid,' Fleet said.

Before Lydia could get properly annoyed, she realised that Fleet was widening his eyes at her, trying to communicate. He picked up the kettle. 'Tea?'

Neither of them drank tea at home.

She joined him at the sink. 'Sounds good.'

With the tap running to fill the kettle, Fleet leaned in and spoke quietly into her ear. 'House could be bugged.'

Lydia went to find Charlie's file box with the dog-eared index cards. There wasn't much of a system, but under 'S' she found a card marked 'security' and a number. She flashed the card at Fleet and said, for the benefit of anybody listening, 'I'm going for a run, clear my head.'

He nodded, playing along. 'I'll make us some food.'

She walked to the bottom of the road and called the number from the card using a burner.

The phone rang for a long time before it was answered by a man. 'You did security work for my uncle. Charlie Crow.'

'I did,' the man agreed. 'How can I help?'

Lydia outlined her concerns, and the man assured her that there weren't any surveillance devices in Charlie's house. In fact, he sounded affronted at the suggestion. 'Charlie's been gone a while,' Lydia said. 'Could someone have come in and installed something in the interim?' It wasn't the kind of question the head of the Crows should ask. It made her appear weak, as if her presence wasn't the deterrent that Charlie's had been, but she was past caring about appearances. Ember was missing. He might have been taken. Her heart hammered and her chest tightened so that she had to shove the thought back into the little box she was using to lock it up. She had to keep functional.

'I installed a checker,' the man said. 'I'm looking at the logs right now, and there have been no breaks. Nothing. The house is clean.'

'You're monitoring the house?'

'It's a failsafe. No monitoring of audio or video,' the man's voice had gone nervous. 'I can show you. It just sends an alarm if it detects anything transmitting from the property.'

'And there's nothing doing that?'

'Clean as a whistle.'

Sometimes, there was a person you wanted to talk to, but you knew that the moment you did, the bad thing would become unbearably real, so you put it off. Lydia knew she couldn't keep avoiding the truth, but she stared at her contacts list for a long moment before pressing the call button.

Emma answered straightaway. Lydia could tell that she was on speaker and that Emma was driving. 'I lost the kid.'

'Oh God,' Emma said. 'What happened?'

Lydia hesitated. Now that she had to say the words, she realised she didn't want to. It sounded so bad. It *was* so bad.

'I'm on my own,' Emma said, letting her know that there weren't small people strapped into the backseat, ears wide open and young minds ready to be corrupted.

Lydia swallowed. 'I told him he could stay with me and Fleet. I said that if that didn't work out or he didn't want to, that we would find somewhere else within the family. I promised I wouldn't involve social services.'

'You shouldn't have done that.'

'He was terrified of it happening.' Lydia was defensive. 'I was reassuring him.'

'You must never promise things you can't be certain of,' Emma said with utter conviction. 'That's why parent-speak is full of "we'll see" and "let me discuss it with your dad" and "I'll think about it". We're not being withholding dicks, we're trying to make sure we don't rashly promise something we can't deliver.'

Lydia heard the rebuke. 'We' meant parents. People who had earned the right to look after vulnerable human beings. Not crime bosses who had grabbed up a child and decided they needed to be watched over in some way.

'Sorry, sorry.' Emma was still speaking, and Lydia could hear the emotion in her voice. 'I'm grumpy about that at the moment.' She proceeded to tell Lydia about an acquaintance who was continually threatening conse-quences to his kids and not following through, making promises for treats that were never honoured. 'He's just teaching them that whatever he says means nothing. And kids need to trust their caregivers. They need to feel that security.'

'Is that why Ember ran? Security?'

'Maybe,' Emma replied. 'Sorry.'

'But how could he think being homeless is safer than being with me?' What Lydia wanted to ask was 'Am I really that bad?'.

The sound of an indicator ticking. And a pause that Lydia didn't enjoy. Then: 'You don't know what his experience of the world has been so far. He may well not trust adults at all. It's not personal. How long has he been missing?'

'Not completely certain,' Lydia said, hating that she hadn't kept better tabs on the kid. 'Getting on for twenty-four hours, though.'

Emma made an indrawn sound. 'Bloody hell. You've got to find him.'

CHAPTER SEVEN

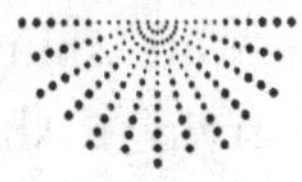

She was in the garden at Charlie's house. The hornbeam tree at the bottom of the garden was silent, and a sliver of moon rode the sky. It usually held at least one corvid, but the tree stood empty. It was winter, and the empty branches were bare, with no leaf cover to soften their twisted shapes. Shapes that seemed to have grown longer and more convoluted than they were in real life.

Despite the quiet and empty garden, she had the unshakeable feeling that she wasn't alone. 'Who's there?' Her voice echoed as if she was inside a cavern, not outside. That's when she realised that she was dreaming.

The eerie silence didn't change, and there was no movement in the frozen air. But the presence that Lydia had known was nearby was suddenly visible. An enormous crow. Easily the size of the tree that it had, impossibly, replaced.

The crow wasn't just huge. Its feathers were dusty-looking and pale grey in places. Was it a sign of age? Or was the bird ill? There was something definitely corrupt. The feeling of decay beneath the surface that reminded her of the image she had seen in the British Museum. The picture of the night raven that was half-rotted away.

The urge to fly had her stretching her arms out. As she did so, the monstrous bird inclined its head to look down at her. Its eyes were shiny black pebbles, and Lydia stared into them, trying to show she wasn't afraid.

'Foolish child,' the crow said.

Lydia didn't hear the voice out loud. It echoed inside her mind, but she had no doubt that it was the crow that had spoken.

'Who are you?' Lydia was trying very hard not to look at the sharp beak, the claws that were digging into the lawn. This crow could kill her with a single slashing blow. That beak would rip through her human flesh like a knife through butter, but somehow she knew it wouldn't even need to touch her to cause her harm. The power emanating from this creature was truly supernatural. This aged crow wasn't a large bird. It was the essence of her Family. It was the original Crow.

And it was staring right through her, as if it could see everything. As if it was judging her and finding her wanting. It tilted its head, considering. The shiny black eyes fixed upon her face.

It opened its beak as if it was going to speak, but the voice she heard was Ember's.

Lydia woke up all at once, like a switch being flipped. She immediately got up and walked through the house. She knew that she would have heard Ember if he had come home during the night. Charlie's alarms would have sounded for starters, but still she looked systematically, room-by-room, as if Ember was a possession she had carelessly misplaced. A set of keys that would turn out to be in the last place she expected to find them.

She expected to find Jason on his laptop in the living room, but he wasn't in the house either. He might have been out and about, chatting to local ghosts or just taking a walk through the dark streets, but she felt a tingle of apprehension. It seemed as if he was disappearing more than usual.

She made a couple of coffees and took them upstairs. Fleet was sitting up in bed, rubbing a hand over his face. He yawned extravagantly as she walked in and took the coffee gratefully. The threads of the dream had fled, but she knew she had heard Ember's voice. She didn't know what he had said, it was a memory that she couldn't bring into focus, just that it had been his voice. It had sounded so young. Her chest squeezed.

Lydia perched on the end of the bed, cradling the mug in her hands. 'Can you see Ember? In a vision, I mean?'

Fleet looked at her for a beat. 'It doesn't work like that.'

'You saw him before. When he was in danger.'

'I know, but I don't control that. I don't choose what I see.'

Lydia pushed down her frustration. It wasn't Fleet's fault. Just another so-called power that turned out to be borderline useless.

'I'm sorry,' Fleet offered, looking miserable.

'Maybe it's a good sign,' Lydia said, not sure who she was trying to comfort more. 'Maybe it means he's safe.'

Thinking about the last time Fleet had seen Ember in a vision reminded her of the need for him to get a scan at the hospital. Dr Walker hadn't been concerned, but she didn't have X-ray vision. Maybe the scan would show some abnormality. Panic gripped her and squeezed her chest. 'You saw him die of a cardiac arrest. What if he does have a weak heart?'

'I saw him collapse,' Fleet said. 'I thought it was a heart attack, but I might be wrong. Could have been any number of things.'

'You said heart attack at the time.'

'Like I said, that's what I thought.' He shrugged. 'But the kid seems fine. Seemed fine. Who knows what was in the pill? Maybe it was a bad batch. We stopped him from taking it, and that means he's out of danger. I've not had any more,' he waved a hand around his eyes to indicate visions.

'We need to find him,' Lydia said, not for the first time. 'He's just a little kid.'

'We will,' Fleet said, taking her hand. 'But he's been looking after himself for a long time. He's probably staying at a friend's house. I'm sure he's fine.'

Lydia didn't have the impression that Ember had a lot of friends, but she knew that Fleet was trying to be reassuring, so she let it go.

'I'm not in work until two, so I'll drive around first.'

'Thank you,' she said.

He squeezed her hand. 'We'll find him.'

WHEN EMBER DIDN'T TURN UP BY THE AFTERNOON, and Aiden reported that nobody in Camberwell had seen him and he hadn't returned to his old flat, Lydia widened her search. She messaged Paul and asked for a meeting.

Since she was asking for a favour, she was willing to go to his territory, but the Fox made things uncharacteristically easy on her by suggesting Tower Bridge. On the way she had a message from Fleet, confirming that he hadn't seen Ember on his drive around. He said he was in meetings for the rest of the day, but that he would call her when he could.

He had his back to her and Lydia enjoyed the freedom to look at him without being observed.

'Got an eyeful?' Paul said without turning.

Feathers. 'Thank you for meeting me.'

His shoulders seemed tense, and it occurred to her how well she still knew Paul Fox. Or how well she felt she knew him. Her instincts told her she could read his body language, that she knew how he was feeling by the way he was standing right now, but her head reminded her that he was a Fox. Unknowable. Untrustworthy. His body could lie as well as his words.

He turned around, and all thought emptied out. The left side of his face was heavily bruised, his eye swollen shut.

She took an involuntary step forward. 'What happened?'

'It doesn't concern you.'

'Okay.' Lydia dropped the arm she had automatically raised. He was untouchable, and she didn't know what to say. Who would dare to punch Paul Fox? And were they still breathing?

A lop-sided smile, made on the unbruised, still-handsome half of his face. 'Are you going soft on me, Little Bird? If you're not careful, I'll start to think you like me.'

Lydia snorted. 'Like' wasn't a word that came into her mind when she thought about Paul Fox. 'I'm just taking a professional interest.'

'So, what professional matter brings you to the river on this fine day? It seems you can't get enough of me.'

'A missing kid,' Lydia said.

She appreciated the way that Paul straightened up, the playfully sly smile dropping from his lips. 'Who?'

'Ten-year-old called Ember Williams.'

'Is he one of yours?'

Lydia nodded, unable to speak for a moment. The guilt was a wave and she was going to drown. 'Last seen on Saturday, at the house. I got up on the Sunday and he was gone. He's skittish, so I figured he had gone for a walk, maybe back to his home. But he wasn't there.'

'Where's home?'

Lydia gave Paul Ember's address. 'He's not there,' she said again. 'And I've got someone watching in case that changes—'

'Good,' Paul said. 'I'll put the word out. You got a photo?'

Lydia sent over the school portrait, complete with the photographer's logo across the front. Ember hadn't bought it, just saved the small digital proof that came with the order form. She didn't know if his gran had still been alive when the picture was taken, whether she hadn't been able to afford the photo, or whether she had never seen it. She could imagine Ember protecting her from something he knew she couldn't do, trying to stop her from feeling guilty. There was just something decent about the kid, thief or not. It wasn't just his sunshine glow, there was something fundamentally good about him, something that reminded her of Fleet.

Paul checked his phone, nodding when he opened the digital image. 'Leave it with me.'

'Thank you,' Lydia said. She hated sounding so vulnerable in front of Paul Fox, but it didn't matter. Not when there was a child lost in the woods. On her watch.

CHAPTER EIGHT

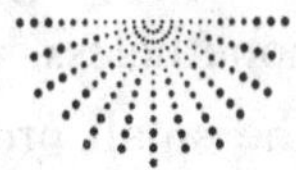

Sandwiched between the chambers and courts beyond Chancery Lane, where the Silver Family held sway, and the good-time clubs, illegal poker games, and cobbled streets of Whitechapel, where the Foxes ran to earth, there was the financial district. The distinctive shining structures of The Gherkin and The Shard were set against the old-money neoclassical buildings. These blinding white edifices, with their columns and colonnades, wide stone steps and grand entrances, had once all been banks. British institutions that had seemed as timeless as the Thames. Now, many of them had been converted into luxury hotels and restaurants. Just as the old banks had been superficially open to everyone, these new institutions curated their clientele through high prices and member's clubs. Lydia felt like an urchin as she walked into the high-ceilinged lobby. Chandeliers the size of small cars illuminated the marble interior, and a sharp-suited man stepped from behind his desk to greet her. Or maybe escort her from the premises.

Maria Silver wasn't alone, but Lydia didn't let that stop her. She wanted to look Maria Silver in the eye and see if she got any kind of sense that the woman was holding something over her. The head of the Silver Family was unlikely to know about Ember, let alone threaten the truce by kidnapping him, but she felt the need to check on her nonetheless.

She intercepted the small group of suited Silvers, greeting Maria as loudly and brashly as she could and enjoying the way heads turned, lips pursed in disapproval. She almost hoped Maria would call security to try to throw her out.

'Ms Crow,' Maria said, her blood-red lips curling in distaste. 'What an unexpected pleasure.'

The sharp tang of Silver filled Lydia's sinuses, and her head began to ache. 'Mazza,' Lydia said. 'How's it hanging?'

Maria glanced at the one man who wasn't giving off 'Silver'. Their client, Lydia realised. Someone important, she hoped. 'Sheik Naquib. Please excuse me for a moment.'

It wasn't a question, and within seconds, Maria had steered Lydia a few paces across the shiny floor. Next to a gigantic stone urn, spilling over with flowers, Maria bared her teeth before snapping. 'What?'

'Have you got it yet?'

'Got what?'

'Your invitation to the wedding of the year.'

'Of course.' Maria looked at Lydia as if she had lost her mind.

'What are we going to do?'

'We aren't going to do anything,' Maria said. She looked over her shoulder, checking on her client. 'I give it a year.'

'You think a divorce is less of a problem than a wedding? This could threaten the truce.'

'I really am very busy,' Maria said. 'This can wait for our next Family meeting.'

'That will be too late.'

Maria's gaze snapped to her. 'What do you suggest we do? They are adults and this is a free country.'

'I suggest we share information. What do you know about the bride to be?'

Maria checked on the sheik again before replying. 'Very little.' She didn't sound happy about it. 'Isn't investigation your area of expertise? Why don't you run along and put together a nice report. I'll be very happy to read it.'

'I don't work for you,' Lydia said. 'But we can pool resources. Have you heard anything else I should know about? Rumours?'

Maria waved a hand in dismissal. 'Don't start listening to gossip, you'll lose your mind.' She paused. 'Well, what's left of it.'

'Let me know if you hear anything. Share information. It's in both of our interests. Where has Scarlett sprung from for starters? You have powerful clients, yes?' Lydia laid on a bit of flattery. 'Knowledge and power go hand in hand.'

Maria flicked an invisible bit of fluff from her sleeve.

She spoke as if expecting to be recorded. 'I think it highly unlikely that I will be party to any kind of information pertaining to criminal or even immoral activity. However,' she met Lydia's gaze, 'I agree to share anything which corroborates your theory or pertains to the forthcoming Fox-Pearl wedding.' She bared her teeth again. 'Without compromising my good standing with those Families, of course. Officially, I am delighted for the happy couple.'

It wasn't much, but Lydia could recognise it was the most Maria was going to say. She thanked her for her time and left things on a cordial note. Smiling, smiling, smiling, while planning to bribe at least one member of the Silver Family. It was just like old times.

LYDIA WALKED DOWN CHEAPSIDE, HEADING FOR Blackfriars station. She was satisfied that Maria wasn't high on her list of suspects. She knew that the woman had a Silver tongue, but she was convinced that her gut would've picked up 'smug' vibes if Maria was keeping leverage as important as Ember. Besides, Maria wouldn't wait to make demands if that was the situation. Lydia hated to admit it, but it had been reassuring to experience 'business as usual' with the head of the Silver Family.

The clock that hung on the outside of St Mary-le-Bow reminded her that she had told Fleet she would let him know if she would be home for dinner. She pulled out her phone to call him when a blast of cold air hit her right side. Hours of training with Charlie had paid off, much as she would've hated to admit to her uncle, and she leapt to the left just as a piece of broken glass arced through the fabric of her loose hoodie. This was why her leather jacket was superior. Better protection against psychotic ghosts.

The spirit staring at her with a horrified expression was young, male, and almost completely transparent. The broken piece of glass that had nearly opened up her biceps clattered to the ground. His mouth opened as if he was trying to speak. The ghost was wearing a shirt and tie with some sort of knitted vest over the top and trousers that looked like they didn't fit very well. It was hard to tell much else in the bright sunshine, and Lydia's knowledge of fashion through the ages was sketchy at best. Her knowledge of ghosts was better, though. This one was barely a shimmer in the air and shouldn't have been able to hold an object, not as far as Lydia's experience told her. 'It's all right,' she said, 'I'm not going to hurt you.' Which was odd, considering he had attacked her.

The spirit was wide-eyed, staring at her in confusion. He opened his mouth as if trying to speak, then disappeared.

The pavement was fairly crowded and a couple of people had looked up from their phones when she leaped away from her attacker.

It probably looked like she had stood on the shard of glass that was now lying on the ground. She smiled reassuringly in their direction, and they returned their gazes to their phones, before moving off. Say what you like about our addiction to tech, but it did make it easier to move through the world without attracting attention.

Although Lydia realised she had spoken too soon. A young woman with blonde hair and a fuzzy purple monster dangling from her shoulder bag was staring in her direction. Not just at her, Lydia realised a second later, but at the fallen glass shard. And then around, as if scanning for something.

The blonde girl had moved closer to the steps of the church and was still staring. Her faced was creased in a frown, and her lips moved as if she was speaking to someone. Maybe on a phone that Lydia couldn't see.

'Are you okay?' Lydia was distracted by a light touch on her shoulder and a deep Scottish voice. A studenty-looking guy with a neat dark beard, brown skin, and kind eyes. 'Did you get stung by a wasp or something?'

That was an excellent explanation for jumping back and looking freaked out. 'No, thank goodness,' she said, channelling unthreatening and embarrassed. 'One was there,' she gestured vaguely. 'And I hate them so much.'

He smiled. 'Got to watch out for those stripy wee bastards.'

By the time he had moved on, the blonde girl had gone.

BACK AT THE HOUSE, LYDIA WAS SURPRISED TO FIND Fleet. She had already checked her arm and knew she wasn't hurt, but knew he wasn't going to react well to her shredded hoodie. 'You're home early,' she tried for deflection, but his gaze was on her arm. 'What happened?'

She filled him in on her ghostly attacker as quickly as possible, showing him the scratch on her arm. 'Barely got me. I'm fine.'

'Someone is coming after you.' He held up the ruined hoodie, his expression carefully calm. 'This could have been serious.'

'I'm fine. Any news about Ember?'

He shook his head. 'But someone sent him. I'm guessing whoever sent Mary after those men.'

'You think someone fired a ghost at me, like a bullet?'

'Unless you pissed off some guy back in Victorian times and forgot to mention you could time travel, it's the most likely explanation.'

'But why send a spirit with a broken bottle after me today? Just because I was on my own? It wasn't a very convincing attack. That spirit was weak.' Lydia shrugged. 'Not that I'm not grateful, but it wasn't exactly the same level as Mary.'

'Opportunity?' Fleet suggested. 'Maybe they just grabbed a chance because you were there alone? Or they're experimenting with the ghost control. It might not be perfectly accurate.'

There were a lot of possibilities. All of them involving someone wanting to hurt her. Fabulous.

Fleet hadn't finished. 'Or they were just looking to spook you. No pun intended.'

'Maybe this was an unrelated incident. Just an unhappy ghost that I happened to look at funny.'

'Ghosts don't usually attack people randomly—' Fleet broke off. 'Do they?'

Lydia wanted to say 'yes', to have this just be another fun side effect of living in London, but she wasn't going to lie to Fleet. 'No.' And there was something else. 'He was so thin,' she said. 'See-through, I mean. I'm not sure if he was all the time, it happened really fast, but I think he got thinner immediately after he sliced at me. Like he used up his energy doing that one thing. And when he disappeared, he looked like he was crying. Upset, not angry.'

It was still hot, and Lydia didn't feel hungry, but Fleet insisted on dinner. 'Don't bother,' she said when he went to put leftover lasagne in the microwave. 'I'll have mine cold.'

'Animal,' he said affectionately, and poured two red wines. 'For the shock,' he said, handing her a glass.

The wine helped with the faded adrenaline, and Lydia found she was ravenous once she started eating. They chatted about Fleet's day, the community trust-building events he had on his roster, the endless meetings that were sapping his soul, the forthcoming knife-amnesty, avoiding the topics of psychotic ghosts and their missing child.

While Fleet cleared up, Lydia went to talk to Jason. He was at the bottom of the garden, looking at the horn-beam that Lydia now thought of as 'Mary's tree'. It also made her think of her dream, so she greeted the crows that were sitting on the branches and asked Jason to come inside to talk.

She told him about the ghost attack, but not that the man had looked frightened.

'It's the NewRipper,' he said. 'Got to be.'

'We need a new name for him,' Lydia said. 'I don't like using the one he chose for himself. It's playing by his rules.'

Jason agreed. 'The GhostBotherer?'

'The PainInTheArse?'

'HomicidalIdiot99?'

They smiled at each other. Then Jason straightened up. 'I've been looking for signs of Ember, but he didn't use social media, and I haven't found mention of him on his classmates' socials. Seems like he kept himself to himself. I accessed the databases for his school and all people associated with it, but it didn't throw up anything obvious.'

'Obvious?'

'Parents on the sex offenders register,' Jason said flatly.

Hell Hawk. Lydia had been so focused on her own world, the danger she might have put Ember into by bringing him into her Family, that she hadn't thought of the other dangers in a child's life.

'Thank you for looking,' she patted his arm.

'I've looked into Scarlett, too, like you asked.'

'Great, thank you.'

He shook his head. 'There's nothing.'

'Nothing?'

'In modern terms, yes. No social media. And I haven't found her in any of the address, banking, NHS or credit check databases either. Next layer is HMRC and the police, but that's significantly trickier. And more illegal. You happy with that?' Jason wasn't asking whether Lydia was morally concerned, she knew, he was checking that she was happy to justify it to Fleet, should he find out. These days, she didn't think he would bat an eyelid.

'Do whatever it takes. She must have some kind of past. She didn't just blink into existence.'

The tailors on Savile Row was not the usual environment for Paul Fox but, somehow, despite his black eye, tattoos and air of coiled violence, he seemed to fit right in. Lydia flung herself into one of the high-backed velvet chairs and watched as Paul looked at himself in the mirror. He smoothed a hand over the front of the suit jacket. 'This one,' he said to the tailor.

'Very good, sir. I will bring the fabric samples, and you can choose the lining material.'

Paul frowned. 'I'll have this one.'

'Excellent choice,' the tailor continued, not missing a beat. 'May I pin the necessary adjustments now?'

While the tailor worked, Paul holding his arms out as instructed, he eyed Lydia in the mirror. 'I'll take cash.'

'What?'

'For a wedding gift.'

'Worried about keeping your new bride in the lifestyle she's accustomed to?'

Paul bared his teeth, and the tailor's hands faltered. 'Hardly.'

'This is all a bit new, though,' Lydia indicated the shop. 'Thought you would have bought local.'

'This is Scarlett's choice,' Paul said easily. 'What she wants, she gets.' His eyes met Lydia's in the mirror. 'For now, anyway.'

'You really want me there?' Lydia had been surprised to receive an invitation.

'Naturally. You and Maria must be there. I know how these things work. If you don't witness the ceremony, you won't believe it.'

He talked as if it was a business meeting.

'I won't insist you join in the celebrations after, but you'll be missing out.' He gave her a Fox smile, and heat rushed through her body.

'How did you two meet, anyway?' Lydia had plenty of practice at ignoring the Fox effect, but she knew she was blushing. It was annoying.

Paul didn't answer for a few minutes. The tailor finished pinning the suit, and she thought that Paul would head back into the changing room. She got up to leave, assuming that their meeting was over.

'Wait for me,' he said.

She sat back down. The tailor eyed her with a professional politeness that managed to feel like an insult. There was a glass decanter of amber liquid and some glasses on a wooden sideboard. 'May I?' Lydia said, pouring herself a generous measure without waiting for the reply. How much did suits cost if you got complimentary single malt? It was a different world to the one the Crows knew. She knocked back the drink and used the burn to refocus her mind. Seeing Paul Fox in a beautiful suit had made his wedding real. What did that mean for the Family?

When Paul emerged in his usual clothes, she felt a sense of relief. He had seemed like a different man in the suit. It was unnerving how much a change of outfit could alter a person. It was a kind of magic trick, and one she didn't understand.

The tailor led Paul to an array of ties and silk squares. He shook his head. 'Not for me.'

The tailor's eyes altered slightly, indicating concern. His skin was remarkably uncreased as if it was rarely folded. Lydia didn't know if he was just professionally expressionless or had been topping up with a bit too much Botox. 'It is usual for a wedding suit to—'

Paul shook his head. He had produced a folded banknote, and he transferred it to the man's hand. 'I'll send someone to pick up my suit on Monday.'

Outside, the sun was beating down on the pavements, and the smell of hot tarmac joined the usual London bouquet. They passed designer shops selling high fashion and Swiss watches. Liberty's wasn't far away, which made Lydia think of Emma, but Paul was leading her in a different direction. Before she could ask, he slanted a look at her. 'Hungry?'

Her stomach rumbled as if obeying Paul Fox. Worrying. 'I could eat.'

They were going to Chinatown, she realised. This was neutral territory for the Families, so there was no conflict, but her insides were knotted up nonetheless.

With the Qing dynasty-style gate and the strings of red paper lanterns crisscrossing the streets, it was clear when they had arrived. When Paul walked into a dim sum place and secured a table for two, Lydia realised the source of her discomfort. This felt disturbingly like a date. She and Paul Fox met in parks. They circled each other like the predators they were. They argued in meetings. They didn't go out for dim sum in buzzy little places with red napkins and chopsticks.

Still. She ordered a Tsingtao beer and waited. He would have a reason for this apparent friendliness, and she needed to find out what it was. That was part of her job. Handling the other heads of the Families. So why did she feel a creeping sense of guilt?

'What are we doing here?'

'Eating,' Paul said.

Lydia gave him a look and waited.

He put his beer down and leaned back, looking around the restaurant as if avoiding eye contact. 'We're being friendly.'

'We're friends now?' A sudden panic gripped her heart. Was he being nice because he'd found Ember's body?

'I said "friendly". Don't get carried away,' Paul was saying, but Lydia barely heard him through the rushing in her ears.

'What?' he said, frowning. Understanding dawned on his face, and when he spoke, his voice was gentle. 'I haven't got any news about your missing kid,' he said. 'Sorry.'

'Okay,' Lydia said, regrouping. She looked at the menu and realised that she was starving.

Once the waiter had taken their order and filled their water glasses, Paul put his elbows on the table. 'I did have something to ask you.'

'If you want me to be a flower girl, I'm going to have to decline.'

He smiled. 'Hilarious. Are the Crows intending to come to the wedding?'

Lydia put down her beer bottle. She wanted to produce her coin, to flip it over her knuckles for comfort, but knew that Paul would see it as an act of aggression. 'Of course,' she said. 'We're not going to risk the truce by insulting the Fox and the Pearl Families.'

Paul didn't move. He was looking directly into her eyes, and she felt the heat of his gaze. After a moment, he said mildly, 'It's important to Scarlett'.

Their food arrived, and there was a quiet moment while plates of won ton and spring rolls and chicken satay sticks were placed onto the table between them. Lydia tried to marshal her thoughts, and Paul didn't take his eyes off her. He thanked the waiter without looking at him, and then raised a single eyebrow. Spill it, the eyebrow said. He knew when she wanted to ask him a question.

'Not important to you?'

He shrugged. 'Not in the same way. Scarlett is very...' He paused, clearly searching for the right word. 'Fervent about our Families. She believes that we're superior.'

'She believes the Fox Family is superior to the Pearls, Silvers and Crows?'

'She's going to be my wife,' he said, as if that was an answer. 'But that's not what I meant. She believes all of the Families are superior. To ordinary people. That's why the big wedding is important to her, she wants it witnessed by people she respects. She wants to consolidate the truce. Bring us closer together.'

Lydia digested this. 'How do you feel about it?'

Paul shrugged. 'I'm more interested in whether you're going to make trouble.'

'I'm a little busy right now.'

Paul's eyes softened. 'Your missing kid.'

She nodded, a sudden lump in her throat.

'Are you going to give me any more information about that?'

'What sort of information?' Lydia wondered if this was Paul's true reason for taking her out, softening her up. The Fox could be looking for an angle he could work, a way to use her weakness against her.

'Details that will help me to look for him.'

'I don't know much,' Lydia said. She narrowed her eyes. 'And why are you being so helpful? Not that I'm not grateful, of course.'

'How grateful?' The leer was automatic, but no less effective.

'You're engaged to be married,' Lydia reminded the Fox.

Paul shrugged easily. 'The kid?'

'We saved his life. He doesn't have any family of his own. Now he's ours.'

'Okay,' Paul said. 'I approve.'

'Thank you,' Lydia said drily.

'It's nice to know that you don't leave kits to fend for themselves.'

'Crows aren't monsters,' she said, stung. 'Of course we don't abandon children.'

Walking away from Chinatown, Paul heading in the opposite direction back to Whitechapel, Lydia found herself studying the crowds, scanning for Ember's face. As if it would be that easy. The kid just popping up, as if nothing had happened. She wanted that to happen. She wanted him to have been playing a massive prank, or punishing her and Fleet for taking him away from his gran's flat, or any number of scenarios, as long as they ended with him alive and unharmed.

Thinking about Ember had her reversing direction. There was a massive comic book store on Shaftesbury Avenue. The chances of him happening to be there were slim-to-none, and she didn't actually know whether he liked superheroes and that kind of stuff, but it seemed a reasonable place to flash his picture, ask whether anybody had seen him.

The store was bright and busy, packed with figurines, costumes, backpacks, books and comics. She approached a member of staff in a black T-shirt with a slogan that probably meant something to a particular fandom, but was lost on Lydia. The young woman didn't recognise Ember's picture but, as she pointed out, gesturing helplessly at the vast numbers of browsers crowding the shop floor, 'I see a lot of faces.'

Lydia collared another three workers, leaving her card with her number. She felt deflated as she left and a little stupid for getting her hopes up. It wasn't going to be that simple.

Her phone buzzed as she walked up Shaftesbury Avenue toward the bus stop on St Giles High Street. It was an unknown number, and her heart leapt. Maybe one of the staff had remembered something. 'Hello?'

'Lydia Crow?'

The voice was female. Young-sounding and warm. 'Yep,' Lydia said. 'Speaking.'

'You don't know me, but I saw you experience something that you might have difficulty explaining. I can help fill in some blanks.'

Lydia started to ask what the woman was talking about, when it hit her. The ghost attack by St Mary-le-Bow. The blonde who she had caught staring. Lydia wasn't getting 'Family' over the phone, but she wasn't taking any chances. The stranger could be one of Scarlett's plays for dominance. Not to mention a Silver or Fox. As always, knowledge was power. 'I'm happy to talk,' Lydia said, 'but face-to-face.'

'Much better,' the woman agreed with suspicious alacrity. She named a restaurant. 'It's on neutral ground.'

Lydia was going to ask how she knew about neutral territory, but she decided to save it for the meeting. She was just about to ask the woman's name, but she had already hung up.

CHAPTER TEN

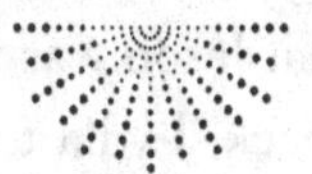

Lydia spotted the young woman as she walked past the restaurant. She was sitting outside, early for their meeting, which made Lydia think she was cautious or liked control. Or, she might just have liked to be respectful of other people's time. Lydia spent so much of her life trying to second-guess other people's motives and examining their behaviour, she was willing to admit it might have warped her a little bit.

Lydia breezed past the menu stand, waving away the member of staff in charge of seating. Her contact had wavy blonde hair and a heart-shaped face and was even younger-looking than Lydia remembered from her brief glimpse. Lydia assumed the woman was an adult, but she could have passed for sixteen. She was slurping on a bright blue slushie and scrolling on a phone, which was in a bedazzled candy pink case, which added to this impression. She jumped up when she saw Lydia and moved as if she was going to hug her. Lydia took an instinctive step back.

'Sorry, sorry. No touchie. Got it.' She smiled prettily, not looking especially regretful. 'I'm just very, you know, tactile. I'm Megan.'

'Right,' Lydia looked around the outdoor seating area. Megan was in Lydia's preferred position: in the corner, with her back to the fake-hedge that bordered the dining space. Glad that Jason was with her and he could keep an eye on her back, Lydia took the chair opposite the blonde who was noisily finishing her drink.

'You said on the phone that you had information.'

'Straight to it then,' Megan said. 'I guess you're super-busy. You seem very calm, though. Does that go with the territory?'

Lydia wasn't entirely sure what Megan meant by that. 'You rang my public number,' she said, playing for time, 'I assume you looked me up?'

'You're Lydia Crow. Investigator. But you're not asking me if I know that.'

She wasn't. Lydia was wondering whether Megan was familiar with the Families, whether the name Crow meant anything to her.

'I have heard of the Crows,' Megan continued. 'Of course.'

Lydia started to speak, but Megan barrelled on. She looked suddenly horrified. 'I'm not trying to, what's the word,' she snapped her fingers, 'ingratiate. I didn't call because you're a Crow.'

'Okay—'

'I'm going to tell you something, and I want you to take me seriously, even if it sounds a bit "out there". Can you do that for me?'

Lydia pressed her lips together to stop herself laughing out loud.

Megan leaned forward, an earnest expression on her heart-shaped face. 'That bit of flying glass that nearly tagged you on Cheapside? That was actually being held by a deceased person, a spirit.' She stared at Lydia intently, as if waiting for a response.

'Okay,' Lydia said.

'I'm being serious,' Megan said. 'Ghosts are real. There are loads of them in London, and I kind of look out for them. The one you met, Tom, has been acting up, and I was following him and then I saw him... do what he did. So I looked into you and—' she broke off, gesturing between them, 'here we are.'

A waiter appeared and did a double-take at Megan's slushie cup. 'You shouldn't be consuming food from outside.'

Megan smiled winningly at him. 'My bad.' She drained the dregs of the drink with a noisy slurp and then handed him the cup. 'I'd like an espresso. And a chocolate brownie. With ice cream. Do you have salted caramel? Can I have that instead of the vanilla, thanks.'

Lydia ordered a double-shot coffee from the visibly irritated server. Once he had moved away, she tried to steer the conversation. She had met people who had claimed to be able to see ghosts, but never one she had believed. It seemed as if Megan had truly seen the ghost attack her on the street, but Lydia was still wary. 'What do you want from me?'

Megan looked confused. 'You're just blowing past "ghosts are real"?'

'At great speed,' Lydia said. 'So, you are familiar with the ghost that attacked me? How familiar is that? Is he usually violent?'

'No!' Megan said. 'Tom wouldn't hurt a hamster.'

'I think the expression is "wouldn't hurt a fly".'

'I'm aware,' Megan said. 'And it's stupid. Tom would definitely swat a fly, but that doesn't make him a monster. Hamsters are a better gauge.'

'Fair enough.' Lydia tried to steer them back on track. 'So you don't know of any reason why he would suddenly try to stab me with some broken glass?'

'No. I wanted to ask you if he spoke to you.' Megan shook her head. 'I really thought it was going to be a bit trickier to get over the ghost bit. Do you have any idea why he attacked you?'

'I don't know him,' Lydia said. 'And I don't know why he went for me.' She wasn't going to tell a complete stranger that she had an ability to power spirits up.

'Okay.' Megan went quiet for a few seconds, clearly digesting this. 'Do you have questions for me? Don't know if I know stuff that you don't know. I'm guessing you already knew they exist. I thought you might be freaking out, might want an explanation, but that's clearly not the case. Hope I'm not wasting your time.' She frowned briefly as she spoke, as if genuinely concerned about this.

Megan's wall of words was wearing Lydia down. Her apparent openness and desire to help was impossible to resist. Even Lydia's cynicism was crumbling. To her surprise, she found herself speaking. 'There's a rumour that someone is controlling them. Manipulating their emotions to get them active.'

Megan absorbed this for a moment. 'When you say rumour, you mean it's your working theory? You've seen a ghost go violent before?'

Lydia glanced around instinctively. Their nearest neighbours were a couple of tables away, but Megan hadn't spoken quietly.

'It doesn't matter,' she said, noticing Lydia's discomfort. 'Nobody is listening. And if they are, they'll just think we're talking about a TV show.'

'People know I'm real,' Lydia said tightly.

'Some people do, fair play,' Megan agreed. 'But not as many as you think. No offence. It was a woman, right?'

Lydia tensed. 'How do you know that?'

'Just a guess,' Megan said.

'Explain.'

Megan sighed as if being asked whether the sky was blue. 'Fury is a biggie, right, in psychic power terms. But frustration, that's even bigger. And unfairness is way stronger than both of them. It, like, amplifies negativity. Turns it right up. That's not gender specific on its own, but in my experience the female spirits tend to have been treated in an unjust way during their lives, and that means the strongest ones I meet are usually women. You need a strong one to be popping around Whitechapel shanking men—'

The waiter arrived with their order, and Megan continued smoothly.

'... so that's season one. What about the arc for season two?'

Once the waiter had gone, they continued. Lydia didn't see any reason to withhold the details from Megan, so she didn't. 'You know the Ripper rip-off murders?'

Megan nodded, eyes wide.

'The killer died in the late Victorian period. Far as we could work out, she was murdered by her suitor. We believe it was a man who went on to kill many others, and was even suspected of being the Ripper for a time.'

'Suspected?'

'Not anymore. Discredited theory.'

'Plenty of those,' Megan said. 'People go mad for the Ripper, don't they? Weirdos.' She sampled her ice cream and then shovelled a forkful of brownie into her mouth. Her eyes closed, and she made a sound of pleasure. 'God, that's so good. You want to try?'

Lydia didn't know if this woman was the real deal or whether she was living in a fantasy world, but she was certainly a believer. And she was either an excellent actress, or she was completely sincere about wanting to help. 'Your turn. What have you heard?'

'Nothing much.' She licked her spoon. 'But I can ask around. For a fee.'

Lydia felt daft for not seeing that coming. 'You want money?'

'We've all got to make a living,' Megan said. She waved a spoon. 'Ice cream isn't free. And I'll tell you about my last conversation with Tom right now. As a bonus.'

Lydia weighed it up. 'How much?'

'A ton.'

'Hundred quid? You're laughing.'

Megan shrugged. 'Up to you.'

Lydia didn't like starting a relationship with a source with money. And she especially didn't like starting at a hundred. Prices always went up, that was a given, and in her experience, they tended to go up fast. But there was a chance that Megan might be telling the truth about her contact with 'Tom the ghost'. And she needed to find the NewRipper fast, ideally before they sent another homicidal ghost to attack her.

Her back went cold, signalling that Jason had moved close. She turned slightly to confirm it was him, while making the movement look natural. She feigned looking around the dining area, as if trying to locate the waiter.

'All quiet,' Jason said. 'I think she came alone.'

Megan's head cocked, as if she was listening. Before Lydia could work out whether that was a coincidence, she looked directly at Jason and then at Lydia. 'So he's with you, then? I did wonder.'

CHAPTER ELEVEN

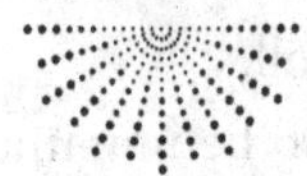

I t took Lydia a second to regroup. Megan might have looked like a children's TV presenter, but she was the real deal. 'You're not Family.' She hadn't got any sort of gleam from Megan. Or sensed any of the four Families.

'Nah. I wasn't born this way.' Megan ran a finger around her plate, collecting the last dregs of melted ice cream and brownie crumbs. 'I nearly drowned when I was six. When I woke up, I could see them.'

'And talk to them?'

Megan flicked her gaze to Jason, who had gone stock still next to Lydia. He was watching Megan with a hungry expression. Lydia realised that this was the second alive person to see him, really properly see him, since he had died.

'Nice suit,' she said. 'Retro.'

'I died in 1985,' Jason said.

'You look good for your age.'

Wait. Was Megan *flirting* with Jason? He was

standing a little straighter. Lydia tried to get things back on track. 'You'll ask around. Find out if anyone knows anything. Call me first. Here's my card.'

'Payment up front,' Megan said. She held her phone out. 'I take Apple Pay.'

Lydia gazed at her for a beat, using the dead-eye stare that worked so well.

Megan appeared to be immune. She dug in her bag and produced a flat white box. 'Or you can use a card. I sell jewellery. One of my side hustles. Card reader comes in handy for all sorts, though.'

'You think I'm stupid?'

'Where am I going to go with your cash? You think I'm going to stiff Lydia Crow? I'm not an idiot.'

Mollified, but also aware that Megan was saying exactly what she knew she wanted to hear, Lydia checked the amount on the phone screen and then tapped her card to the screen. 'Your info had better be stellar.'

Megan checked her phone. 'I'll email a receipt.'

'You said you were going to tell me about Tom.'

Megan turned serious. 'He hadn't been around for my last couple of visits. I do the rounds, check on them all regularly.'

There was more Lydia wanted to ask about that, but now was not the time. 'He's been disappearing?' She didn't look at Jason, but could feel his attention sharpening.

'I don't know,' Megan said, frowning. 'He wasn't making a lot of sense when we spoke. He seemed thinner than usual. More see-through, you know? And he was really upset.'

'About anything in particular?' Lydia asked, at the same time as Jason said: 'Where did he go?'

Megan glanced between them. 'He said he had been somewhere dark. And that it smelled really bad. It reminded him of the way the river used to be. He said there were candles and a pretty brooch.'

'A brooch?'

'No.' Megan shook her head, correcting herself. 'He didn't say brooch. He said cameo. I looked it up, and they're this old sort of jewellery. Usually made into brooches, which you definitely don't see these days. I wonder why that is? Just fashion, I suppose. And now people go for pin badges instead. I love a good pin badge.'

'Anything else?' Lydia said quickly, hoping to stem the tide of Megan's ocean of random thoughts.

'Like I said, he was pretty thin, and we didn't talk for long. Thanks for the brownie,' Megan said, slipping her phone into her pocket and getting up. 'Lovely to meet you both. I'll be in touch.'

BACK AT THE HOUSE, JASON MADE A BEELINE FOR HIS preferred spot on the sofa and opened his laptop. Lydia did a quick walkthrough of the house, in the hope that Ember would just be chilling out in his room. She would give anything for him to look up at her with a 'what's your prob-lem' expression. Once she had confirmed that he hadn't come home, she pushed down the rising panic. She felt like she was choking, but she forced a few deep breaths before heading back to the living room to find Jason. She would be no good to anyone if she couldn't function.

'He's not back?' Jason said, seeing her expression.

The urge to cry was back, and her throat closed up. She fought for control and Jason silently handed her an unopened can of Coke. 'I'm sorry,' he said.

She shook her head, still unable to speak.

'He's been living on his own for a year, right?'

She knew Jason was trying to be reassuring. It wasn't his fault that she wanted to scream. She popped the tab on the can and sat behind her desk. 'What did you think of her?'

Jason accepted the change of subject. 'Megan? She could see me. For real.'

'Are you looking her up?'

He shook his head. 'That would be rude.'

'Okay.'

He frowned. 'You want me to?'

Lydia thought about it for a second. 'No. I think I'll trust her.'

He nodded.

'At least until she gives me a reason not to,' she amended, realising how sappy she sounded.

Jason grinned. 'She was pretty likeable.'

'Shut up.' Lydia glowered at Jason, which only encouraged him. 'What are you doing then?'

'Cameos,' Jason said, fingers tapping as he spoke.

Lydia thought about doing her own research, but she knew Jason was better at it. So she took a swig from her can and closed her eyes for some thinking time. She tried to bring the ghost, Tom, into her mind. He had tried to speak, she could see his mouth opening, forming words, but she hadn't heard anything. Had he been silent, or had the London noise drowned him out?

'I actually don't feel so good,' Jason said, breaking into her thoughts. He closed his eyes. 'Maybe I overdid it today.'

'You need to rest?'

Jason didn't need sleep, but she assumed he felt tired at times. She had never thought to ask.

'I don't know. I'm going out for some fresh air.'

He left the room and Lydia had time to feel relieved that he hadn't just disappeared, when Fleet returned. He had rolled up his shirt-sleeves and there was a sheen of sweat on his face, showing that he had walked fast from the station. She didn't have a chance to tell him about her concerns for Jason or the news that there was another bona fide ghost-whisperer in London. And that she was possibly the perkiest person Lydia had ever met. Fleet had news of his own. 'Look.' He handed her a piece of white paper, the size of a Post-It note. There was a string of numbers written in the middle in black pen.

'Where did you find it?'

'In my pocket. Someone must have slipped it in during the amnesty.'

'You didn't notice?'

Fleet shook his head, clearly annoyed by that fact. 'It was busy. Lots of people.'

'Lots of knives?' Lydia asked. She was trying to make

him feel better about not noticing somebody getting close enough to put something in his pocket. There had been distractions.

'That too,' he smiled briefly. 'But the community also turned out to talk. To ask what we're doing about the criminals who have no intention of volunteering their weapons.'

'That's fair.'

He acknowledged her point with a lift of his chin. 'And to talk about the bin collections, the graffiti, littering, neighbour disputes, noise pollution—'

'I get the picture.' She squinted at the numbers on the paper. 'It could be a mobile number minus the zero.'

Fleet was already shaking his head. 'Tried it.'

'Map coordinates?'

'That's my guess. There are too many numbers, though.'

'If it's directing you to a place, maybe the other numbers are just the date.' She felt a choking sensation and the urge to spread her wings. 'Is this about Ember?' She wanted to say 'ransom note' but couldn't bring herself to voice the words.

Fleet was still, thinking. 'No. Too cryptic. A kidnapper would have no reason to obfuscate. Ransom demands are clear and to the point.'

Lydia wanted to be comforted, but if the NewRipper was playing with them, all bets were off.

They sat in the sticky heat of the kitchen with the glass doors open, drinking cold beers and puzzling. There were ten numbers. 'X and Y coordinates are twelve numbers, longitude and latitude sixteen.'

Lydia was on her phone. 'The UK Ordnance Survey grid reference number is nine. With a couple of letters. There's a six-number version, though.'

After twenty minutes and the rest of their beers, they agreed that the most likely meaning was a grid reference that pointed to Russell Square in Bloomsbury. The remaining numbers were unlikely to be a date, so they went with seven in the evening.

'Tonight then.' Fleet looked at his watch. 'Fancy a trip across the river?'

RUSSELL SQUARE SAT CLOSE TO THE BRITISH Museum, and the area around the impressive Greek-revival edifice was thronged with people. The museum had closed an hour earlier, but the nearby pubs and coffee shops had people spilling out onto the pavement, and there were still parties of tourists with brightly coloured sunhats being shepherded by guides working overtime. There was a fountain in the middle of the park and several benches. Not knowing who they were looking for, Lydia and Fleet split the area into a grid and took it methodically. 'What if it's not a person?' Lydia asked after they were halfway through, with nobody running up to introduce themselves.

'Could be a dead drop,' Fleet said. 'We can go back through, checking the bins, under the benches, around the trees.'

'Lovely.' Lydia had been momentarily distracted by a man in a bright blue T-shirt, who appeared to be paying them attention, but then she realised he was just checking Fleet out. And who could blame him?

'It might be you,' Fleet was saying. 'Whoever it is, they're just expecting me. We should split up.'

That made sense. If the contact was skittish, they might wait until Fleet was alone. Or, Lydia looked around at the busy pathway and the people lazing on the grass, they could have already bolted. The crowd ahead shifted, and her gaze snagged on a bench. There was a lone man sitting on it. He looked different to most of the people enjoying the park in the summer evening. He was elderly, for a start, and wearing more clothes. A jacket over something knitted, either a jumper or vest, and a tie. And a flat cap. If it hadn't been so obviously well worn, it might have looked like a costume. Lydia nudged Fleet and dipped her chin.

Lydia hung back and let Fleet approach the bench from the front. As Fleet sat down, she circled around the back to the other side of the man. If he tried to run, she would tackle him. Very gently, of course. She didn't want to break his hip.

The man's hair was white, and his head was tilted down, as if he was studying something in his lap. The folded newspaper, perhaps.

'Oh shit,' Fleet said.

'What?' Lydia abandoned her post. From the front, she could see instantly that something was wrong. The man was very still. Too still. The peak of his cap was obscuring his forehead and eyes, but she bent down and got a look. Eyelids drooping over pale blue irises, filmed over and very obviously dead.

Fleet was feeling for a pulse. He shook his head.

Lydia was already patting him down, checking pockets. She found his wallet and flipped it open. Sixty pounds in cash, debit and credit cards in the name Magnus Henriksen, plus a staff ID card for University College London. 'Not a robbery,' she said, replacing the wallet. In his jacket pocket, she found a phone. An old model with a crack across the screen and scuffs on the case. She looked at Fleet, who had his phone in his hand. He appeared to be hesitating. 'What is it?'

'I should call this in,' he said, but didn't move.

After a beat, when Fleet still hadn't moved, she asked: 'You're not calling it in?' Any moment, somebody else was going to notice that the man was deceased. And that Lydia had just rifled through his pockets.

He looked unhappy. 'I can wait for you to leave, and then it's just on me, you won't be involved, but I don't know...'

Lydia was itching to move, to do something. There was a dead man sitting in front of them, and they were just standing there. It was unlike Fleet to be indecisive. She realised she was still holding the man's phone. She put it into her own pocket to examine later.

He spoke quietly. 'I have a very bad feeling about this. I was directed here. What if I'm considered a suspect?'

Lydia was shocked, but she didn't have time to react.

He took her arm and they walked away from the body. 'You have CIs?'

'What?' She was still trying to process Fleet's words. He was a copper. He had never worried about coming under suspicion before. Things were worse at his work than she had realised.

'People you use for surveillance. Information?'

'Yes.'

'People who aren't Crows.'

'Yes,' she said again. 'Why?'

'Can you get one of them to call in an anonymous tip?'

They had reached the park exit. 'You're serious. You're really not going to call it in?'

'I don't trust the Met,' Fleet said after a moment. 'Not entirely. Not when it comes to myself.'

This was huge. Fleet had always trusted the system. In the past, he had bent rules to keep her safe or to give her investigative leeway, but he had never stepped outside the legalities altogether. 'I think I might have been a bad influence,' she said lightly.

CHAPTER TWELVE

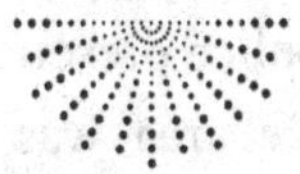

Back at the house, Lydia slipped Henriksen's phone to Jason. 'It's locked with a PIN number. Don't know if you can get into it?'

Jason looked at the device with interest. 'It's not a new model, so there's a good chance tech isn't high priority. Hopefully that means he's lazy with his security. I've got access to lists of most-used PINs.'

'That's terrifying,' Lydia said. 'And useful.'

Jason made finger guns. 'Bang on.'

Lydia wasn't sure how Fleet would react to her taking Henriksen's phone. She had compromised a possible crime scene, but then he hadn't called in the death directly. The next morning, he surprised her again.

'Magnus Henriksen was an associate professor in Scandinavian Studies at UCL. If we go now,' Fleet said, 'we might get into his office first. The body would have been identified straight away, but they would speak to his next of kin first. It's not my section, but we're all stretched. I'd be surprised if they've assigned a visit to his work already. It might not even be on the action list.'

Lydia and Fleet arrived at the department building before nine. There were plenty of staff and students about, but no sign of police presence.

The administrative area was on the second floor. Notice boards lined the corridor, and there was a list of office hours on the door, as well as staff names. Fleet flashed his warrant card and separated off one of the admin staff to show them Magnus Henriksen's office. A middle-aged woman called Susan Osano, who wore red-framed glasses and had the frighteningly efficient manner of all office administrators.

'Am I allowed to ask what this is about?'

Fleet and Lydia moved the woman away from the open door to the office.

Fleet said quietly. 'This information hasn't been officially released, not until we have located his family, but I'm sorry to tell you that Mr Henriksen is dead.'

'Oh my goodness,' Osano said, putting a hand onto her ample chest.

'You need to keep this information to yourself for now,' Lydia said.

'Of course,' Osano said quickly. She glanced back at the office door and Lydia wondered whether their visit would be the subject of departmental gossip before lunchtime.

Forestalling questions about the nature of the death, Fleet explained that he couldn't give further details but that there was an active investigation. 'We need to see Mr Henriksen's office as a matter of urgency.'

On the short walk there, they found out that Henriksen had a grown-up daughter who lived in Florida with her husband and three kids and a brother who was in a care home in Brighton. 'Vascular dementia,' Osano explained. 'Very sad.'

'Was he in a relationship with anyone?' Fleet asked.

The woman shook her head sadly. 'I wouldn't think so. He practically lived here.'

'Did you like him?' Lydia asked.

She coloured. 'Not in that way. But he was always polite.' She glanced down the corridor as if expecting someone to be listening. 'Not all of them are.'

'Thank you for your help,' Fleet said, after she had unlocked the office door. 'We'll take it from here.'

'Right.' She hesitated. 'Would you like tea?'

Fleet smiled at her, his easy charm smoothing the situation as always. 'That would be great, thank you. Just milk for me.'

'And me,' Lydia said. 'Thanks.'

Once the woman had moved away, Lydia opened the door. If she had been asked what she expected of an academic's office in the university, she would have included rather more wood-panelling and bookcases, but the piles of books of all sizes and ages, filing cabinets, and musty smell of paper and pipe smoke were all spot-on. The latter had to be pretty strong to have lasted past the smoking ban, unless Henriksen was a rebel who lit up behind his closed door.

Fleet moved to the desk and began searching

through the piles of papers. There were academic journals, letters, student assessment forms, and large-size art
books, as well as chunky tomes on Old Norse, Scandinavian Romanticism and 'Sociolinguistic Modalities in the
Modern Nordic Region' whatever that might be.

On the corner of the desk, there was a desk diary
perched on a surprisingly up-to-date laptop. Lydia
flipped open the diary to the last couple of weeks. It was
sparsely filled in the tight sloping handwriting that she
already recognised as Henriksen's. Faculty meetings, a
Zoom with a professor in Bergen, and a lunch with 'P'
which had then been crossed out.

Fleet finished with the papers on top of the desk and
began opening drawers.

'Will you get into trouble for this?'

'Probably. But I don't care,' Fleet said, pulling A4
paper and notebooks and copious pencils from the desk
drawers. 'This was a message for me.'

It was such a non-Fleet sentiment that Lydia
stopped looking through the filing cabinet and gave him
her full attention.

'He wanted to speak to me and now he's dead,' Fleet
said, flipping through the stack of blank paper. 'Whatever he had to say or show me made it worth murdering
him.'

'We don't even know the cause of death, it might
have been natural. Just a coincidence.'

Fleet didn't dignify that with a response. 'Look,' he
said, holding up a printed catalogue from the British
Museum. 'Close to the meeting place.'

'He's a professor, working in this area of London. It

would be weird if he didn't visit the British Museum on the regular.'

He acknowledged the point.

'I know you feel responsible,' she tried. 'You shouldn't.'

Fleet didn't respond. He opened another drawer and pulled out a sheaf of file folders.

Lydia closed the cabinet and started with the stacks of books.

They worked in silence for a little while, but then Fleet stopped. 'It's not that exactly...' He put his hands on his hips and stared into the distance for a moment, clearly trying to organise his thoughts. 'I'm angry. And I want to know what he was going to tell me. And I feel guilty that both those impulses are bigger than feeling bad for the man. I know it's compartmentalising and essential for my job, but--' He broke off, seeing that Lydia was distracted. 'What?'

Lydia was looking at the topmost book in the second teetering pile. She had been flipping through the pages until something made her stop. A reproduction of a painting that made her skin go cold. 'What if Henriksen didn't have a message for you?'

'He did. He wanted to meet me.'

She angled the full-page illustration so that Fleet could see it. 'What if he was the message?'

At that moment, the door opened and the office administrator came in with two mugs of tea. 'I'll just put these here. Let me know if you need anything else...'

Fleet thanked the woman. She hovered as if suddenly unsure about leaving them alone in the office.

'I know you can't tell me anything,' she said, 'but was he in some kind of trouble?'

Lydia wanted to say 'clearly, he's dead', but luckily Fleet was doing the talking. He explained that Henriksen's death was unexpected and so it had sparked an investigation. 'We're obliged to investigate all sudden deaths, but there's no cause for alarm. It's routine. There is every chance that we won't find evidence of foul play, but it's important to be certain. You understand, I'm sure.'

Osano frowned. 'There will be gossip flying around. You know what universities are like.'

'What do you think people will say?' Fleet asked, smiling as if he wasn't being entirely serious. 'Was he well-liked? Any big academic spats we should know about?'

'I don't agree with the gossip. A man has died, it doesn't feel right to speak about him.'

'Ah, but I'm police,' Fleet said, 'and I'm asking. It's not prurient curiosity, it's my job.'

She straightened. 'Of course. In that case...' She shot a glance at the half-closed door, as if expecting someone to barge in. 'Some of Professor Henriksen's academic colleagues were getting a little frustrated with him of late. Nothing serious, you understand? Nothing...' She trailed off, but Lydia heard the unspoken words 'nothing that would suggest they were considering killing him'.

'What kind of frustrations?'

'He had been a little negligent with his teaching responsibilities, I know there was some friction with the department head over that.'

'And?' Fleet prodded.

'I believe that his field of study was drawing some criticism. But I don't know any more than that. He was always polite to me. A gentleman.'

ON THEIR WAY BACK TO DENMARK HILL, LYDIA HAD tried to put the picture from the book out of her mind. She had failed. The raven's feathers had been dull and dusty, with the suggestion of something decaying underneath. The hole where the raven's eye ought to have been had been impossibly black and Lydia had felt herself tipping forward as she looked into it. Superstition. Old stories, told in childhood, coming back to haunt her adult self. There would be reasonable psychological explanations for the effect the image had on her. Reasonable, sane explanations.

'If the murder is a message for you, it's not very clear,' Fleet said, clearly also unable to stop thinking about Henriksen. 'Is the professor significant or is it just meant to direct you to look at your history?'

'Not my history,' Lydia said sharply. 'I am not my Family.' She felt feathers in her throat. 'Not entirely,' she amended.

JASON WAS STILL WORKING ON OPENING Henriksen's phone, so Lydia put off telling Fleet about it. There was no point in making him complicit in the crime until it had given them something useful. If Jason couldn't unlock it, she would deliver it anonymously to the Met. No harm done.

Fleet bolted some food and a large coffee. He had to go into work that afternoon and was clearly not relishing the prospect, cursing loudly when he dropped some food onto his shirt.

Lydia wanted to talk to him or, at least, to give him a chance to air his feelings. But he was buttoning up a new shirt with an air of unhappy determination.

'Are you okay?' she ventured. She knew he had got sick of that particular question when he was struggling with his visions, but this felt different. He was fizzing with energy and a simmering frustration.

'Let's see if I've still got a job,' he said with false cheerfulness, heading out of the door at a smart clip. He promised to keep in touch if there was any news on the Henriksen case, but warned her that he might be stuck in meetings for the rest of the day. 'Or a cell. If they find out about our unauthorised trip to the university.'

'Don't joke about that,' Lydia said.

Fleet flashed a grim smile. 'Who says I'm joking?'

Lydia spent the rest of the day checking in with the team watching Ember's flat, roaming the streets on the off-chance that she might see him, and speaking to what felt like every single resident of Camberwell to see if he had been spotted. Ember had been missing for four nights, now, and even though he had been living alone for a year, she knew that had been different. Had he fled London? Was he living on the streets in another city? Had he been taken?

With nothing to show for her searching, except for a stomach that was sore from too many bad cups of coffee and a yawning hole in the middle of her chest, she rang Emma to give her the bad news.

'I know you don't want to involve the authorities, but—'

'I know, I know,' Lydia said. 'If I thought it would help, I would have done it already. If he doesn't come back tonight, I'll think about it.'

'I'm sorry,' Emma said, the sympathy in her voice making Lydia's throat close up. 'He may well be staying with a friend. Playing video games somewhere while you worry.'

'I hope so,' Lydia said with feeling.

After talking to Emma, Lydia felt as if she was drowning. She wanted to believe that Ember was safely holed up with a pal, maybe even laughing at her and Fleet. She had been trying to take comfort from Fleet's lack of visions. If Ember was in danger, wouldn't he see it? Like he had before?

The fear was seeping into every part of her body and brain and she could feel herself freezing in place. You stop, you die. Crows kept moving.

Instead of going back to the house, she headed to Burgess Park to outrun her feelings. A solid plan.

It usually helped to clear her head, but today her tangled thoughts refused to sort themselves into neat piles and she felt just as jumbled as when she had set out. Glimpsing Scarlett ahead of her in the park wasn't exactly a welcome surprise.

She slowed before reaching Scarlett, making sure her breathing was under control before she arrived in front of the immaculately-made-up woman. Scarlett looked like she had stepped off a red carpet, making Lydia feel even sweatier and more scruffy than usual. She pulled at the jersey shorts that were stuck to her thighs, and pushed her damp hair off her forehead.

'You waiting for me? Or is this just a weird coincidence?'

Scarlett bared her teeth. 'You think I would come to Camberwell just for fun?'

'It's Crow territory,' Lydia put a flat authority into her voice, ruined slightly by her sweaty hair falling back into her eyes. 'You need a reason.'

'I heard that Paul was in the area and I wanted to find out why. Are you meeting him?'

'No,' Lydia said truthfully. 'At least as far as I know. Sometimes he turns up. Usually when he wants something.' She didn't bother to elaborate that she meant that in a purely professional sense. She was being childish and couldn't find it in herself to care. There was an entitled air to Scarlett, an expectation that everyone would fall in line. It ruffled Lydia's feathers the wrong way.

'I know who you are,' Scarlett said. Her gaze raked over Lydia's face like claws.

Lydia was fascinated. Scarlett's entire demeanour had changed. She was still alluring, of course, but it was the shiny distraction of a predator. 'That's good. You don't have a concussion.'

A sour face. 'You destroyed the court.'

'What makes you think that?' Say nothing. Admit nothing. Wait for more information.

'Ellie told me.'

The little girl with tangled blonde hair and multiple strands of colourful jewellery around her neck and thin wrists stepped out from behind the large oak tree. Lydia fought the urge to fly. She ought to have known better than to talk to a Pearl anywhere near greenery. Last time they had been annoyed with her, they had ripped tree roots from deep underground and tried to bury her in churning, choking earth.

'Hi Ellie,' she said, shooting for calm. Unconcerned. 'Still like your bling I see.'

Lydia didn't know much about kids, but she knew they changed a lot over a short space of time. Ellie ought to be taller, older-looking, but she looked exactly the same.

'You killed my family.' Scarlett's voice was harsh. The sun was dappled through the leaves of the tree and the shadows made her face look suddenly older. 'My ancestors. You destroyed our kingdom.'

'It wasn't all that,' Lydia said. She was hyperaware of the trees, the ground. If she felt a tremor, she was going to start running. Not for the first time, she wished she could fly. 'Trust me, you are better off up here. In your lovely hotel suite.'

'You killed them. My ancestors, my heritage.'

'You didn't even know them. And now you're the all-powerful head of the Pearl family,' Lydia said. 'You're not exactly hurting, so don't come at me.'

'You took everything from me, from my family. And now I'm going to take everything from you.'

Paul loped across the grass and Scarlett shifted in front of Lydia's eyes. She softened, reached out a hand to pat Lydia's arm, as if they were having a friendly chat.

He nodded to Ellie as if he had met her before.

Lydia had been so focused on Scarlett and whether the ground beneath her feet was shifting, that she hadn't noticed, but the tree was full of crows. They had sensed that something unfriendly was going down and were lined up, watching over her. Paul glanced up at the cawing birds filling the branches and frowned. 'You expecting trouble?'

'Always,' Lydia said.

Scarlett turned a bright smile onto Paul. 'We were just getting to know each other.'

Paul smiled and kissed her cheek, but there was a wariness in his stance. 'What are you doing in Camberwell?'

'Getting to know Lydia,' Scarlett said smoothly. 'Paying my respects. I'm visiting Maria Silver next. I know I'm the new girl and I thought it would be political to play nicely. It's a surprise to see you on this side of the river.'

'Missing person case,' Paul said easily. 'I offered to help.'

'That was very neighbourly of you,' Scarlett said, approval thick in her voice. But Lydia could hear the lie buried in her words. 'I assume the truce encourages cooperation.'

'The truce encourages us not to destroy each other,'

Lydia said. 'And not to trespass on each other's territory without invitation or good reason.' She stared at Scarlett in open challenge.

'Can I speak with you for a moment.' Paul had hold of Lydia's arm and was towing her away.

'What?' Lydia said, staring at his hand on her upper arm until he let go.

'No word on your kid. I'm sorry.'

Lydia's antagonism rushed out of her and she felt like she wanted to sit on the grass. 'Thank you for trying. And for letting me know.'

He nodded. 'In return, perhaps you can refrain from scratching at my fiancé.'

'I don't scratch,' Lydia said.

'Darling,' Scarlett said, her voice as beautiful as the rest of her. 'Can we go for food? All this making nice has made me hungry.'

Paul flashed Scarlett a charming smile. 'I know the perfect place.'

'Out of Camberwell, I hope,' Lydia muttered.

Paul didn't bother to answer. He joined Scarlett and they walked away, his arm slung across her shoulders in a possessive gesture. Ellie trailed behind them, looking like their sullen kid. One little happy family. Two ancient powerful Families. Another problem for Lydia to worry about.

CHAPTER THIRTEEN

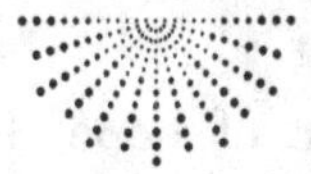

Lydia checked in on Jason's progress with Henriksen's phone, but he shooed her away. And then she spent a little time going through the list of requests from Family members and locals that Aiden had left on her desk. It was hard to focus and there was a pulsing pain in her temples. She kept having to push away images of Ember hurt, lost and frightened, but she couldn't stop herself from picturing his thin frame and the delicate bones of his face. He was so young. Too young to be out of the nest.

Fleet was late in from work and she met him in the kitchen. He looked exhausted and she realised that this had become his default post-work state. He had been so energised and purposeful when they had first met and the change was stark. Of course, he was also worrying about their lost nestling.

'Long day?' Lydia opened the fridge and took out a couple of beers.

'The usual soul-sapping meetings,' Fleet said.

'At least you haven't been arrested for Henriksen.'

They clinked bottles.

Fleet held his beer loosely, not drinking. 'I wasn't in work.'

His expression was sad and Lydia's mind jumped immediately to their missing child. Before she could ask, he said: 'It's not Ember.'

The small bubble of hope she had been nursing popped, leaving an empty hollow in her stomach. 'Where were you?'

'I went to Ember's school and spoke to the other parents, just in case we'd missed a friendship or some other lead. I visited Auntie. You said she'd looked tired when you picked Ember up.'

'She okay?' Lydia was feeling her way through the conversation.

'She's fine,' he said. 'Sorry I said I was going into work. I just wasn't ready to talk about it.'

Lydia waited.

'I've got lots of holiday days.'

'Okay.'

'I got told to take them. The impression I got was that they believe I need a rest and that some time off will benefit my mental health.'

Lydia could imagine how that felt. 'I'm sorry.'

'They had HR in the meeting, so I knew something was up. It's just another step on the path to letting me go.'

'They can't do that, can they?'

He shrugged. 'The worst thing is, I'm not sure I even care.' He took a long drink.

Lydia put hers down, wondering what to say.

'It's fine,' he said. 'I'm fine. Anyway, I did manage to speak to a friend who works the Camden area. She said Henriksen's death hasn't been flagged high priority.' He ticked things off on his fingers. 'No sign of a struggle at the scene. No obvious injuries. Cash left in his wallet.'

'Have we been mentioned?' Lydia imagined a helpful passerby telling the cops that she had nicked a phone from the corpse.

'All clear so far,' Fleet said.

'I've had a thought.' Lydia wanted to say it quickly, like ripping off a plaster. 'What if Ember going missing is part of the game?'

Fleet frowned. 'That seems—'

'The timing,' Lydia ploughed on.

'Who knows about him, though?'

'If they've been watching us, they could have seen him.' Cold fear washed through her body. Ember could be lying dead somewhere. A playing piece used and broken, just to mess with her. She couldn't say it out loud, but knew Fleet was following the same line of thought by the tightening of his mouth, the bleak look that shaded behind his eyes.

He reached out and took her hand. 'We'll find him.'

She stepped into his arms and pressed her face into his chest, eyes tightly shut. Count of five, she told herself. She could fall apart for the count of five, then she had to get her shit together.

Wiping her eyes and picking up her beer, Lydia forced her mind back to Henriksen. If she was right, and Ember going missing was connected to the NewRipper, then he was a solid lead. She pictured the man on the bench, his head bent to his chest. 'We must have got there soon after he died. If we'd been earlier, we could have stopped it.'

Fleet shook his head. 'Unlikely. Post-mortem isn't back yet, but my colleague said it looked like a heart attack. It was quick at least.'

'No puncture wounds?' Lydia was thinking of a syringe carrying an undetectable toxin. Or a bubble of air. A list of ways to assassinate a person scrolled through her mind, like a cursed Instagram feed. 'It would have to be subtle. It was a crowded place.'

'You would think someone must have seen something,' Fleet agreed. 'But Henriksen was old. That makes him pretty invisible.'

'Much like our suspected killer.'

'Ghost?' Fleet said. 'Mary's definitely gone, right?'

'Definitely,' Lydia remembered the expression on her face. The faint scent of lilacs in the hotel room and the sense of emptiness, where before there had been crackling energy.

'This isn't her MO, anyway.' Fleet stretched his arms above his head and twisted. His spine cracked. 'Or the MO of the guy that attacked you. They both—' He made a slashing gesture with his arm.

'Cardiac arrest,' Lydia said, thinking out loud. 'Had to be very quick. No time for clutching his chest or anything. He didn't even keel over.' Henriksen had been seated, head bent down and spine hunched, but in a position that was easy to mistake for a man at rest. 'I need to speak to Jason.'

'Maybe it really was a heart attack,' Fleet said. 'A natural one, I mean.'

As if summoned by her words, Jason walked into the kitchen, Henriksen's phone in his hand. 'I did it.'

For a split second, Lydia thought that Jason meant he had murdered Henriksen. Then her brain caught up, and she realised that Jason was flushed with triumph. He waved the phone. 'Buckle up, kids. The professor was into some weird shit.'

'Is that a phone?'

Lydia looked at Fleet, wondering if he was going to be angry that she had stolen a dead man's phone from a possible crime scene. Of course, from his point of view, he was just watching the device float into the room, and he seemed to be taking it very calmly.

'Henriksen's,' she said. 'I took it.'

He just raised his beer bottle. 'Good idea.'

'Once I'd cracked his PIN,' Jason said, 'it wasn't even a challenge. It's like the man wants to be caught.'

'Caught?'

'His work email is filled with complaints. Sounds like he was going off the rails.'

'What does that mean? Aren't academics supposed to be quirky?'

'He had been missing student advisory meetings, was late with marking, stuff like that. And there were a couple of snooty rejections for papers he submitted to journals and conferences. A rejected research proposal from a grant funding body, stuff like that.'

Lydia leaned against the kitchen units and caught Fleet's eye. 'Career not going so great, got it.'

'And there's this,' Jason peered at the screen to read out an email from one of Henriksen's colleagues at the School of Scandinavian Studies. The sentences were convoluted and filled with unnecessarily long words, making Lydia doubly glad she had never attempted university, but the gist was clear: he was worried about Henriksen. 'The school feels that your focus on the traditional folklore has become diluted by your interest in the current mythology surrounding the Crows of Camberwell. This diaspora, while of tangential relevance, is not a suitable research area for the school, and if you persist, I am seriously concerned that it will affect your prospects. I hope this isn't too blunt, as I am writing as your friend as well as your colleague.'

'Why set up a meeting with me?' Fleet asked, once Lydia had repeated the gist. 'He was clearly more interested in you.'

'That's not the best bit,' Jason said, tapping and swiping like a man who had been born with a phone in his hand. 'Our boy was chatting on some interesting forums on the fringes of the web. Not in his capacity as a respected academic.'

'Crow stuff?'

'Ghosts,' Jason said, looking up from the screen. 'He had an interesting conversation with spectral85 about the rituals required to bind a ghost to this earthly plane. If you did that, it would owe you obedience, apparently.'

Lydia repeated Jason's words for Fleet.

'Holy shit,' Fleet said. 'He could be our guy.' He stood next to Jason, who angled the phone so that he could read it at the same time.

'Lots of people are interested in ghosts,' Lydia said, not wanting to get too excited.

'Spectral85 certainly is. They were interested in an object that could be used to attract ghosts. They asked Henriksen whether he had heard of an artefact called "The Lady of Shadows". They got into quite the debate. A couple of others shared stories,' Jason was scanning through pages, reading stuff out. The other comments didn't seem coherent or relevant. One person had written an entire screed about their grandfather's cursed walking stick. Another said that they were haunted by an evil spirit that made them argue with their spouse and children. Spectral85 and Henriksen, who used the forum handle RavenEye, sounded fairly sane in comparison.

'Is there anything else?' Lydia asked.

Jason smiled radiantly. 'Only Henriksen's research into The Lady of Shadows. His extremely thorough research. With a reference image.'

Lydia went to stand on the other side of Jason, ignoring the cold that spread across that side of her body. There was an image of an old-looking piece of ugly jewellery. It was oval and had the profile of a woman's head, carved in some pale material, stark against a black background. The edge of the oval was gold, studded with red and green gemstones.

'It's a cameo,' Jason explained. 'They've been around since Sumerian times, and they were popular in ancient Roman civilisation, loads were found in Pompeii. They got big again in the seventeenth century and again in Victorian times. According to Henriksen, this one was made in Italy in the late eighteenth century.'

Lydia repeated the information for Fleet, not knowing how much he had managed to read. 'More importantly, Megan said that Tom saw a cameo when he was taken somewhere dark.'

He stared at her. 'Henriksen has research on The Lady of Shadows? An object that is meant to control ghosts?'

Lydia looked at Fleet and Jason. Jason looked at her and Fleet. Fleet looked at Lydia and at the empty air where he could see a mobile phone floating in the air. They all spoke at the same time: 'Henriksen could be the NewRipper.'

CHAPTER FOURTEEN

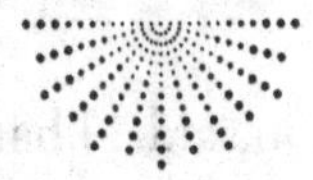

Jason relocated to his preferred spot on the sofa and used his laptop to research The Lady of Shadows. He did an image search and found gold almost immediately. 'There's a piece on the BBC site which has it pictured as one of the pieces that went missing from the British Museum.'

'Missing?'

'Stolen,' Jason said.

'Stolen when?' Lydia was already picturing a masked man dropping through a skylight to avoid motion sensors like something out of Mission Impossible.

'Last year, but it says they have uncovered thefts going back several years.'

'From the museum?' Fleet frowned. 'That's surprising. I thought security is tight there.'

Lydia scanned the article. 'It seems that there's a big cache of uncatalogued artefacts in their storerooms. They were alerted to the thefts when some glass gems turned up on eBay. When they went back through the records, they found that the number of uncatalogued items had gone down by six hundred.'

'That's a lot of stuff to mislay.'

'And they think records were doctored, too, to cover up more thefts. Suspect is ex-curator. He would have had full access to the storerooms, plenty of opportunity over the years.'

'eBay, though,' Jason said. 'That seems...'

'Lame?' Lydia said. 'I don't think of eBay as the most sophisticated place to shift stolen art.'

'Amateur hour,' Fleet agreed, picking up the gist of the conversation from Lydia's side. 'If he's guilty, he ought to be kicking himself for not making more from his crimes.'

'That sounds weird coming from a copper.' Lydia nudged him with her hip.

Fleet shrugged. 'I'm just saying.'

'Do the dates line up?'

Jason nodded. 'It was stolen and sold before Mary became active.'

Looking again at the picture of the cameo known as The Lady of Shadows, she tried to see it as something other than a creepy-looking brooch. The white head and shoulders were carved so that they sat proud from the gold setting. The blank white eyes were disturbing, but the face was clearly that of an attractive young woman. The notes referred to it as a double-cameo. A quick search online suggested this meant that there would be another cameo on the other side. This alternative wasn't photographed or described though.

'What's it made from?' Fleet asked.

'Onyx,' Lydia told him. 'Setting is gold and there are rubies and emeralds on the front and back.'

Fleet whistled. 'That'll be worth a bit, I'm guessing.'

'A lot more than cash to Henriksen,' Jason said. 'He really believed it could control ghosts.'

'So this ghost attractor thing has just been sat in the vaults at the British Museum for years?' Fleet frowned. 'Why wasn't it drawing ghosts to it then?'

'Maybe it was and we didn't know...' Lydia said. Then another thought occurred to her. 'Or maybe it needs to be activated in some way?'

'Rubbed?'

'What?' Lydia checked to see if Fleet was making a filthy joke.

'Like the genie in the lamp,' he explained.

'Could be. Human energy or just the warmth that came from being held by a living creature. If it's a magical object, it could be anything.'

'Okay. So this was used to attract Mary. That's why she kept disappearing?'

'Let's say that's what happened. Is it possible that Henriksen directed her, said stuff that set her off?'

'Like brainwashing?'

'Maybe. Or just talking to her about what had happened to her in life. Enough that it set off her quest for justice. He could have pointed her at the men connected to Cherish's death, although we don't have any connection between the professor and Cherish...'

'But if Henriksen is the Ripper, who killed him?'

'An accomplice,' Fleet said. 'Got to be. Or this Spectral85 geezer. Maybe they knew Henriksen had the Lady and wanted it for himself?'

'You think Henriksen was nervous? That's why he wanted to meet you?' Lydia asked Fleet. 'Maybe he wanted to request police protection. Maybe he fell out with his accomplice, or just realised that he was in over his head.'

WITH THE SUSPICION THAT HENRIKSEN MIGHT BE the NewRipper, Fleet wasn't about to let Lydia visit his home address alone. And Lydia wasn't exactly sad about him tagging along. Besides, as Fleet said, spending quality time together was 'the plus side to being forced to take holiday from work'. Okay, most couples probably wouldn't count potentially dangerous investigative work as quality time, but they were missing out.

Henriksen lived in Camberwell. 'Is this what started his obsession with the Crows or did he move here to be closer to his research?' Fleet asked as they approached the address.

Lydia shrugged. She had little sense of how much a professor earned, but Church Street in Camberwell felt like a long way from Bloomsbury and the rarefied atmosphere of the university buildings. The street had its own fair share of restaurants and takeaways, and the scent of spices and fried chicken made Lydia's mouth water. Henriksen's was a dark blue door next to a falafel place, with an Italian restaurant on the other side.

The main door opened into a dingy hallway. The steep staircase was poorly lit, but they weren't going to get any wiser loitering in the grubby communal area, so up was the way to go. Lydia hated the sense of being trapped. If someone came at them from above, she would only have one direction to escape. Henriksen was dead, but there was a chance he had an accomplice. And even odds that they had offed Henriksen. That person could even be staying at this address, or be there now, picking over Henriksen's valuables. She could feel the tension from Fleet and they both stepped lightly, making as little noise as possible. Not just because they hoped to surprise their quarry, but so that they could hear any movement from above.

The layout of the stairwell and door to the single flat reminded Lydia of The Fork. It wasn't as if that was a unique piece of architecture in this part of London, but the similarity was jarring. Fleet stepped in front of Lydia and she took a side position, out of the direct line of sight. He had been to the letting agency and flashed his warrant card to get a key. When Lydia had asked whether his work would find out when the officers on the case went to do the same, Fleet said that he didn't even know if they would. Henriksen hadn't died at home, so it wasn't a crime scene. And if the post-mortem confirmed a natural cardiac arrest, there wouldn't be any further investigation. 'The Met is stretched with all the obvious assault and murder, they don't need to go looking for more. They'll have informed the next of kin by now, so they might come up to look through his stuff I suppose. Depends on how close they were.'

Or how rich they considered Henriksen to be, Lydia added silently.

Fleet slid the key into the lock and opened the door. It scraped against some mail lying on the floor. A take-away leaflet and charity appeal that Henriksen would never look at.

Lydia couldn't sense any 'Family', but that didn't mean there wasn't somebody inside. Fleet did a quick walk-through and then called for Lydia to join him. She had already stepped in when she heard a crash and a muttered swear word. 'Sorry,' Fleet said as she followed the sound. 'The window's open and the wind knocked this over.' He righted the lamp.

The flat's entrance opened into a large open-plan living space, with clean white walls and an impressive bay window. It had stained glass in the top panes and wooden sashes and was utterly filthy. Built-in bookcases bracketed the window, filled with a mix of books and interesting objects. Ceramics, fossils, and what Lydia sincerely hoped was a replica of a shrunken head and not the real thing. The rest of the room was pretty bare, as if the professor was too busy with the life of the mind to worry about things like furniture. There was a single IKEA Poang chair next to a metal adjustable reading light and a carved wooden side table holding a decorative lamp, now cracked and with its shade askew. No television.

'Don't go in—' Fleet began as Lydia backtracked to check the other rooms. She found a serviceable bathroom and an empty bedroom-sized room before finding the room Fleet had started to warn her off. It was good he hadn't bothered to finish his sentence as she wouldn't be much of an investigator if she'd heeded that kind of warning.

Looking at the wall in the large bedroom, she could see why Fleet's protective instinct had activated. 'Hell Hawk,' she breathed.

'I know. Sorry,' Fleet said, joining her.

'It's classic,' she said, viewing the display. 'You've got to give him that.'

'I need to call this in.' Fleet didn't move.

'Do you?' Lydia turned away from the wall, complete with its psycho-stalker vibes. 'There's no law against pinning shit up. And the guy's dead now.'

'Look at the pictures,' Fleet said gently.

Lydia had. And her brain had apparently refused to take in the details. It had just registered 'collage of photos and some murder-board-style red wool.' It had failed to notice that there were several black and white photographs of her, taken candidly and with a long lens. In one, she was getting out of her car, face averted. Another was the front of Charlie's house and she could just be glimpsed through the open curtains of the living room window. 'This is why I hate working on the ground floor,' she said, tapping the image.

'Lyds,' Fleet said. He was looking at her with a disturbingly sympathetic expression.

'It's nothing new,' she argued, trying not to focus on the images that had been clearly manipulated with image software and printed out. Models and actresses, with her head superimposed, zoomed-in blurred pictures of her face with coins added over her eyes, a dead crow with multiple tiny images of Lydia added to its wings.

'We already knew that Henriksen had an academic interest in the Crows. This just confirms that it went deeper than that. Henriksen really might be our guy.'

'I haven't seen any signs of cohabitation. One tooth-brush and one towel in the bathroom, stuff on one side of the bed only.'

It didn't mean that Henriksen hadn't been working with someone else, of course. There weren't any signs that he had been keeping Ember here either, which was something.

'No sign of Ember,' Fleet said, echoing her thoughts. He was looking at the board. 'No pictures of him here. It's all you.' He glanced at Lydia. 'Why did he want to meet me? If he's the New Ripper, why invite a copper for a cosy chat?'

'To get close to me?' Lydia suggested. 'By proxy.'

'Information gathering,' Fleet mused. 'It's risky, but then he might have felt invincible. If he's controlling ghosts, that might have given him an inflated sense of power.'

'Or it's our possible co-conspirator,' Lydia replied, 'who wanted Henriksen out of the way. But why do it in a public place? And if they're after me, why lure you there and not me?'

'I've been thinking about that,' Fleet said. 'They might have assumed I would call it in, become embroiled in the official investigation. That might have taken me away from you.'

Lydia gave him a long look. 'They think you're my protection?'

Fleet nudged her. 'Because I am.'

'Yes, of course,' she said lightly. 'You're my big strong man and I'm just a helpless little woman.'

'You are pretty short.'

Lydia narrowed her eyes. 'Don't make me hurt you.'

Fleet turned serious. 'Someone could be trying to isolate you. Weaken you.'

'I still don't think we can jump to the conclusion that Henriksen's our guy,' Lydia said. 'Just because he was interested in ghosts and the cameo, doesn't mean he was using it to kill people. That's a big leap.'

'He was certainly nursing an unhealthy interest in you,' Fleet said, scowling at the display of images.

They resumed searching the flat. They were both practised at looking without disturbing things and they worked in companionable silence, rifling through drawers with a light touch, flicking through the books on the nightstand, photographing the stalker board.

Looking at the board again, now that the initial shock had worn off, Lydia couldn't help feel that she was in a scene from a TV series. A board of creepy photographs. Red wool stretched between them, indicating connections. Or just psychopathy. There was something staged about it. Fake.

'I'm not so sure this is—' she was speaking as she walked into the second bedroom, but Fleet cut her off.

'It's him.'

He had slid open the mirrored doors of a wall-length fitted wardrobe and was staring inside. Coats and suits were shoved to one side and the carpet had been pulled up from the floor. White symbols had been painted messily on the exposed boards.

Lydia used the torch on her phone to get a better look. Small objects were spaced around the white symbols. A scrap of fabric. A small cut-out picture of Brad Carter. A used cigarette butt.

'Is this the ritual that controlled Mary? Sent her after Carter and the others?'

'It certainly looks like it.' Fleet turned a shining gaze onto Lydia. 'We found the NewRipper.'

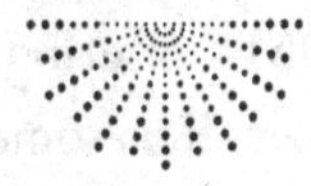

Lydia read through professor Henriksen's published work. That was a lie. She skimmed through the abstracts that were available for free on the various academic research sites and read the blurbs and contents pages for his published works. She didn't know if she was expecting to see something which conclusively proved he was a maniac, harnessing the power inherent in ghosts in order to target and murder individuals, but amongst the incomprehensible linguistics jargon, one piece had stood out. It was a lighter piece, clearly aimed at the lay person, and had been published in its entirety in an online folklore magazine. It was titled 'Scandinavian Folklore and Fact: Where Myth Meets Matter', and it went into startling detail about the Crow Family and speculated wildly about the supernatural powers that may be present in the bloodline 'as recently as the nineteenth century'.

She went back to the university site and trawled Henriksen's department for colleagues. There was a link to the PhD students too, and she went through this list, trying to match any to Henriksen. She fired off a few emails, explaining that she was a private investigator and had some questions. Then, just to be thorough, she found their social media profiles. One woman gave distinctly 'woo' vibes with her profile picture and feed. Lydia slid into her DMs, offering condolences on her loss and introducing herself as someone 'concerned with finding the truth' about Henriksen's death.

Fleet, on the other hand, didn't understand why she was bothering. 'Henriksen is the NewRipper,' he said. 'We found him. He's dead and there was no sign of an accomplice. There's a good chance this is over.'

Lydia opened her mouth to argue, but Fleet was still going.

'He used the cameo and a ritual to send Mary after Carter and the other men involved in Cherish's death. He's obsessed with you and the Crow Family and targeted your house. Maybe he didn't know he was going to get Mary, maybe he just went with that when it happened? He has been interested in the esoteric for years, finding out that ghosts were real and that he could control them had to be a rush.'

'I wonder if he could see Mary,' Lydia mused. 'Or whether he followed the steps from this ritual thing he unearthed and then read about the murder in the paper.' Something had been bothering her. 'Why did he send them after those men? What's his connection to Cherish?'

'I'm sure we'll find it,' Fleet said. 'Maybe he knew her?'

'And why did he ask to meet you? That's asking to be found out.'

'Attack of conscience? Or it was part of his obsession with you. Maybe he wanted to offer a little bit of information, something false to send us on a wild goose chase. Or maybe the goal was just to get close to you through me. Watching you from afar and sending ghosts after you wasn't hitting the spot anymore?'

'And his death?'

'Heart attack. Could have been natural.'

'One hell of a coincidence.'

'Could it have been a consequence of the mojo he was working? My visions aren't exactly restful, maybe doing what he was doing was having a physical effect on him?'

Lydia looked at the pictures that Fleet had printed out from Henriksen's flat. She had image searched for the white painted symbols and not found much, but Jason had taken over. He was wandering the dark corners of the internet as they spoke, hopefully confirming their theories. It would be nice if it all tied together. 'The ghost that attacked me looked really unhappy,' Lydia said, picturing Tom. 'If he's been controlling ghosts, maybe they decided to take revenge? A pissed off ghost might decide to kill the puppet master.'

'Good,' Fleet said. 'That makes sense. So why do you look so unhappy?'

'The cameo wasn't there.'

'Maybe he kept it on him and we missed it. Or it was at his office, we didn't have time to do a proper search.'

These were reasonable suggestions, but Lydia couldn't shake her gut feeling that it had all been too easy. All the evidence for Henriksen, nicely laid out. 'You don't think it's too convenient. You got called to meet Henriksen and then we find all that stuff at his flat—'

'I don't see how—'

'That's because you're a copper, not a Crow. What's the first rule of conning a mark?' Lydia didn't wait for him to answer. 'You make them think they're smarter than you. You make them think they've won.'

Fleet digested this. 'You think we're being set up?'

'We're being set up now?' Jason wandered into the kitchen.

'I don't know,' Lydia said. She caught Fleet's eye and said: 'I think we've been handed the NewRipper on a plate. It feels like someone wants us to feel like we've won.'

'Or we have won,' Fleet argued. 'You found Mary, got her to move on or whatever, now you've found the man who was controlling her. You've stopped the man who was messing with the ghosts. You did it. Can't you just—'

The mug that Jason had just picked up smashed on the kitchen floor.

Fleet flinched. 'What was—?'

'Jason,' Lydia said, staring at the pieces of mug in horror. 'He's gone again.'

. . .

'THAT PROVES IT,' LYDIA SAID. SHE HAD DONE A FAST walk through the house and there was no sign of Jason. He had definitely disappeared. She thought about what he'd said, that it had felt violent. She couldn't shake the feeling that he had been yanked away by the missing cameo.

'Henriksen could have an accomplice. Someone else using the cameo,' Fleet was saying. 'Doesn't mean Henriksen isn't our mastermind.'

'Does he really feel right to you? In your gut?'

Fleet stared at her for a moment. 'I find it hard to trust my gut since—'

His father. His visions. Lydia got it. But she had enough certainty for them both. 'Tom, the ghost that tried to stab me, said that the place he's been dragged to smelled bad. There wasn't an odour at Henriksen's. And why would he have targeted those responsible for Cherish's death? What's his connection to her? Or them?'

'Maybe Mary chose them, was more involved than we think?'

'We've established that she had to have been directed. We can't change that now just because it doesn't fit a suspect that has been handed to us on a plate. We can't ignore the facts just because it's convenient.'

Fleet ran a hand over his head. 'You're right. Fuck.'

CHAPTER SIXTEEN

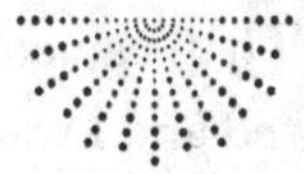

Jason didn't reappear in the next hour, or the one after that. 'He's been pulled to the cameo,' Lydia said again.

'We don't know that,' Fleet replied. Also not for the first time. Although he was losing certainty in the face of Lydia's conviction.

'He knows how worried I am about Ember. We're making strides in the Henriksen case, he wouldn't just leave. Not now. So this must be against his will.' Lydia stared at Fleet, ready for him to bring up the fact that Jason had always disappeared against his will, even before the NewRipper appeared on the scene with The Lady of Shadows. She didn't have a watertight argument against this, just that he did that far less when fully powered up. And that her gut told her that this was different.

The next day Megan called. 'I haven't been able to follow up with Tom,' she explained earnestly. 'He's

MIA. And I haven't got news from any of my other contacts either. I will refund you—'

'That's okay,' Lydia interrupted. There was a relief in speaking to another live person who could see ghosts. Her own fears tumbled out of her mouth before she could stop them. 'Someone is using a ritual to draw ghosts to an object. That cameo you mentioned, we think. They're being used and I want to stop it.'

A beat of silence. 'You want to come with me on my rounds?'

Fleet had a meeting with a copper friend to discuss possible avenues for finding Ember. He promised it would be off the record and that he would keep the chat in the 'purely hypothetical' realm. Lydia didn't care any longer if the police did get wind of his disappearance. She was desperate to find him and willing to use any means.

He insisted on meeting Megan first, though.

'Are you worried about me?' Lydia asked, half-teasing. Fleet was still on high alert after seeing the stalker board. He wasn't as quick to dismiss it as a set-up, but also didn't seem entirely reassured by the fact that Henriksen was in cold storage.

'She was on the scene when something attacked you. I'm curious.'

'I told you, she's harmless.'

Megan bounced up to them, still as blonde and smiley as before. She opened her arms, inviting Lydia to hug her. Lydia took a step back.

'Still not on hugging terms, got it. Maybe next time?'

She turned to Fleet. 'What about you, big guy? Up for it?'

Fleet looked bemused.

'High five?' Megan held up her hand. 'Don't leave me hanging.'

Fleet touched his hand to Megan's and she grabbed hold, turning it into an awkward version of the bro-hug. Then she looked around, her mood dipping. 'Where's Jason? I thought we had a connection.'

'That's what I wanted to ask you about. Have you seen him?'

She shook her head. 'He's missing?'

Lydia hadn't wanted to say the words out loud, hadn't wanted to make it real. She nodded instead.

'How long?'

'He's been disappearing on and off for the last couple of weeks. But I haven't seen him since yesterday and I'm worried.'

She felt Fleet glance at her. He had been gone for longer when The Fork was destroyed. His anchor had gone and it had severely weakened him. But she had brought him back. He was anchored to her and she powered him up. For good measure, she had anchored him to Charlie's house, too.

'He's a strong one,' Megan said. 'Where's his base?'

'Camberwell. He can move around London, but we haven't tested further than that.'

'Could be anywhere, then.' Megan looked worried. 'How do we check whether he's properly missing? Could he just be having a little jolly? Seeing the sights?'

He wouldn't do that without telling her. And he hadn't been himself. Lydia could feel in her bones that something was wrong.

'What about the other matter?' Fleet asked. 'Have you spoken to your contacts?'

Megan looked at Lydia with an unspoken question.

'You can speak freely. Fleet's a copper, but he's one of the good ones.'

'It's been a bit odd,' Megan said. She looked at Lydia with obvious sympathy. 'I don't want to worry you, but some of them have gone.'

'Gone?' Ice trailed over Lydia's spine.

'The ones that can talk. There's a couple of Polish soldiers from WW2, they hang out in Soho. They're more than echoes, maybe because they've got each other to talk to, I dunno, but anyway. They've gone. Betty who stays at the river. She was killed by her boyfriend. He choked her, but she wasn't all the way gone when he chucked her in the river. Water finished her off.'

'Jesus,' Fleet muttered under his breath.

'Betty's always been chatty,' Megan continued. 'Likes to tell me about who she's seen, what the mudlarkers have found lately. She makes up a lot of it, I think, bored out of her skull the poor lamb, but she's always there. Until now.'

'Too many to be coincidence,' Fleet said. 'This sounds ominous.'

'You believe me, Mr Copper?' Megan tilted her head. 'That's a turn up.'

'What about the ones that can't talk?'

Megan shrugged. 'I wasn't focusing on them.

Figured they wouldn't be much help with the gossip. We could go and take a look now?'

Megan's first port of call was a wine bar close to Smithfield Market. There were many plague pits deep under London, and lots still hadn't been discovered. One of the largest was underneath Charterhouse Square, in the same area, and it was home to around fifty thousand victims. The railway discovered it, like they do with so many of London's little underground surprises, and they brought the museum people in to have a gander. Megan explained all of this, before adding cheerfully 'can't get underground at the square, though, they filled it in with concrete and built a park on top, so it's a bust for us.' She went on to explain that she had discovered the ghosts in the nearby bar by accident. 'I worked there for a bit, one of my many side-gigs. Hustle culture, am I right?' Megan didn't pause for Lydia to respond. 'There are too many not to be from a mass grave, and, well, you'll see. They obviously weren't well when they passed...'

'I don't understand,' Lydia said, as they approached the bar. 'I thought ghosts were anchored to where they died. Not where they were buried.'

'People were panicking with the plague, right? You got someone all covered in buboes and unconscious from the pain, you think they're waiting with that body all night, letting the rest of the family breathe in the bad air or whatever they thought was causing it? Nah, mate. That corpse-to-be was out on the cart and being hauled off to the pit quick smart.' Megan went uncharacteristically quiet for a moment. 'Plenty of people took their last breath in the pit.' She gave an elaborate shudder. 'Can't dwell on it.'

'We're going to the cellars?' Lydia asked, as Megan led the way through the bar and down a set of stairs. A sign marked 'toilets' took them past another bar area and further down another flight of stairs. Underground was never her happy place. Crows liked to be able to see the sky.

'There are a few just in here,' Megan said, leading her to a door marked 'private'. There was the scent of cooking oil filtering from the kitchens above and a whiff of mildew. Lydia thought of Tom's description of 'bad smells' and wondered whether they were about to come face-to-face with the real NewRipper. Whether he would be able to use the cameo to control Jason and force him into violence. She pushed the thought away. Jason would never hurt her. He would never hurt anyone.

'They don't speak,' Megan was saying. 'Just echoes. I'm warning you, now,' she said to Lydia, 'some of them cry. It's grim.'

Lydia steeled herself, but when they walked through into the small stone-lined room, there was nobody there. A couple of broken chairs, wooden wine boxes, cleaning supplies and a pile of empty lever-arch folders in the corner showed that the place was mainly used as a storeroom. It was cold, but Lydia couldn't see any spirits.

She didn't need to check with Megan, as she was

looking around the room with undisguised confusion. 'They're gone.'

On their way back from the bar, Megan was uncharacteristically quiet. When she spoke, her usual buoyancy was dialled down by a factor of at least fifty. 'We could visit Peter.' Megan bit her lip. 'If he's there. There is definitely something moving ghosts from their usual hangouts.'

'Worth a look. We might get lucky.' Lydia was willing to take any chance. She had no other leads and a terrible sense that time was running out.

'He's a strong one,' Megan warned. 'Very pissed off. Even if he's home, he might not speak to us. And we need to stop at a bakery first.'

Peter hung out in an old merchant's house near to the river. It predated the great fire of London and boasted an old smuggler's tunnel that led to the water. As well as being a listed building and a site of historic interest, it was yet another bar. Say what you like about Londoners, but they knew how to prioritise having a nice place to have a drink.

The bar consisted of a series of wood-panelled rooms and the staff were more alert than in the last place. When Megan tried to walk into what looked like the old dining room of the house, she was turned away for not having a reservation. 'Don't worry,' Megan said, quietly as they back-tracked. 'We just need to get downstairs.'

Of course, Lydia thought. Hell Hawk.

The barrel-vaulted cellars were lined with brick that

had been painted white. With oak furniture and black-framed photographs, it made a welcoming space for after-work drinks or a birthday celebration. If you ignored the shadowy figure in the corner of the room.

Mercifully, the place was empty apart from the ghost, but Lydia didn't know how long they would have privacy.

'I've brought a friend,' Megan said. 'This is Lydia.'

The shape in the corner unfolded to reveal a large man in dark blue overalls. He had a misshapen head and it took Lydia a beat to realise that it was caved in on one side. The gore was as fresh-looking as the day it had happened and Lydia's stomach turned over.

'I brought you something,' Megan said. She slid a white box from her backpack and opened it. 'Jammy doughnuts. Your fave.'

The smell of sweet fried dough wafted through the air. Peter came close and tilted his ruined head into the box. He inhaled noisily.

'It's good to see you,' Megan said. 'Lots of people missing on my rounds this week.'

Peter continued to huff at the doughnuts as if he could inhale them right into his system.

'Have you seen anything unusual?' Lydia produced her coin and flipped it into the air.

Peter's head snapped up and he stared at the coin.

Lydia felt Megan tense next to her, but she kept her focus on the ghost.

'Shiny,' Peter said. Crystals of sugar clung to his chin and lips, before they seemed to realise that they weren't holding onto anything and flaked away. Peter's tongue darted from his mouth as if to catch them and there was a terrible hunger in his eyes.

'Have you met anyone new? Woken up somewhere different? Blacked out?' Lydia knew how Jason described blinking in and out of existence, but she didn't know if his experience was universal or whether Peter was even self-aware enough to have noticed.

Peter didn't answer. His tongue darted out again and began exploring the skin around his mouth.

'You didn't go anywhere,' Megan said. To Lydia, Megan said, 'Peter always stays right here. He can't move from this room.'

Peter's gaze flickered to Megan and his mouth pulled down in disapproval. 'Shows what you know,' he said, spite filling his voice.

Lydia caught on. 'He didn't see anything,' she said to Megan. 'But that's okay. It's not his fault.'

'Lady,' Peter said, his gaze still fixed on the spinning coin. 'Beau-ti-ful.' He drew the word out in a creepy singsong that Lydia knew she would be hearing in her nightmares for years to come.

'And a man? Old guy with a short beard.' Lydia was about to describe Henriksen further, but Peter was shaking his head.

'The lady had a shiny. Beau-ti-ful. Small lady in her hand. I wanted it but she wouldn't let go and then I woke up at home.' He glanced around as if verifying that he was still in the same place.

'Who was the lady?' Megan asked.

'Small,' Peter said, holding out his hand. 'Pretty shiny.'

'The other lady. The one holding the shiny. What did she look like?'

Peter shook his head, his outline shuddering. His eyes were hungry and his mouth opened and closed. He whispered 'beau-ti-ful' one more time before retreating to his corner and refusing to speak again.

Outside, Lydia gave Megan an appraising look. 'You handled him well.'

Megan beamed with her whole being. 'A compliment!'

'Shut up,' Lydia said, squashing her own smile. 'Do you think the small lady means the cameo?'

Megan turned down the wattage on her smile and stopped her celebratory dance. 'Makes sense. So it really pulls them in. That's worrying.'

'And Jason – and Peter – are strong enough to get away?'

'For now,' Megan said. 'Maybe they'll get tired after a while.'

'We need to find it before that happens.' Lydia had known that Jason was being dragged against his will, but meeting Peter had made it real. The anger was fizzing through her veins and she welcomed it.

'Any idea on the beautiful lady?' Megan asked.

Lydia had seen hunger like that before. She knew exactly which Family incited it.

CHAPTER SEVENTEEN

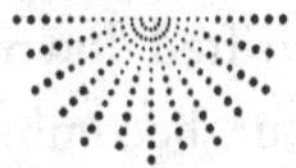

Jason reappeared early that evening. Lydia was at her desk, reading the surveillance reports from around Camberwell and trying to think of where else Ember might have gone when she looked up and saw him in the middle of the room, translucent and shaking.

She got up and went to him. He was gradually becoming more opaque, but it took a while before he was able to hold himself together enough to speak.

'I'm sorry,' she said. He was clearly distressed and she felt helpless. 'What can I do?'

Jason's eyes were wide and he was still shaking. 'Something dragged me out of here. I felt it.'

'I'm sorry,' she said again. 'That must be so scary.'

Jason shoved the sleeves of his suit jacket and tried to smile. 'I'm a ghost, I don't get scared.'

Lydia ignored the obvious lie. She put a hand out, stopping just short of touching him. Right now, her hand would go right through his arm and that wouldn't be comforting for either of them. She could feel the strange electrical buzz of his energy.

When she asked if he was all right, he didn't answer her immediately. 'I don't know,' he said eventually. Then he added, 'I can't be inside,' and floated through the wall.

Lydia followed him outside to the garden. It was still warm, and Jason had drifted down to the hornbeam tree. His form was filling out, becoming less translucent. As Lydia watched, he became opaque and finally stopped vibrating. Three crows were sat on the upper branches, staring back at him with great intensity.

He held up his hands and studied them in the early evening sunlight. 'I'm here.' He glanced at her then. 'I'm here, aren't I?'

Lydia reached out and clasped his hands in hers. They were cold, of course, but felt solid. She squeezed his fingers. 'You're here. You're okay.'

'It's bad,' Jason said uncomfortably. 'Wrong.'

'Wrong how?'

His face twisted in distress. 'I don't know. I was pulled, like before, but then I felt like I was being squeezed. There was this intense pressure all around. Like I was in a space that's too small and it was getting smaller. I couldn't move. I couldn't breathe, I know I don't need to, but it hurt—'

'I'm sorry. That sounds horrible.' The cold from their clasped hands was spreading through Lydia's body, but it was nothing to the dread that had settled in her stomach. 'Do you remember seeing anything? Was there a person there?'

Jason shook his head quickly.

'Any detail at all would help,' she pressed. 'Sounds? Smells? Anything?'

Jason stared up into the hornbeam tree for a minute and the crows stared back at him. Lydia forced herself to wait quietly. She wanted to pace the garden, to hit something, but she knew that kind of energy wasn't going to help Jason. There was something very vulnerable about being dragged somewhere without consent. She could only imagine how frightened he must be.

'Bad drains,' he said eventually.

'Okay, that's good.'

He pulled a disgusted face, looking more himself. 'Really bad drains. Like sewage.'

'Got it. Good. Do you hear anything?'

Instantly, his expression closed down. 'No.'

'I wanted to ask you something else,' Lydia decided to plough on. Jason was upset, but this was too important to put off. Her gut told her that Henriksen wasn't the NewRipper, which meant there was a strong possibility that whoever set him up also arranged his death. 'If you wanted to kill someone without a weapon, how would you do it?'

A pause. Lydia wasn't sure if Jason was offended, or thinking. After another moment he said, 'I could try and scare them. But most people can't see me, so it would have to be moving objects around them and hoping that was enough to freak them out. I could take their hand. They would feel the cold and that might scare them?'

'What about when you entered me?' There was no way to say that without it sounding filthy, so Lydia just rolled right past it. 'You were weaker away from The

Fork and it was just your soul riding along with me, but what if you did it when you were stronger? Would you be cold enough to lower my body temp that way? Dangerously? Or could you, I don't know, grab my heart and stop it beating?'

Jason was staring at Lydia in horror. 'Why are you asking me this? I wouldn't kill someone.'

'I don't mean you,' Lydia said. She didn't say that if he was being controlled by the NewRipper that neither of them knew what he might do. 'Henriksen died in a public place, no struggle, no weapon. I'm trying to work out how it was done.'

'Or he had a heart attack.' Jason was shaking. Unhappy. 'He was old, it happens.'

'Henriksen was directed to the same meeting place as Fleet. I don't think his death was natural.'

'Motive?'

Lydia explained about Henriksen's research. 'Maybe he had contact with our killer, gave them information, not realising they were going to use it in such a practical sense. He might have just been sharing research, theories, stories, and have had no idea they were true.'

'And the killer saw him as a loose end? Wanted to off him so that he couldn't identify him?' Jason nodded, his vibrating had calmed as he focused on the case. Lydia could relate.

'But why do it in a public place? And why bring a DCI to the scene?'

'Fleet thinks they wanted to incriminate him. Maybe get him arrested.'

Jason's eyes widened. 'Was that a possibility?'

'His reputation at work isn't great,' Lydia said. 'He says that management thinks he's about to go off sick with mental health issues and most of his colleagues either distrust or pity him.'

'Still.' Jason noticed he was hovering above the grass and moved down fractionally so that he was standing on the ground. 'It's still a stretch to believe him a killer.'

'Fleet thinks they just wanted him distracted. Tied up with work, one way or another, so that I was alone.'

'He thinks you're the next target?'

Prickles spread across her skin. 'It's possible.'

'I don't think you're next,' Jason said musingly.

'Why?'

'That would end the game.'

LYDIA ENCOURAGED JASON BACK INTO THE HOUSE. She sat in the kitchen, keeping him company while he poured her a bowl of cereal she didn't want, and chopped up some fruit she was unlikely to eat.

'I think I was underground,' Jason said. He put down the knife and turned to face Lydia. 'I didn't see anything, but there's something about it that makes me think that.'

'Maybe the way sound was echoing or the temperature?' Lydia knew what Jason meant. There was something intangible but unmistakable about being underground. Your mind just knew you were in the depths.

'It hurt so much, I think I was crying. I might have been screaming. It's hard to remember anything except the pain, but it did smell bad.' Jason closed his eyes. 'Backed-up toilets, stagnant water, mildew.'

'That's good,' Lydia said. 'We can start searching.'

They relocated to the office and Jason's preferred spot on the sofa.

He opened his laptop. 'I'll start with a one-mile radius. Let's assume that whatever is affecting me is nearby. If distance isn't an issue, we might never find it, but—'

'We may as well try,' Lydia finished.

She didn't have high hopes, but seeing Jason energised with a sense of purpose was reason enough.

Ten minutes later, she heard Fleet arrive home and called out for him to join them. Her slim hope that his friend had provided them with some new lead on Ember was extinguished the moment she saw his face. He looked defeated.

She got up from the sofa and hugged him. 'Jason's back,' she said, probably unnecessarily. He couldn't see Jason, but she guessed from Fleet's perspective it looked like the laptop was suspended a few inches above empty sofa cushions, the keys clicking of their own accord.

She was just filling Fleet in on her trip with Megan and everything Jason had told her, when Jason made a noise of triumph. He had a list of underground spaces within Camberwell.

'Why is it always underground?' Lydia said out loud, without entirely meaning to.

Fleet gave her a sympathetic look.

'I can mark these on the map,' Jason was saying,

staring intently at his screen. 'But I think this one is the most likely—'

Without warning, he blinked out of existence. His laptop fell onto the sofa, bounced and landed on the floor.

'Feathers.' Lydia scooped it up. The screen looked intact, but it had gone into sleep mode. 'I'm going to have to get one of those bumper protector things.'

Fleet was staring at the space where Jason had been. 'Is he all right?'

'I hope so,' Lydia said, fear uncoiling in her stomach. 'Whatever is messing with ghosts, it's dragging Jason along for the ride.'

'So they're doing something right now?' Fleet asked. 'We can use that.'

Lydia didn't like to think of Jason being dragged to the cameo as an opportunity, but there was a chance to interrupt the culprit in action.

Once they had the document open, Lydia scanned Jason's list. She saw immediately the location he meant. It wasn't well known, there was a high chance of old drains and bad smells, and it was likely deserted for most of the time.

THE SOUTHWARK COLD WAR BUNKER HAD BEEN built to be used by the government in the event of a nuclear attack. It had been constructed underneath a health centre, but once the centre was closed by the council in the nineties, the building was demolished. 'Apparently kids were breaking in,' Lydia said. She widened her eyes at Fleet in mock surprise. 'Imagine that?'

The bit of waste ground had been developed by locals into a small community garden, but the council had filled in the main entrance to the bunker with concrete and padlocked the metal doors shut.

Lydia asked around and found someone who lived in the estate nearby. He was a responsible father of two, but had played in the bunker as a kid. 'Last time I went down there it had flooded. You could see the water marks up high,' he held a hand above his head, 'put me off.'

Lydia wasn't going to think about drowning underground. He showed Lydia and Fleet where there was an emergency exit hatch with a ladder straight into one of the rooms below. Lydia thanked him and handed over some cash. 'No need to chat about this with anyone, okay?'

The man thanked her politely, but clearly couldn't wait to get away. Once he had left, Fleet unpacked his supplies. High-power torches, thick gloves, and various tools. The hatch was covered with a heavily rusted panel, but was easy enough to lever up with a long-handled chisel.

'You want to do this?'

'Want is a strong word,' Lydia said. 'But Jason might be down there. Whoever is doing this might be priming him to become a killer. Working their ghost control on him.'

'More to the point, your stalker might be down there,' Fleet said. He had been over his objections on their way to the site and clearly wasn't convinced. 'They might be armed with more than just a brooch.'

'I'm willing to take that chance,' Lydia said. 'They're clearly keen on getting someone else to do their dirty work, doesn't suggest they're used to confrontation or violence themselves.'

They were both whispering. The top of the ladder was visible, but the daylight didn't reach far into the narrow shaft.

'I'll go first,' Fleet said, giving up the argument.

For a moment, Lydia wasn't sure if his broad shoulders would fit, but then they did. He tested each rung before putting his full weight onto it, moving slowly and carefully.

Without letting herself think about it too hard, she followed.

THE SMELL HIT LYDIA BEFORE THEY REACHED THE bottom. Bad drains didn't really cover it. Human sewage provided the dominant notes, but once Lydia's boots splashed onto the concrete floor, a thick layer of decay was added to the bouquet. Fleet had clicked on his torch and was aiming it at the base of the ladder so Lydia had a good view of the murky water that covered the ground to a depth of an inch or so. There was stuff floating in it that she didn't want to study in any detail.

The light played around the space, revealing a large room with a structural support pillar in the middle. Wooden debris was piled against the walls, and there were the remains of charts and signage, showing its intended purpose as a command centre. Lydia couldn't see any ghosts. It felt cold, but that might have just been because they were underground.

'Clear,' she whispered, pulling out her own torch and switching it on.

They moved cautiously through the bunker. The next room smelled even worse and Lydia wondered if they were getting closer to the toilets. She had expected to see rats, but the place was eerily silent.

With the light from the torches moving on the walls and the splashing of their feet in the disgusting water, Lydia felt every hair on her body standing to attention. While the place had clearly been trashed on at least one occasion, with broken furniture strewn around, there was a surprising lack of graffiti. It suggested that not many people had been down here in the decades since it was mothballed.

The high water marks on the walls were a good reason for that, she supposed. Most casual vandals weren't interested in being entombed in a watery grave. Well that was a fun phrase. *Feathers*. Her brain was misfiring. She slipped her spare hand into her pocket and squeezed her coin. She wasn't going to lose it in this creepy concrete hellhole. She was Lydia Crow and she was going to complete an efficient sweep of the area, see if she could find her friend. Or the psycho who was trying to weaponise ghosts.

Bolstered by the reiteration of her mission, Lydia took the lead position through the doorless exit and into the next room. Another large space with some broken desks and cabinets. The floor was drier, at least, and the smell was either getting better or she was becoming immune.

'Just how big is this place?' Fleet asked in a low voice. His torch beam played over the walls, revealing a mildewed map.

'What was that?' Lydia stopped moving, every sense straining to try to pick up on the stray sound.

'I don't hear anything,' Fleet whispered after a moment.

'I don't now either, it's—' She broke off as she heard the sound again. Someone was crying. It wasn't Jason, thank Feathers, but it was awful nonetheless.

She moved toward the open doorway. As she got closer a stream of cold air hit her skin. 'They're here,' she whispered.

The crying got louder.

Once she was close enough, she angled her light through the gap in the wall, illuminating the room beyond. It was packed with ghosts.

For a moment, Lydia's brain struggled to process what she was seeing. The ghosts were crowded into the room, standing on the ground or just above it, in the way that Jason did. They were in a variety of states of solidity, though, with some more-transparent spirits wedged in between the more solid ones, overlapping each other in a jumble of limbs and faces that made Lydia feel nauseous. She scanned faces as best she could, looking for Jason.

Heart pounding, she tried to look beyond the ghosts, to see through them to what else was in the room or who else was there. She thought there might be markings on the floor, but it was hard to see through the mass of shifting spirits. More kept appearing, too, popping into existence before her eyes, filling the room more tightly with every passing second.

'Jason?' Lydia didn't want to step into the room, her fingers were already numb from the cold.

'What is it?'

'You can't see them?'

'It's bloody cold,' Fleet said. 'Ghosts?'

'So many,' Lydia said, still searching the room for Jason.

She felt Fleet's arm around her shoulders and she leaned into him for warmth. 'Can you aim your torch into the room?'

He did so. The ghosts seemed to be attracted to something in the centre of it, they were standing so closely packed that they were overlapping each other. Lydia tried to focus on the ground, to see if she could spot the cameo, but it was impossible. The torch light, the shuddering spirits, and the awful wailing were over-whelming. And more ghosts were still appearing. The air felt electric with their combined energy.

'Can you see anything?' She assumed he would have said if he had seen a person, and he wouldn't be distracted by the ghosts, but it was getting harder to think straight. She was so cold. And the ghosts kept multiplying. They were standing on top of each other, inside each other, lying on the floor and floating up by the ceiling. Some were silent, many were crying, and they were all vibrating. Her head hurt and her own torch beam wavered as her hand shook.

'Jason?' She called again.

The crying increased. It was scraping the inside of Lydia's mind. Her eyes were watering and it was either the strange energy of the room or she was crying. She couldn't tell.

'You see him?' Fleet's voice seemed to be coming from far away.

'No,' Lydia said. 'I don't know...'

Another shift in the mass of ghosts and another wave of nausea. If she was going into the room to look for Jason, it had to be now. Before she lost her lunch.

She stepped away from Fleet and plunged into the room.

If she had been cold before, it was nothing to the experience inside the room. The freezing air burned, and her lungs instantly seized. She backed out of the room as quickly as she could, but her limbs were jerky and uncooperative. She had just enough time to think that this had been a monumentally stupid idea when the crying increased sharply in volume before there was a bright flash of light and she felt herself knocked back. An explosion.

The awful wailing of the ghosts had been abruptly silenced and the electric in the air had gone. Her skin was burning.

'Lydia!'

Blackness. She didn't know if her eyes were open or shut. She knew that had been Fleet shouting. He had sounded panicked. Her brain was scrambled and she struggled to remember where she was. She felt an arm around her waist and she was lifted, moving through the air. She glimpsed the room as she was hauled away, her fingers still gripping her torch as if it was a lifeline. The room was completely empty.

'Come on, come on,' Fleet was saying. He didn't sound like himself. Fleet was so rarely scared, she thought. A fractured thought that fell through her confused mind.

She didn't feel the pain yet. That was coming.

CHAPTER EIGHTEEN

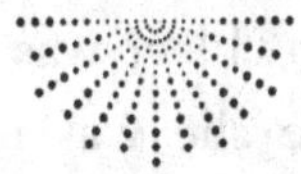

Lydia barely remembered climbing the ladder out of the underground bunker. She knew Fleet had been behind her, his arms caging her and stopping her from falling if she lost her grip. He had pushed her, too, hands on her backside, helping her up and over the edge. She had been able to walk for most of the way back to Denmark Hill, but close to the house her legs had given way and Fleet had carried her. She hurt all over, skin buzzing, but there was a particularly painful patch on her neck and she concentrated on that. If she focused on that sharp pain, maybe she could keep herself conscious.

Her brain had started functioning in the fresh air. At least in part. She knew they had been in the Camberwell Bunker. That she hadn't found Jason. She remembered the ghosts and their awful crying.

'Come here,' Fleet said, pulling her quickly through the bathroom doorway. They were upstairs, but Lydia didn't remember getting up the stairs. Her thoughts were coming in staccato images. Disjointed.

He stepped into the bath and got the overhead shower running.

She was shaking from her scalp to her toes. The adrenaline that had flooded her body had burned out and she was left feeling as weak as a hatchling. 'They were so frightened.'

'You need to strip,' Fleet was saying, but his voice sounded strange. Like she was underwater. No such luck. Water would be nice right now. Cooling water, liquid relief. Her skin was tingling painfully. It felt like thousands of needles being jabbed into her arms and legs, the neckline of her top. And that burning centre of white-hot pain on her neck. The worse of the stuff must have landed there, she realised. She tried to lift the edge of the fabric, tried to pull it up to get it over her head, but her fingers weren't obeying instructions.

He grabbed the thin material and yanked, ripping it almost in two and threading her uncooperative body through the head and arm holes. 'Jeans,' he said.

Can't... She had intended to say it out loud, but something was paralysing her throat. Her vocal cords weren't vibrating. Her lungs only getting shallow sips of air. There wasn't enough breath to make sound. That was panic, probably. The detached part of her mind that liked to step back and observe was still online. That was something.

The stuff was over Fleet, too, she realised. His grey T-shirt was splattered with dark patches. She felt a sudden spurt of fear for Fleet and that cut through her strangely dissociated state. Hell Hawk. This was bad.

'Get in,' he lifted her over the edge of the bath and

held her under the spray. 'Sit,' he said. 'I don't want you to fall.'

She sank down to a crouch in the tub and propped herself against the back of the bath, the drops of water mixing with the needle-stabbing feeling. She closed her eyes and heard, rather than saw, Fleet leave the room. Moments later he was back.

'You need to be in here,' Lydia mumbled. He had to clean off the stuff, too. He had to be in pain. She certainly was.

'I will,' Fleet said. He crouched down and helped her to stand. The water had drenched his clothes, but he was entirely focused on her. 'Lean on me,' he said.

He had brought scissors from the kitchen and she realised he intended to cut her jeans to get them off. 'I can take them off, it's okay,' she said.

She braced her hands on his shoulders and tried not to cry out as the fabric peeled away from her skin. It burned even worse than the needle-spikes.

Fleet tugged the fabric down over her thighs and she balanced by holding onto him to step out of each leg. He was working quickly, but it still seemed to take a long time. Lydia knew that some of the liquid sluicing over her face was her own tears. Feathers, it hurt.

Fleet's hands were still on her. He had lathered with his shower gel and was smoothing over her skin in a rhythmic fashion, rinsing away every trace of the muck. 'Fleet,' she managed. 'You have to get it off you.'

'Hang on.'

Lydia was steadier on her feet. Now that the pain

had receded and she was no longer panicking, she felt stronger. 'Let me help you.'

'Can you lean against the wall for a sec?'

As soon as her hands were off his shoulders, Fleet pulled his T-shirt over his head. He couldn't prevent the hiss of pain as the fabric ripped away patches of skin. Then he stood up and reached one arm behind the shower screen to snag a towel. He stepped out of the tub and leaned in to help Lydia. As soon as she tried to lift one leg to get out of the bath, a wave of dizziness over-took and she fell. There was no impact. In a split second, Fleet had put his arms around her body and scooped her up. He wrapped her in the towel and carried her to the bedroom.

Once she was sitting in the middle of the mattress, pillows behind her and another towel draped over her legs, he headed back to the bathroom, unbuckling his jeans as he went.

'I can help,' Lydia said.

'Stay,' Fleet replied, giving her a firm look. 'Please.'

It was the 'please' that did it. She let her eyes close and listened to the water running as Fleet showered. Exhaustion had come for her and she fought to stay awake. Her skin was on fire in places and she wondered if it was blistering.

After a few minutes, Fleet was back in the room. Lydia forced her eyes open and then snapped fully alert. He had a towel around his waist and she could see angry red weals across his chest where the stuff had burned through his T-shirt.

She sucked in a breath. 'That looks bad. Should I call a doctor?'

He approached the bed. 'You know a GP that's gonna do a house call?'

'Sort of. Should I?' Lydia's aversion to seeing Dr Walker was warring with the sight of Fleet's damaged skin. She didn't even want to know how hers looked. The pain had receded from the dizzying levels but she didn't feel exactly comfortable.

He winced as he sat on the edge of the bed. 'It's okay.'

'It's not okay.' Lydia wasn't good with medical stuff, but she remembered her mum using stinging antiseptic cream on every scrape and cut she'd had as a child. 'We need to make sure we don't get infected.'

Fleet smiled at her. 'I don't think ghosts carry diseases.'

'Sepsis,' Lydia said, not smiling.

'Okay. Do you have a first-aid kit?'

'Don't know.' Since moving into Charlie's house, Lydia had seen inside all of the cupboards, but she hadn't made a thorough inventory. She'd been pretty distracted with other things.

'I can go to the pharmacy,' Fleet said.

His tone was low and the words were slower than usual. Lydia could see her own tiredness mirrored in Fleet.

'You can sleep first,' she said. Good sense was being chased away by wave after wave of weariness. Uncon-sciousness was creeping up behind her with a heavy weight in its hand.

Fleet moved cautiously onto the bed, wincing as he moved. 'I'll just close my eyes for a few minutes and then I'll go...'

'It's a plan,' Lydia murmured. Her last thought was to wish that Jason was here. She had been managing not to think about him, not to consider the possibility that he might have been in the bunker with the other ghosts and that whatever happened to them had also happened to him. She wanted to see his face, to know that he was okay. She wished she believed in a higher power and could say a prayer for his safety. Then sleep coshed her over the head and all was black silence.

Lydia opened her eyes to a drilling pain in her head and sharpness over her body where the covers touched. At some point in the night, she had unwound from the towel and ended up under the duvet. She moved gingerly, setting off a fresh wave of prickling pain over her skin. Fleet wasn't in bed and, as if summoned by her thoughts, he pushed the door open a few moments later. He was wearing jersey shorts and nothing else and Lydia felt sympathy pain for the red welts across his chest.

'Breakfast of champions,' Fleet said, putting the tray he was carrying onto the bed. Glasses of water, cans of Coke, painkillers, antiseptic cream, and toast with chocolate spread. 'I was going to head to the bakery and get pain au chocolat, but I didn't want to leave you.'

Or wear a T-shirt, Lydia guessed. She was already dreading putting on clothes over her sore skin.

'It's fine,' he said, seeing her looking at his chest. The wounds looked as if they were sealed with a translucent layer of fresh skin. That had to be a good sign.

'I put the antiseptic on. Let's see yours.'

Lydia struggled to a sitting position. Fleet sucked in a breath through his teeth when the cover fell from her chest and arms. A quick glance of her own confirmed that her white skin was streaked with red weals. 'They're healing quickly.' This was more hope than certainty, but she felt the need to be chipper in the face of Fleet's distress.

'Maybe you should call that doc you mentioned.'

Lydia shrugged and managed not to hiss in pain at the movement. Progress. She popped some painkillers from the packet and took a bite of toast. Her stomach rolled in complaint, but she forced down half a slice and most of the water. 'It's fine. Just need to rest up today and let them scab over. More importantly. We need to work out what happened.'

'What could you see?'

Lydia frowned. 'Ghosts packed in. I don't know how many, but more kept appearing. They were stacked on top of each other, pushed inside each other. They were being dragged there, I could feel it. And the energy in the room...' she trailed off, trying to work out how to describe it. 'Electric. But also like a huge pressure. It's really hard to explain.'

Fleet reached out to hold her hand.

'Could you feel it?' Lydia asked.

'I couldn't see anyone. But it was really cold and that made it hard to think.' He ducked his head. 'I felt weird.

Sort of drugged. I might have missed something. There could have been something small. It wasn't easy to scan thoroughly with the torch.'

'Did you see a bomb?'

Fleet shook his head. 'Sorry. No.'

A pause. 'Was it a bomb? It really felt like an explosion and then there was that stuff everywhere. On us, I mean.'

Fleet took painkillers and drained his glass of water. He pushed the plate of toast closer to Lydia. 'I thought so.' He swallowed hard. 'For a moment there... I thought that was it. A bomb would have collapsed the bunker. And nobody knew we were there. Game over.'

'There was a bang?' Lydia thought that she remembered a flash of light, but her memories still felt jumbled. Uncertain.

'And a burst of light. And that stuff was flying everywhere.' He closed his eyes briefly. 'I felt the burning instantly and started running.'

'Good thing you did.' Lydia didn't want to think about how much worse their injuries would be if Fleet hadn't got the stuff washed off them so quickly. She picked up the antiseptic cream and began applying it to the worst of her broken skin. It stung like a bastard.

'I'm thinking a small explosive attached to a quantity of corrosive substance,' Fleet continued. 'It might have been detonated remotely or there could have been a trigger wire or pressure pad that we activated.'

'A defence? What could that have been hiding?'

'Or a trap. Maybe we were meant to go into the bunker?'

'We weren't exactly pointed to it, though. You think that was meant to kill us?'

'It could have. If we'd been moving faster, we would have been closer to the source and would have been covered in the stuff.'

Lydia remembered how hesitant she had been. Her senses had been screaming that something was wrong. Maybe Fleet's foresight had been activated, too.

'The cold was brutal,' Fleet said. 'Was that just the spirits?'

Lydia nodded, still thinking. 'That many, all together. I've never been so close to a group like that. They looked unhappy and some were crying.' She pictured the group, their mouths opening. 'It was like they were speaking, but I couldn't hear them. And that's it.'

'Were they angry? Like Mary?'

Lydia closed her eyes again. And it came to her. What had been so very wrong. 'They didn't look angry,' she said. 'They looked terrified.'

CHAPTER NINETEEN

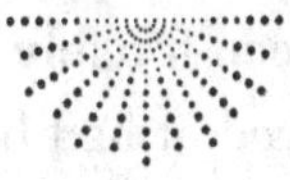

Lydia wanted to rest. She also really didn't want any clothing to touch her burned skin. But Ember was still missing. She had made a pact with herself that if she hadn't found him by now, it was time to go to the police, the secret service, and maybe even the Silvers. If she offered a cash reward, Maria Silver might be stirred to tap her resources.

Her only comfort was that if he had been taken, there would have been a ransom demand by now. Which meant it was more likely that he had run away. Things were truly bad when that was the better option. She called Emma to update her on the lack of news. And to hear her comforting voice.

What she really wanted to do was to go back to sleep, to pretend that none of this was happening, but that wasn't an option.

'There aren't any dishes of cereal out,' Fleet said, coming back into the bedroom. 'Does that mean Jason isn't back?'

Lydia swallowed her nausea. 'I'll look for him,' Lydia said. She hadn't seen Jason in the bunker and was steadfastly refusing to believe he had been there. That he might have been hurt. The thought of losing Jason was unacceptable. She needed to function, so she simply wasn't going to consider the possibility. When she had thought that he had been forcibly 'moved on' when The Fork had been destroyed, it had been like losing a limb. She wasn't going through that again.

After a walkthrough of the house, she went out to the garden. It was cloudy today, but still warm. Next to the tree that Lydia tried, and failed, not to think of as 'Mary's', Lydia closed her eyes and willed Jason to return. Something might be dicking about with ghosts, pulling them in and spitting poison into their minds, twisting their essence or spirit or whatever, but she was Jason's friend. And she was Lydia Crow. 'Hell Hawk, Jason,' she said out loud. 'Get your arse back home.'

When she opened her eyes, she almost expected to see him standing in front of her. But instead it was just the tree. And a couple of crows in the branches, giving her beady eyed looks that managed to appear sarcastic.

'Good morning,' she said politely. 'I'm looking for Jason. I'm worried about him.'

One of the crows flapped its wings and moved along the branch. Either they were getting closer to listen to her, or it was a coincidence. She did feel stupid, though. Why hadn't she asked the crows for help earlier?

She dug into her pocket for her phone and thumbed to the school photo of Ember. 'This child is missing. He isn't a fledgling, he shouldn't be out of the nest.'

The crows tilted their heads, as if listening.

'Please could you look for him?' Lydia held her phone out, tilting it toward the branches of the tree where the crows were perched. They hopped along the branches to get closer, peering at the screen with shining black eyes and then back at Lydia. Questioning.

'He's important to me,' Lydia said.

They cawed in response and took flight.

BACK INSIDE THE HOUSE, FLEET WAS SITTING IN THE kitchen. Despite the injuries, his torso was still very pleasant to look at. Lydia thought briefly about climbing onto his lap, but then remembered the searing pain of anything touching her. Feathers. 'Coffee?' She offered instead.

'We really should get checked out,' Fleet said. 'Medically.'

'I'm fine,' Lydia said. 'Already healing.' She had always been pretty robust. Another gift of her Crow heritage, she assumed, along with her ability to down whisky in large quantities. Whisky. Now that sounded tempting. She re-routed from the coffee machine to the drinks cupboard in the living room.

Charlie had a dedicated sideboard with bottles of booze, crystal glasses, cocktail shakers, and bar tools. While she still hated living in his house, drinking his booze was somehow quite satisfying. It had to be the teenager that apparently still controlled a good part of her brain.

She turned around with two bottles in her arms and

almost dropped them as a waft of cool air tickled her skin. She heard a faint voice. She looked around, desperate for a glimpse of Jason. The voice was still speaking and she thought it might be him. Still too quiet to catch the words, but it was definitely speech. 'Jason?'

The voice got a little louder. She stood stock still, stretching out her senses to listen and feel. 'It's okay,' she said to the cold air. 'You're safe. I'm here.'

After a few minutes, she could see a shimmer and it slowly coalesced into the shape of her friend. His voice got more distinct with every second until she could hear him reciting something mathematical, seemingly to calm himself.

'Thank Feathers.' Lydia wanted to hug him, but knew he was too incorporeal for that. She stepped closer and tried to convey her relief and happiness through vibes. She knew that most adults would use their words, but she was frightened that if she spoke, the sobs that had been rising up through her sternum would burst out.

Gradually he became solid enough for Lydia to make out his expression. It was confused.

'It's okay,' she managed. 'You're okay.'

'I was just—' he began, and then stopped.

The vibrating had subsided and his feet were on the floor and not floating above it. Lydia began to breathe properly and was able to push down the urge to cry. 'I was so worried.'

Jason eyed the booze. 'Drowning your concern?' Then he noticed her injuries. 'What happened? You're hurt.'

She gave him the rundown, including the corrosive

goo that had hit her and Fleet. 'I look worse than I feel,' she lied.

'You were looking for me?'

'Of course,' she said.

They looked at each other for a beat.

Jason cleared his throat. He was looking more solid now, and Lydia could no longer see the sofa through his body.

'I was yanked away from here,' he said. 'I know that. There was that bad smell and feeling of being underground. It's hard to remember properly, I've just got flashes. But it didn't feel right and people were crying.' He stopped. 'It was a bad scene.'

Lydia's stomach clenched. He had been there.

'I could feel myself being held, trapped, but I knew I had to get away. I managed to pull myself away, but not back here. I couldn't just, you know, blink back or whatever. I was on a street for a bit, I think, and I could feel this force still pulling and pulling. I didn't want to go back underground, so I kept moving in the other direction. Away. One step after another until I couldn't see my feet or my body or anything.' He shook his head.

'You were strong enough to pull away from the bunker. That's good.'

'Only just,' he said, looking at himself as if for reassurance. 'I was getting weaker, I could feel it. And then everything was blank. And now I'm here. And I feel like shit. I don't know if I can do that again.'

'It's okay,' Lydia said. 'I'm going to find whoever is doing this and I'm going to stop them.'

'Ideally before I get exploded into toxic goo.'

Lydia stopped. 'You think the ghosts themselves exploded?'

'We've got to be made of something,' Jason said. 'Or, at least, we're energy. That doesn't just disappear.'

'You disappear all the time,' Lydia argued.

'I disappear from your point of view. But I actually move to another physical location. We don't know what would happen if I actually died. Disappeared. Was destroyed.' He ran a hand through his hair. 'I don't know what term to use.'

'Mary moved on. That's like dying for you guys. What if the cameo doesn't just pull ghosts in? What if it forces you to move on?'

'And being forced like that isn't natural. It's violent.' He glanced at the sofa, where his laptop was lying on the cushions.

'You want to research it, don't you?'

He gave her a crooked smile. 'Come on. Of course.'

JASON HAD REGAINED ENOUGH CORPOREALITY TO work his computer and she could tell he wanted a moment to himself. Lydia took her bottles into the kitchen. She no longer felt the urge to drink, but whisky was good for taking the edge off physical pain.

'Jason's back,' she informed Fleet. 'He's okay.'

'That's good.' He clocked the bottles. 'Day drinking?'

She opened the Talisker. It was an eighteen-year-old and probably a couple of hundred quid. She took a hit straight from the bottle and then offered it to Fleet. He shook his head, then reconsidered, grabbing juice glasses from the cupboard.

'Was he there?'

'Briefly,' Lydia said, pouring generous measures. 'But he managed to save himself. This time.'

'What do you mean?'

'He thinks the explosion wasn't a bomb. That the ghosts themselves exploded.' Lydia ran through the theory. That the ghosts were being forced to cross over to the other side or wherever they went. But because it was happening violently, suddenly, and not through achieving resolution, in the way that Mary had, their energy was transformed into something physical. And toxic.

'Ectoplasm?' Fleet asked.

'Ghost goop.'

He took a sip of his whisky, his expression still serious. 'I did take some samples.'

Lydia was surprised. She hadn't been thinking all that straight after the bunker. Intense pain had a way of clouding one's thought processes, she found. Fleet had thought to cut a couple of samples of their goo-splattered clothes before bagging and binning the rest, and he produced two repurposed jam jars, one with T-shirt scraps and one with a small smear of goo. 'I scraped that off,' he said.

'Very make do and mend,' Lydia said, indicating the jars.

'I thought the stuff would probably melt through a plastic evidence bag.'

Now, he held out a jar to Lydia and she took it gingerly, holding it up to the light.

'Are we really talking ectoplasm?' Fleet asked.

Lydia had been trying not to think about Ghost-busters. That was just silly, but it was difficult not to. The stuff was sitting in a jam jar.

'Matter doesn't just disappear, does it? That's physics,' Fleet said. 'If ghosts get used up or damaged or moved on, this is what that energy converts to. It makes sense.'

He didn't look happy. 'What's wrong?'

'I didn't get a vision. What is the point of them if they don't warn me?'

Lydia didn't know the answer to that. 'Did that woman explain?' Fleet had spent time with a fortune-telling woman called Bee. One of the Three Sisters who lived on a supernaturally warded island off the north-east coast, on the border with Scotland.

'She helped me control them. I couldn't tell what was real and what was vision. You remember?'

Lydia did. It had been terrifying for her, so feathers-only-knew how bad it had been for Fleet.

'She calmed them down, helped me shrink them down into something manageable. I can see them, but they don't overwhelm my mind anymore. But she didn't tell me how to control them. Summon them or whatever.' He rubbed his face, stubble scratching.

'You could visit her again. See if you can get more answers.'

'I could try harder,' Fleet said. 'I've been sort of

pushing it down. Keeping the volume on mute and trying to ignore it.'

'That's understandable.' Lydia had always known she wasn't a normal human. She could imagine the last couple of years had been shocking for Fleet.

'Not really.' He shook his head, looking like he wanted to hit something. 'I've been a coward. Working out how to use this ability,' he tapped his head, 'might have helped loads of people. How many people have died because I haven't been trying harder?'

'And how many have been saved because you're functional enough to do your job?' Lydia countered. 'There's always more that any of us could technically do. There's always more that's needed. You're always telling me that.'

He smiled, then. 'Yeah. But it's different when I'm telling you.'

She walked around the kitchen counter and reached up to cup his cheek with her least-damaged hand. 'You're good, Fleet, but you're just one person. You can only do what you can do.'

'I know,' he mumbled, arms bracketing her body, but not touching. 'I just wish I could do more.'

'You do plenty,' Lydia went onto her toes and kissed him.

His hand grazed her side and she sucked in a breath.

'Sorry,' he moved away instantly. 'I hurt you.'

'It's just tender,' she said, looking at the offending wound. Before he could say something else, she held up a hand. 'Don't suggest hospital again.'

'What about the doctor you mentioned? The one the Crows use. Doesn't she do house calls?'

Dr Walker, speaking gently to Ember, as she examined him. The memory flipped through her mind and she wondered, with a blinding flash, how she had been so stupid?

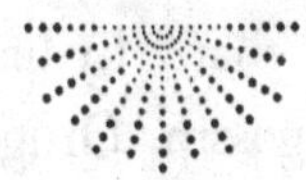

When she wasn't attending on site, Dr Walker worked out of an old tanning salon on Peckham Road. Lydia had her home address, though, thanks to Jason and his skills. The doctor roosted near Ruskin Park. It was a Victorian terrace which had been tastefully renovated, with the ubiquitous extension at the back to form an open-plan kitchen with bifold doors onto the small garden. Jason had shown Lydia the particulars of the house from when it had been sold three years ago, which meant that Dr Walker had dropped a cool two million and was doing all right for herself.

There was a hefty premium on the good doc's services, but the Crows didn't pay that kind of money. Of course, they didn't have exclusivity either. Walker could be patching up gang members from surrounding Brixton and Peckham and maybe even further afield. It hadn't concerned Lydia until this moment. She had assumed that Walker knew to keep her mouth shut.

'Inherited wealth?' She asked Jason, just checking she wasn't jumping to conclusions.

He shook his head, eyes on his screen. 'Not as far as I can see. Attended a comprehensive in Essex. Qualified at Barts and worked at The Royal London until she was struck off in 2011.'

'I think I knew that,' Lydia frowned, trying to remember the Family gossip. 'Drug stuff?'

'I can find out,' Jason said, fingers dancing over the keyboard. 'It's public record at the medical tribunal service. Hang on.'

A moment later he had it. 'Fraud. Crem forms, prescriptions, time sheets.' He looked up. 'Dr Walker was versatile.'

'Crem forms?' Lydia had asked before her brain had time to catch up. She wasn't sure she really wanted to know.

'Ash cash. Docs get paid for filing the paperwork for crematoriums. They have to verify that body is safe to be burned or something like that. Don't know if that's still a thing, but back in 2010, Dr Walker conned sixteen grand with that scheme. I wonder how she did that...' He trailed off, fingers tapping again.

Lydia left him in his research bubble and went to call Aiden. It didn't seem as if Dr Walker had a motive, or the skills, to kidnap Ember, but she certainly appeared adept at spotting opportunity. Her gut told her that the doctor had most likely sold information about Ember to the highest bidder.

Another unwelcome thought: what if the highest bidder had been the NewRipper? They were playing with Lydia, so it wasn't beyond the realms of possibility that they would be paying for information on her and her Family. She felt sick.

Forty minutes later, they were in Aiden's car, parked down the street from Dr Walker's address.

Lydia had Aiden and a Crow called Leon. She knew Aiden had been training him up and thought it was time he got more involved. Plus, a bit of extra muscle was always handy. Lydia didn't know if Dr Walker lived alone, for starters. The woman kept her private life private, which was smart given her line of work.

'Let's go,' Lydia said.

Leon just nodded, barely managing eye contact. He hadn't managed to say a single word out loud to Lydia so far and she wondered if there was such a thing as too much hype. What had Aiden been telling the Family? She didn't want her own people to be frightened around her, however handy it was for leadership.

There was a black Lexus SUV on the monoblocked driveway and a state-of-the-art security system on the house. 'Window alarms,' Aiden said quietly. 'And three cameras on the front.'

Leon vaulted over the locked side-gate and headed to the back, while Lydia and Aiden took the front. She went for the doorbell, which set off a vicious barking from inside.

Aiden widened his eyes at Lydia. 'Guard dog, too. This woman is paranoid.'

'Sensible,' Lydia corrected. 'Think about her clientele.'

They waited for a minute, Lydia imagining Dr

Walker peering at them through the cameras and deciding not to open up. If she thought about slipping out the back, she would meet Leon. And she had to know that she couldn't avoid Lydia forever. It would be better to open the door now.

As if the doc had come to the same conclusion, the dog stopped barking and Lydia heard a lock clicking. When the door opened, Lydia saw fear in the doctor's eyes and she pushed down her empathy. This woman might be responsible for Ember being taken. And even if she wasn't, she was clearly making extra cash from somewhere.

'This is a surprise,' Dr Walker said. 'I don't work from home.'

'Put the kettle on, doc,' Aiden said, breezing in and making it clear that they wouldn't be chatting on the doorstep.

Dr Walker stepped back instinctively. 'I don't bring my work home.'

A low growl started. It came from the Bullmastiff that was pressed protectively against Dr Walker's side. The growl became a snapping snarl and the dog tensed low, as if readying to jump.

'Call off your friend,' Lydia said, keeping her voice pleasant. 'I would hate to have to snap its neck.'

Lydia would never hurt a dog, but Dr Walker didn't know that and she hastily pulled the dog back, issuing calming commands.

'Shall we,' Lydia indicated the hallway that led to the kitchen.

Aiden appeared in the doorway. 'All clear,' he said.

'What is this about?' Dr Walker's voice was steel and Lydia couldn't help but be impressed.

'Is Ember okay?' She asked. 'I told you I couldn't be a hundred per cent without a full—'

'I definitely want to talk about Ember,' Lydia said, hustling the doctor into the kitchen.

Leon was standing in front of the bifold doors, arms crossed bouncer-style. He had the muscles and scowl to match, so it was an impressive sight.

Dr Walker's gaze flicked from Aiden to Leon and back to Lydia. 'I did what you asked. I could only do a basic health check, I told you—'

'I'm rather more interested in your mouth,' Lydia said. 'As in, who have you been talking to?'

The doctor stopped speaking. A crease deepened on her lined forehead. 'What?'

'You told somebody about Ember, and I want to know who,' Lydia said. 'We can get to the "why" and the necessary reparations later.'

'Ember's missing,' Aiden said. He was standing closest to the doctor and she winced when he spoke. The colour had drained from her face.

'I didn't... I would never...' Dr Walker visibly pulled herself together. 'I am aware of the importance of discretion.'

'I believe that's true,' Lydia said. 'You wouldn't have lasted this long in your profession otherwise. But someone knows about Ember. And that someone took him.'

Dr Walker's white skin went even paler.

'You should sit down,' Lydia said. She didn't want the doc passing out before she had answers.

Aiden closed a hand over Dr Walker's shoulder and steered her onto the bench seat that stretched along the dining table.

Lydia stepped closer, looking down at the doctor and allowing no mercy to show in her face. 'There's a very short list of people who were aware of Ember and his importance to me. I trust everyone else on that list, which leaves you.' Lydia pointed at Walker. 'So, talk.'

'I...' Dr Walker closed her mouth. Her eyes took on a resigned expression. It was one that said 'I am in deep shit, but I'm not saying a damn thing.'

'Who are you afraid of?' Aiden asked, his voice as cold as the ocean. 'Apart from us.'

Dr Walker shook her head.

Lydia sighed. She produced her coin and held it up in front of Dr Walker. The woman didn't flinch, but her eyes went wide.

In her peripheral, Aiden was smiling. Leon had a blank expression, but she saw the interest in his gaze. She could feel their attention as if it was alive. She was holding the room and it was intoxicating. The coin flip was as natural as breathing and the shining disc turned in the air with dazzling, supernatural slowness.

Dr Walker watched it, transfixed.

'Now,' Lydia said. 'Who did you tell about Ember?'

'A woman,' Dr Walker said, without hesitation.

'Name?'

'I don't know.'

'Give me her name.'

Dr Walker didn't move her gaze from the spinning coin, but her body began to shake. 'I don't know. She didn't tell me.'

Satisfied that Walker really didn't know the name, Lydia tried a different direction. 'She approached you?'

A nod. 'A year ago. Said she would pay for any information on you.'

Lydia took a slow breath to calm her fury. 'I hope it was a lot.'

Tears were leaking from the corners of Dr Walker's eyes. She was hardly blinking, but Lydia didn't care. She was too angry. 'How did you contact her?'

'Number. Phone.'

'Have you been paid?'

'Yes.'

'How?'

A shuddering breath. 'Delivered by courier.'

'But you met her once? The initial contact. What does she look like?'

Dr Walker swallowed. 'Older than me. Tall.'

'And you just agreed to sell me out. Just like that?' Lydia should have given up being surprised by people a long time ago, but apparently not.

A little fire in Dr Walker's eyes. 'She said she would have me put away if I didn't comply. She knew all about my work.'

'Put away? She was police?'

A tiny head shake. 'I think she works for the government. National security.' She looked pleadingly at Lydia. 'I didn't have a choice.'

. . .

Lydia left Dr Walker with strict instructions to carry on as normal. If she was informing on her other clients to Sinclair she could continue, but if she ever passed on information about the Crow Family she would lose everything. Starting with her fingers.

Back in the car, Aiden had been silent. Lydia could feel his judgement but guessed he wasn't going to question her in front of Leon.

Once they were back at Charlie's, he dismissed Leon and turned in his seat to face Lydia. 'You're letting her get away with informing.'

'She's a good medic. And now we know she's compromised. We will be extra careful not to let anything slip around her.'

'But she will know when we're hurt,' Aiden argued. 'We can't hide that if she's patching us up.'

'True,' Lydia said. 'It's not ideal, but if we had to find someone new, we wouldn't be sure they're trustworthy. And she is scared of us. She owes us.'

'It's a mistake,' Aiden said. He was looking serious. 'I'm sorry, boss, but she's too greedy. She'll sell us out to the highest bidder.'

'What would you do?' Lydia was tired. 'Decent docs that are willing to work outside the system don't exactly grow on trees.'

'Right then,' Aiden said, giving the question due consideration. 'We have to keep her working for us?'

'I think it's best.'

'Set fire to her house for starters,' Aiden said promptly. 'Public retribution so everyone knows what happens if you cross the Crows. And let her know we keep a file on her work. She's been practising illegally for years, that's a lot of blackmail. I'd bleed her funds dry and stop her working for anybody else. Clip her wings good and proper.'

Lydia looked at her second in command for a moment. 'You're good at this.'

CHAPTER TWENTY-ONE

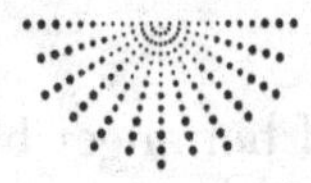

Back at the house, Lydia found the leaflet with Sinclair's contact number. Despite the urge to burn it, she had shoved it into a desk drawer, and now she was grateful to her past restraint.

If you walked directly toward the Thames from Camberwell, following the new road and passing Kennington Park, you hit Vauxhall Bridge and the blocky Lego-style MI6 building. Lydia didn't know exactly where MI13 roosted, but she wasn't going to cross the river for Sinclair.

The woman was waiting on the appointed bench on the Vauxhall embankment, swathed in her signature look of drapey knitwear cape and with a sharp pair of heeled black boots.

'Bit warm for that get-up, isn't it?' Lydia said, plonking herself down on the bench.

'Linen,' Sinclair said. 'You'd be surprised.'

'I suppose you feel the cold at your age.'

A thin smile. Bright eyes assessing her over a hawk-like nose. It hadn't occurred to Lydia before now, and she kicked herself for it. Sinclair was a predator. She abandoned any plans to be diplomatic. 'You have Ember.'

If she had expected equivocation and deception, she was bang out of luck.

'He is quite safe.'

The white heat of her anger blazed so brightly, she was amazed Sinclair couldn't see it. 'If he is harmed in any—'

'He is unharmed and I have no interest in doing so.'

The truth was sinking in, but Lydia couldn't quite believe it. 'You kidnapped a child to get my attention?'

Sinclair glanced around. 'We should discuss this elsewhere.'

'I disagree. We should discuss this right now.' Lydia raised her voice to demonstrate just how little she cared about Sinclair's precious low profile. 'You brought this battle, so let's have it.'

'I do not wish to fight with you. We have bigger concerns than your misgivings about my profession and the activities of my predecessor. There has been another death and I would value your input. In return, I can offer you the resources of my department. We should work together, this is what I've been trying to convey—'

'Take me to him.'

Sinclair shook her head. 'I don't think you understand how leverage works.'

'I don't think you understand how leverage works with me. You take me to Ember right now and release him to my care and I will consider your request.'

'I really would prefer we talk elsewhere.'

'You started this,' Lydia said, not budging.

Sinclair waited until a middle-aged suit with a brief-case walked past and then said: 'I would like you to look at some remains. In situ.'

'And?'

'And give your professional opinion. As a Crow.'

'You want me to tell you if there's Family involvement?'

'I want you to tell me everything you can glean.'

'Done.'

Sinclair nodded briskly. 'We can go now.'

'Not until you've given me Ember.' Lydia forced herself to lean back, to plant herself on the seat and demonstrate that she wasn't going to move. 'I will not cooperate until I have Ember. That is the deal.'

'You expect me to trust you that you will hold up your—' Sinclair broke off. She must have seen something in Lydia's expression. After a moment, she tried again. 'Be reasonable. I want to deliver the child back into your care at the earliest possible moment, but what would you do in my position?'

Lydia didn't like it, but she had to accept that Sinclair was holding the better cards in this round. 'Fine,' she said. 'But I need to see him.'

Sinclair took a phone from her pocket and dialled. After a quick exchange, she hit a button to change to video and held the screen so that Lydia could see a kitchen. At the small table, Ember was visible. Alive. Not speaking or looking at the person who was presumably holding their own phone to capture the video, but shovelling spoonfuls of cereal into his mouth with a mechanical efficiency.

'This isn't over,' Lydia said, her gaze drinking in the sight of him until Sinclair took the phone back. 'There will be repercussions.'

'You want your child returned. I want a favour. We can both walk away from this happy.'

If Lydia had her way, Sinclair would never experience another moment of happiness again. Keeping that thought to herself, she said: 'Let's go.'

SINCLAIR MADE A CALL AND WITHIN FIVE MINUTES, a black SUV pulled up nearby. Lydia eyed the car with some trepidation, but she got inside anyway. She didn't have a choice. Being inside the blandly expensive vehicle reminded her of Gale, Sinclair's predecessor. Which didn't help her mood.

Sinclair was running through the details and Lydia had to force herself to concentrate. She kept seeing Ember in her mind's eye. He had looked physically healthy, but she knew he had to be frightened. It made it difficult to concentrate. 'Say that again,' she said, when she realised that Sinclair was looking at her expectantly.

'I understand that you are unhappy with my methods,' Sinclair said, making the understatement of the century, 'but it was the only way to get your attention.'

'Your agent just died?'

Sinclair nodded.

'You took Ember almost a week ago.' Lydia couldn't stop thinking that Ember had been imprisoned and frightened for all this time. 'If your agent only just turned up dead, why did you take Ember before?'

'There was another matter.'

Lydia's jaw was clenched and she forced herself to relax enough to speak. 'Tell me.'

Sinclair looked at her, lips pursed as if considering. 'You remember that I had lost contact with my agent? And I was interested in any intel you would be able to provide concerning the fifth Family?'

Lydia had been thinking about this since Sinclair had first told her about it. 'You know that Gale was very interested in the four Families? People told him all kinds of stories, he at least had the sense to know when someone was spinning a line.'

'But some of those tall tales turned out to be real. And they turned out to have value to the service.'

Lydia assumed Sinclair was referring to Gale's assassin recruitment. That hadn't ended so well for her cousin Maddie. Or the people Maddie killed before Lydia threw her off a roof.

But Sinclair wasn't talking about assassins. 'The intel suggested that the fifth Family has the ability to create instant disguises, something that could be of great utility to the service. It has caught the interest of those higher up the chain, and I've been tasked with verifying it. Then I heard that you had taken in a child. I assumed that wasn't just a random act from the goodness of your heart.'

Lydia thought for a beat. 'You thought Ember was a member of this mythical fifth Family?'

'It seemed like a possibility. A new person, installed

with the head of the Crows. I thought that if he did have this fifth Family ability, we might get a chance to observe it.'

Lydia pushed down the fury at Sinclair running an experiment on a child. Even if she hadn't laid a finger on Ember, she had terrorised him. 'It's not real,' she said, keeping her emotion in check and her voice cold. 'Gale was cracked. You agree, so don't pull that face.'

'Nevertheless. He believed there was a fifth Family. One that could change their appearance at will. It's in his notes. And now I have corroboration from an agent in the field. An agent whose body we're about to view, which makes me wonder if he was killed for sharing this information.'

Lydia didn't have a smart answer for that. All she knew was that there wasn't a fifth Family. In all the bedtime stories her father told her, he had never so much as hinted at one.

'Disguises are a hugely important part of covert ops,' Sinclair was saying. 'We use glasses, clothing, facial hair to alter appearance, and even prosthetics and the CIA developed full-face masks.'

'Like in Mission Impossible.'

'Yes, but they're extremely expensive and difficult to make, they have to be bespoke for the individual so are effectively single-use, and while they're pretty bloody good, if someone starts looking for one, they're going to find it. Imagine if we had the ability to truly transform appearance? In a completely undetectable way?'

'You actually believe it's possible?'

'Gale certainly thought so.'

'I'm not asking about him.'

Sinclair looked out of the side window at the passing traffic. 'It seems unlikely. But...'

Lydia waited.

After another moment of silence, Sinclair met her gaze. 'Let's say I've learned to keep an open mind.'

THE CRIME SCENE WAS A DISUSED COMMERCIAL building in Hackney that had recently been the site of an illegal party. The squatting movement of the seventies and eighties might not be in its heyday, but the network of squats throughout the fringes of London was alive and well. Sinclair was telling Lydia that the service kept tabs on the squatting scene, as it had ties to anarchist groups and other subversive movements. Nice to have her resources, Lydia supposed. But it did involve a pact with the devil, so there was that significant downside.

They had tabs on the illegal party and had an undercover agent do a drop-in, nothing untoward reported, but a homeless gentleman, looking to sleep in the building after the party had disbanded had called the police after he found the corpse of a man.

The building was a low-rise office block with unlovely seventies architecture. 'Council owned,' Sinclair said as they got out of the car, 'and disused for the last twelve months due to a planning cock-up.'

Lydia got out of the car, squeezing her coin tightly in her palm. She would honour her word to Sinclair for this one job, but she wasn't going to make it easy on the woman. 'Tell me again why I'm here?'

Sinclair shot an exasperated look. 'I want you to use your specialist skills.'

'And what might they be?'

'I want you to tell me if the Fifth Family were involved.'

Inside, the unmistakable odour of stale sweat and human waste, plus something artificially sweet. If Lydia had to guess, she would say about a thousand candy-flavoured vapes. The walls were covered in fresh graffiti, including anarchist symbols and anti-capitalist slogans. The ground floor was one large space and had probably been intended as an open-plan office. There wasn't any furniture and every supporting pillar had been covered in spray paint. The edges of the room were littered with empty plastic bottles, squashed cans and used needles. Someone had got really annoyed with one of the walls and bashed a ragged hole in the plasterboard.

'Upstairs,' Sinclair said, leading the way. The second floor had an empty kitchen, now covered in unmentionable substances, several offices, plus a smaller open-plan space. This had a few abandoned sleeping bags and more party detritus. Apart from a couple of desks, both of which had been attempted to be lit on fire, and some broken wheelie chairs, there wasn't much to note. Except for the one intact wheelie chair which had a dead body lashed to it with thin rope.

Lydia had seen few corpses in her time, but never one that looked quite like this. There was a sunken aspect to the skin and flesh, as if it had collapsed in on itself, and there were deep lacerations on his bound forearms. A knife, Lydia thought, distantly, the part of her brain that always seemed to be able to process the details without getting overwhelmed by horror, had kicked into gear. The smells of the squat party vied with the unmistakable undercurrent of death, but the top note of iron overshadowed everything else.

'Go ahead,' Sinclair said. 'My people have been over the scene. We're going to clean this up.'

'You won't be informing the police?'

'He was an agent,' Sinclair said. 'We want it kept quiet.'

'What does it matter now?' The ropes had cut into the man's wrists. Livid marks were visible where he had tried to move. He had been alive when he was tied up, she knew that much.

'We don't want chatter about spies. Too many other groups who might get twitchy about exactly who is in their inner circle. Paranoia is a dangerous thing and I don't want it spreading.'

Lydia pulled on plastic booties and got closer to the body. Her boots squelched unpleasantly into the squishy surface of the short-pile office carpet. It was saturated. Her stomach turned over, but she took a couple of shallow breaths and squeezed her coin until the urge to hurl subsided.

'We think this happened after the party?'

'Yes. Time of death is around eight this evening.

Locals say that the last of the party-goers moved on by ten in the morning. The Collective, that's the name the anarchist group goes by, probably heard about it on the grapevine and thought it would make a good place for...' Sinclair waved a hand. 'An execution.'

'Nobody heard anything?'

'Nothing reported.'

'So they had time,' Lydia said. 'Peace and quiet to carry out this.' She indicated the blood. 'Bleeding out isn't a fun way to go. Was this a punishment? Torture?'

Sinclair's mouth tightened. 'We're assuming that they realised he was undercover. Whether they knew he was an agent or assumed he was police, doesn't really matter. They clearly didn't want him to feed back any further intel. Maybe this was a way to send a message to the others in The Collective, warning them to keep their mouths shut.'

'You worried that he told them he was service?'

'No,' Sinclair said. 'He was trained to resist coercion. And this doesn't look effective.'

Lydia's stomach was getting rebellious again, so she focused on the carpet.

Sinclair was musing out loud. 'He would have passed out quickly. The cuts are deep and blood loss would have been severe and fast. Either it wasn't torture, or it's an amateur making a mistake.'

Aware of Sinclair watching, she touched the ropes that looped over the unfortunate man's wrists. If the man was Family, he wasn't a main bloodline. This close to the corpse, she would usually be getting some kind of signal. Trying not to think about that too much, Lydia got closer to the body in the chair, stretching out her senses. There was a light tug of desire.

'You tested the blood? No hepatitis or anything?'

'Squeaky clean,' Sinclair said, frowning slightly.

Lydia dropped to a crouch, ignoring the wave of disgust that rolled through her body as she got closer to the blood-soaked carpet. The iron was catching at the back of her throat and she took shallow breaths. Before she could overthink it, Lydia peeled off the vinyl glove she had automatically put on and pushed her palm against the sodden weave. The top layer of blood was brown, but some dark red liquid rose around her fingers as she applied pressure. She closed her eyes and concentrated. The signature was faint, but unmistakable. Pearl.

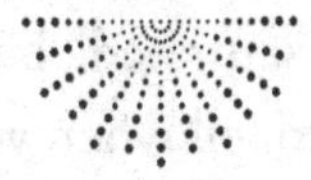

Sinclair kept her end of the bargain. Which was good news for everyone. On the way to what Sinclair called a 'safe house' on the edge of Camden, Lydia mulled over the crime scene. In itself, Sinclair's spook being a Pearl wasn't a surprise. The Pearl Family was diluted to the point at which thousands of Londoners probably had a bit running through their veins. Besides, the Pearl traits certainly leant themselves to spy work. They could charm people, seduce them, ingratiate themselves into groups and manipulate from within. Crows also had their value, as evidenced by Gale and Sinclair's campaign to recruit Lydia, and Gale's training of Maddie as an assassin. Crows had power, and they could be vicious. Lydia doubted that Foxes had been used by the service. They had all the requisite skills, a combination of the other three Families with an extra dose of sexual chemistry that would weaken the toughest soldier or seduce the most pious political leader. Paul Fox flashed into Lydia's mind. He could probably turn a carved statue into a pulsing, writhing body in heat, and extract every secret from their stone mind before they knew what was happening. But the Foxes were untrainable. Unrecruitable. They held allegiance to their blood, their pack, but weren't fans of hierarchical organisation.

'The carpet was saturated, but is that all of it? I assume you'll be able to tell when you process the scene.'

'Of course.' Sinclair said, picking up the thread of Lydia's thoughts. 'Why?'

'I'm wondering if the blood was the point.' One of the forum discussions that Henriksen had taken part in had debated the use of human blood for rituals to reveal, attract and bind ghosts.

Sinclair's mouth tightened. 'If there's something you're keeping to yourself...'

'As I said, there was a faint note of Pearl. Which means your agent probably had some in his family history. In London, that's not all that unusual, and it probably helped him in his work.'

'The agent told me that The Collective had knowledge of the fifth Family and a power that allowed them to transform themselves into another human being. A disguise so convincing that it would fool a biometric scanner and could be applied and removed in seconds.'

'I told you. There isn't a fifth Family.'

'You've asked around?'

Lydia decided not to respond to that. Sinclair seemed to be wilfully ignoring the last few times she had stated the fact and she wasn't in the business of wasting her breath. 'I got no hint of an unfamiliar Family signature,' she said, referencing the crime scene. She tried to change the subject. 'You said the group was considered low risk?'

Sinclair hesitated. 'The dynamic seems to have changed rapidly. About a year ago, as far as we can tell, things got serious. Five was aware of them, but had handed them to us. Proof, if you were looking for it, that they were considered a low-level threat.'

'We inherited the agent from Five along with the case. As soon as he mentioned a Fifth Family, they couldn't pass it along quickly enough. Fairy tales as far as they're concerned.'

'But why did Five have an agent in a peaceful group?' People had a right to gather and protest. It wasn't right that they had been under state surveillance.

'Best way to keep an eye on a group like this is to have actual eyes and ears on the ground. Plus, you never know who else they will come into contact with. The Collective appeared harmless, but radical groups attract radical people.'

'And you think that's what happened?'

'I think a new leader changed the remit of The Collective. Decisively.'

Lydia flipped her coin over her knuckles. Her stomach was clenched with anxiety. She knew that she would see Ember in a matter of minutes, that he was relatively safe, but the traffic seemed worse than usual, the car crawling toward Camden with cruel slowness.

Sinclair broke the silence in the car. 'I want to be honest with you. You know from my somewhat drastic actions that this is important.'

The urge to do something violent rushed through Lydia like the wind through trees. It left her steady. She smiled. 'You want me to listen to what you have to say?'

Sinclair eyed her warily. She was giving every impression of a person who was going to reveal some big truth, but the woman was a consummate liar.

'I think we should work together,' Sinclair tried. 'Until we find the fifth Family.'

'You kidnapped my child.' The words were stark and she hadn't expected to say them.

Sinclair smiled thinly. 'How's your research into Scarlett going?'

Lydia frowned, momentarily thrown. 'What's it to you?'

'I could help you out.'

The audacity of the woman was breath-taking. 'You never stop, do you?'

'I know why you haven't been able to find out much about her background.'

Lydia stared at Sinclair. 'You hinted that there might be a spy in our midst. Before. Are you telling me that you know Scarlett is a spook?'

'No,' Sinclair said. 'Not to my knowledge, at any rate. Like I said before, I can't vouch for five and six. I'm not on their Christmas card list right now.'

'So what then?'

'You ready to work together?'

Lydia forced herself to wait before responding. She squeezed her coin and fought for calm. Scarlett was a problem. Sinclair might know something important. She might also be dangling a promise as false as the fifth

Family nonsense. 'Take me to Ember,' she said, knowing that every unnecessary second in Sinclair's presence was bringing her closer to a violence she wouldn't come back from.

The safe house was a modest little terrace that looked lived-in, but nondescript. The woman who let them inside looked to be in her sixties. She had silvery-grey hair pulled back into a bun, a polka-dot apron, and the posture of a ballet dancer. 'I've just come on shift,' she said to Sinclair, leading them back through the house. 'No problems.'

The kitchen was part of the original house and was small. There wasn't room for a table and the cabinets looked tired. The woman went back to stirring a pan on the stove. She gave Sinclair a very succinct rundown on Ember's activities for the day, his mood and food intake. She might have looked like a motherly figure from central casting, but Lydia was left in no doubt that she was a professional member of the service.

Lydia could feel her wings wanting to stretch out, the urge to fly. She wanted to snap at Sinclair. She wanted to punch someone.

'I'm Penny,' the woman said, wiping her hands on a checked tea towel before holding one out for Lydia to ignore.

'And I'm Lady Gaga,' Lydia replied. 'Where's Ember?'

Her eyes flicked to Sinclair. 'He's in his room.'

'Locked in?'

The woman calling herself Penny sighed. 'Of course not. You can go on up. First door on the left.'

'Stay here,' Lydia told the two women. She had no idea if they would obey, but she took the stairs two at a time and burst through the door without knocking. If someone was inside with Ember, she wanted the element of surprise.

Ember was sitting on the bed, his backpack next to him and a pack of playing cards in his hands. He looked whole and alive. The relief thudded through Lydia in a sledgehammer blow and, for a moment, she was unable to move or speak. Her eyes flicked over him, taking in bitesize details. His hands, holding the cards, his trainers, laces trailing on the carpet, his eyes, tired.

'I knew you'd come,' Ember said. He wasn't smiling, but his sunshine glow poured out and bathed the whole room in warmth for a few seconds, before it dimmed again. Footsteps behind Lydia. She turned to find a middle-aged bald man in a shirt with pit-stains and a cheap tie looking at her with unabashed curiosity.

'What?' Lydia snapped.

'He said you'd come,' he said. 'I wanted to see the famous Lydia Crow for myself.' The man was layering on the sarcasm, but Lydia could detect something else in his tone. Truth.

She spread her hands, the movement like opening her wings. 'In the flesh. And who are you?'

'Marty,' the man said without missing a beat.

'Of course,' Lydia said. 'Marty the spook. How nice. Tell me, Marty, what the hell are you doing with my kid?'

'I'm not a kid,' Ember piped up. He was shuffling the cards with what looked like a nervous tick. It made Lydia want to set fire to things.

'Your kid?' Marty said at the same time.

Lydia didn't reply. Her coin was in her hand and she rubbed her thumb over its surface, focusing on the sensation so that she stayed calm. Ember had been terrorised enough, he didn't need to see his new caregiver lose control.

'You will be briefed,' Marty said pompously.

'I have no doubt. I hope, for your sake, that it goes well.' Lydia put the certainty of the Crows behind her words and enjoyed the way Marty blanched. She turned to Ember. 'Did they hurt you?'

He shook his head, eyes big.

'You want to come with me?'

A nod. He immediately slid the cards into their battered cardboard case and unzipped his backpack to stow them safely.

Lydia smiled. More relief. There had never been any doubt that she was walking out with Ember, but she was glad she didn't have to force him.

He was standing up, slinging his backpack over his skinny arms.

'You can't go,' Marty said, recovering a little.

'Step aside,' Lydia said, her voice even.

'Leave them,' Sinclair's voice floated up the stairs. For a second Lydia wondered how she had known what had been said, but then she realised that the room would be bugged. Sinclair would have been monitoring the situation, watching Lydia and Ember's reunion, trying to glean every morsel of information possible. Her stomach clenched in renewed fury. The house was superficially a home, but it was nothing more than a cage. A cage they had put Ember inside.

Marty moved out of the doorway and Lydia paused to let Ember go in front.

Sinclair was in the downstairs hall. 'Goodbye, Mr Williams.' she said to Ember. 'Obviously this safe house is burned,' she added to Lydia. 'I thought it was worth it to demonstrate that we had been taking good care of your charge. I'm not a monster, don't forget that.'

Lydia turned to face the woman. She flipped her coin into the air and let it spin lazily. 'I won't forget anything about this.'

CHAPTER TWENTY-THREE

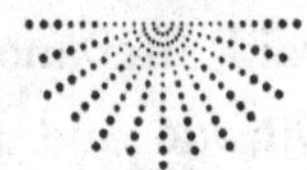

Lydia had booked an Uber as soon as she had arrived at the safe house. Once she had Ember in the car, Lydia took a moment to message Fleet, Emma, Aiden and Paul. Her phone rang straight away. Fleet.

'Is he alright?'

'We're on our way. Are you home?'

'I'm at the flat.' He meant his flat. 'I'll head to Denmark Hill.'

Back at the house, Ember didn't make any move to unbuckle his seatbelt. Lydia glanced at him, registering his blank expression and the telltale tension lines around his eyes and mouth. 'Do you want to go in?'

He shrugged. It was a small movement, but she was pretty sure she detected an increase in his anxiety.

'I hate this house,' Lydia said, 'so it's okay if you do too.'

He shot her a startled look. 'You hate your house? It's well big, though, innit?'

'It is big,' Lydia said. 'Must have cost my uncle a packet. But I still hate it.'

'Why do you live here, then?'

'Good question,' she said. 'But we don't always get what we want. I'm guessing you are well aware of that one.'

'I'll go in,' Ember said, after another moment.

Once they were inside and Ember had shed his backpack, Lydia checked that there was ready-made food in the fridge and told him to help himself to whatever he wanted.

'Anything?' Ember asked with a small smile.

'Anything except alcohol.'

'I could have a beer,' Ember said immediately. 'I'm old enough.'

'You're ten,' Lydia said. 'What kind of guardian would I be if I didn't make you wait until you were at least fourteen?'

Ember brightened at that.

Lydia didn't expect to be in charge of a fourteen-year-old Ember, so she congratulated herself on dodging a bullet.

Once Ember had made himself a sandwich involving several cold meats, sliced cheese and a handful of crisps and popped the tab on a can of Fanta, he seemed to relax a notch. Lydia took a can of Coke from the fridge and pressed it to her neck and forehead. The doors to the garden were wide open, but the air stayed stubbornly still. London in a heatwave brought the term 'close' into stark, sticky reality. Every breath was like inhaling warm soup.

'I didn't run away,' Ember said, the words a bit muffled by his sandwich.

Lydia carried on assembling her own snack plate. Grapes, cold from the fridge, cheese, and salted crackers. 'Okay.'

'I didn't.'

She looked at him, then. 'I believe you.'

He swallowed the last of his mouthful. 'I did leave. I just needed to... Dunno. Get out for a bit. I walked to the park and sat on the swings. Not playing,' he said quickly, 'just thinking, you know?'

'I know.'

'I was going to come back, but I just wanted to... stay out a bit longer.'

Lydia heard the words that he wasn't saying. He had wanted to weigh up his options. Maybe make them worry a bit or lay down his own ground rules. Make it clear he was staying with them of his own free will and not because they had plonked him in a room and told him it was home. She got it. Kid hadn't survived this long without a healthy dose of independence. Not to mention scepticism.

'This sus guy started talking to me.'

'At the park?'

Ember shook his head. 'Street. He said he had a job for me and I could earn a lot of money. Five hundred quid.'

'And you went with him?'

'Ick. No,' Ember said. 'You think I'm stupid? I did a runner.'

'Good for you,' Lydia said.

'Not really.' Ember's face fell. 'Set-up, wannit. I was too busy running from the creeper and didn't see the car. Two geezers got me into the back before I knew what was up.' He shook his head. 'Proper embarrassing.'

Yes. A child should've been able to fend off three adult secret service operatives, Lydia thought drily. But she kept the thought to herself. 'Did they take you straight to the house?'

He nodded, the spark of animation dying in his eyes as the memory came back. She tried not to think about how scared he must have been. Her fists were clenched and she made an effort to uncurl her fingers. 'What happened then?'

'That lady, Penny or whatever, she made me tea. I wasn't gonna eat it, thought it could be poisoned or have, like, sleeping tablets in it, but it was fish fingers. The branded ones,' he made a complicated hand gesture that Lydia assumed meant good. 'Bangin' chips, and all.'

'Was it?'

'What?'

'Drugged?'

'Nah. The fake-gran was the main person I saw and we watched a bit of TV. No streaming, though, so nothing on. Just one of them property things where they're looking at big houses in fields. I went to bed.'

'Right. Okay.' Lydia wanted a list of every person he had interacted with, a recording of every conversation, every moment. She knew Ember was putting on his brave face, but she had to know the details, had to know just how much Sinclair was going to have to pay. They had taken him. They had caged him. He had been frightened. These were not easy facts to stow and Lydia would be the first to admit that she sometimes had problems with her anger. Right now, she wanted to set fire to MI13. Instead, she asked: 'Fake gran?'

'Yeah. I figured that was her bit. Make me feel safe or whatever. Stop me kicking off. And it would look good if anyone official came knocking. Although,' the thought clearly just occurred to him, 'I guess they're not too worried about official.'

'I don't think they are,' Lydia said. 'One rule for us, another for them.'

Ember nodded. 'True dat.'

'What about the rest of the time?'

He shrugged. 'More of the same. Fed me all right. Frosties and Cocoa Pops in the morning.'

Lydia was out of her depth. If Emma was here, she'd know whether Ember was secretly traumatised and hiding it behind the details of breakfast cereal. She had no idea. Maybe branded food really had been enough to make being kidnapped seem fine. And what did that say about his life to this point?

'I'm sorry,' Lydia said. 'They shouldn't have done this. They used you to get to me.'

Ember tapped the side of his empty drinks can. 'That sort of thing happen a lot?'

'No.' Lydia put all of her Crow certainty behind the word and she saw Ember's eyes widen slightly.

'That's good then, innit,' Ember said.

That night, Ember went to the spare room early. He left the door open a little way though, and Lydia stopped in on her way to bed. Standing in the doorway, she waited until he looked up from his phone and acknowledged her.

'Did you have that before?'

'Picked it up on our way out,' Ember said casually. 'It's a piece of shit.'

She felt a rush of affection for the light-fingered boy who was putting up a very convincing front. Nicking a phone wasn't as good as punching them all in the face, but it was something. 'I'm sorry about what happened,' Lydia said. 'If I hadn't brought you back here, you wouldn't have been taken.'

'It's a'ight,' Ember said, not looking up.

'It's not all right. You must have been very scared. Anyone would have been. You've been very brave.' She didn't know what to say, but she tried to channel her own mother and Emma, tried to think what they would say. 'You don't have to be brave now, though. We can talk about it, or I can book a counsellor or—'

'It's a'ight,' Ember said, seeming a bit annoyed. 'I told you.'

'But—'

'I wasn't that scared. I knew you were gonna come and get me. That nothin' really bad was gonna happen.'

'How?'

Another little shrug and he returned his gaze to the phone. 'I saw it.'

THE NEXT MORNING, AFTER A NIGHT IN WHICH Lydia got up to check that Ember was still in his room, sleeping soundly, at three and six in the morning, she downed a large coffee and wondered how on earth Emma functioned.

'You said that you knew Lydia was coming to get you,' Fleet said. 'You saw it?'

Ember nodded. He had made himself one of his enormous sandwiches and was taking big bites, his jaw only just able to open wide enough to get the stacked filling into his mouth. Either the kid was having a growth spurt, or he was stocking up on food while it was available. The habits of a child who never knew when he would next go hungry.

'I see things that are going to happen, too,' Fleet said.

Lydia was surprised. This wasn't the kind of thing that Fleet usually mentioned to people. His candour with the kid gave her a warm feeling that she couldn't quite define.

Ember chewed silently, regarding Fleet with evident scepticism.

'I get visions. They just happen, like a TV has switched on in my head, and I'm watching it. For a while it was a bit scary. They happened all the time and I couldn't stop them.'

Ember still seemed to be deciding whether Fleet was trying to trap him. 'Sounds cracked. You should see a doctor.'

'I did get help, as it happens,' Fleet said easily. 'And now I've got some control. I can,' he paused, clearly searching for the right words, 'turn the volume down? Only it's not just the sound. I kind of make them quieter and smaller, so they are clearly predictions and not reality. It's much easier to cope with. And they don't run all the time, either. It's not exactly silent up here,' he gestured to his head, 'but it's not as loud as it was.'

'Cracked,' Ember said again, but he was watching Fleet carefully.

Fleet shrugged. 'I just wondered if you had the same thing.'

Ember's sandwich lay on the plate, momentarily forgotten. 'I don't get that,' he said. 'What you said. A TV.'

Lydia wondered if the description had thrown him.

'It doesn't just happen, neither.'

'How did you see me coming to get you?' Lydia asked.

'I asked, didn't I?'

Lydia forced herself not to glance at Fleet. Didn't want Ember to feel like this was an interrogation.

'I dunno how it works, but if I ask a question, I get an answer. And it's right. So I asked if I was gonna get hurt. And then I asked if I was gonna get out.'

'That sounds useful,' Lydia said.

'Sometimes. It's hard to ask the right question, though.'

'Can you show us?' Fleet was leaning against the counter, but Lydia could see the sudden tension in his body.

Ember got up and left the room.

Fleet raised an eyebrow. 'Too fast?'

'Maybe,' Lydia said. 'Or he just needed a break. He's probably sick of being asked questions.'

'He doesn't trust us—'

Ember walked back into the room. He had his box of

playing cards. 'I use these,' he said, tipping them out and placing the stack onto the breakfast bar.

'Like using tarot cards?' Lydia asked. She leaned forward to get a better look.

'I dunno.' Ember flicked a glance in her direction. 'Not used them.'

'You ask a question about the future?'

Ember looked blank for a second and then he shook his head. 'Any question. But it's not like Google. You have to, like, word it right. Not too specific and not too,' he waved a hand.

'Vague?' Fleet asked.

'Yeah. That.'

'Sounds tricky,' Lydia said, eyeing the cards dubiously.

'I'm pretty good at it now,' Ember said, a touch defensively. 'But it's hard to explain. It's more like vibes. I just know when it's a good one.'

'How do the cards work?'

Another slight hesitation. Lydia could see a struggle behind his eyes. He clearly wanted to talk about this, but he was scared. How many times had he been called weird? Or had he always kept this to himself and now it was bursting to come out, shaken-up soda fizzing out of a can. 'Gran told me never to talk about it.'

'You're safe with us,' Fleet said, surprising Lydia.

'We won't think you're weird.' Lydia produced her coin and held it out to show Ember. Not to hypnotise Ember but to demonstrate that she wasn't exactly normal herself. She flipped the coin and made it dance

in the air, swooping and spinning until she caught it
back in her hand.

'Got a question?' Ember asked.

'You don't have to prove anything,' Lydia said.

He shrugged.

'Will I stay a DCI at work?' Fleet asked.

Lydia looked at him in surprise.

Ember shuffled the playing cards and then laid out
three cards, face down. He dealt another three, face up,
on top of these and stared for a moment. The six of
hearts, king of spades and a three of clubs. Then he dealt
another card above. The jack of hearts.

Tarot cards had detailed pictures and a whole set of
lore. Each card had a specific meaning. Lydia wondered
if Ember had assigned meaning to each of these cards in
the same way, through trial and error of asking questions
and receiving answers. Or whether it was just, as he had
said, based on a feeling he got.

Ember swept the cards back into the pack and, for a
moment, she wondered if he had been unsuccessful.

'No,' Ember said. 'You won't.'

'Does that mean I'll get promoted or demoted? Or
that I won't be in the police at all?'

'That's what I meant about asking the right question,' Ember said. 'I did warn you.'

'You did,' Fleet said. 'I'm not asking you to do this for
me, but can you ask follow-up questions? To clarify?'

'Dunno,' Ember said. 'I can, like, ask in a different
way. But sometimes they feel like they're dead.'

'Dead?'

'I dunno how else to say it. Switched off. I can just

tell they aren't... they aren't on anymore. And sometimes they won't help at all.' Ember flicked his gaze between them. 'I can just tell. They're, like, switched off.'

Lydia thought about the simpatico feeling she had with her coin, like it was an extension of her own body. That was hard to explain out loud, too.

CHAPTER TWENTY-FOUR

The next morning, Lydia showered and got dressed in jersey shorts and a vest top. She had bought a fan for her office and was looking forward to sitting in front of it.

Ember's door was ajar and Lydia could hear snoring from within. She stood in the hallway and listened, enjoying the reassurance. He was safe. He was alive. While Lydia knew that he hadn't been living an ideal, safe existence before he met her, the thought that she had put a child in danger had weighed heavier on her than she had realised. And she had thought it had been pretty weighty.

Fleet would usually have left for work by this time, but he was still fast asleep and Lydia saw no reason to wake him. Fleet had loved his job. It had been part of his identity. Now it was sucking the life out of him.

With a fresh coffee and a plate of buttered toast, Lydia sat behind her desk and tried to corral her thoughts. Sinclair's field agent had been drained of their blood. Either in a botched attempt at torture, or because someone wanted a pint or three of his blood.

That agent had infiltrated an extremist group called The Collective. They had been waving tambourines, producing leaflets, and talking about alternatives to capitalism, when a new leader had stepped in and changed up the agenda.

Before the agent died he had fed information to Sinclair about a fifth Family and the magical powers of disguise that they possessed. This echoed some information from Gale's files on the Families, along with the idea that the fifth Family would show up when there was an important Family gathering. Like a wedding.

Now Sinclair was convinced this Family and this power existed and was on a one-woman mission to find it and take it back to the service. A prize that would, presumably, move her up the ranks and out of the dunce's department of MI13. Perhaps she had her eye on a desk in MI5 or MI6. Perhaps this was her golden ticket?

Whatever Sinclair thought, it was enough to make her kidnap a ten-year-old boy and hold him for several days. Ember had turned up in the Crow's roost after there had been news of the Fox-Pearl wedding. Clearly, Sinclair had hoped Ember would change appearance, reveal himself as part of the mythical fifth Family. Using him as leverage to get Lydia's help was a happy by-product. Sinclair asking Lydia to work with her was probably a sign of how badly she wanted to impress MI5.

Lydia finished her second piece of toast and licked

her fingers. She called Aiden to come and keep an eye on Ember for a couple of hours. He was still fast asleep but she didn't want him to wake up to an empty house. Then she called Angel and requested a food delivery, explaining that she was looking after a ten-year-old for the foreseeable future.

'No problem,' Angel said, but there was something in her voice. A hesitation.

'What is it?'

'I've got a new job,' Angel said. 'New place opening on Brixton Road.'

'That's great.' Lydia had been paying Angel to keep her stocked with food and it was very handy. But the truth was, it was mainly to make sure that Angel wasn't out of pocket after The Fork had been destroyed, taking her livelihood with it.

'Are you okay to do today's delivery? No worries if—'

'No, no. I can do it. Last one, though?'

'Last one.' Lydia congratulated Angel again and then headed out. She couldn't account for the light feeling the call had given her, but there was a sense of getting unstuck. Angel was moving on. Maybe she could too?

Henry Crow was in the garden in a striped canvas deckchair. Lydia remembered it from her child-hood, although the material was sun-faded now, and the man occupying it was a little faded too. He had a news-paper open and resting over his face, which was as close to sun-safety that Henry Crow got.

Lydia had timed her visit to avoid her mum. She

knew that her dad was more likely to talk about the Crows if her mum wasn't in earshot.

Just as she was trying to work out how to wake her father up without giving him a heart attack, he spoke.

'Hello, love.' Then he removed the paper and raised an eyebrow. 'You've been busy.'

Lydia didn't know if that was a question or a statement of fact or a not-so-subtle dig about her non-attendance at the last couple of family gatherings. She settled for simplicity. 'A bit. Yeah.'

'You need help.'

Another non-question. 'If that's okay?'

He smiled. 'Anything for you, love. You know that.'

She smiled back. Henry Crow might have been the heir to the Crow Family with all the raw power that entailed, but he was her dad. He had always been her dad, first and foremost. And he had thrown away the politics and power of the Family for her sake, to give her a choice in life and to keep her safe for as long as possible. Whatever her mum had hoped, Henry had always known that he couldn't keep Lydia safe forever.

'Pull up a pew,' he said.

The deckchair that her mum must have been using earlier was over in the shade near the house, but their wooden picnic bench was nearby. Lydia perched on the bench seat and rested her elbows on her knees. She cut straight to it. 'Were there always four Families?'

'That's an interesting question,' he said, peering up at her from his reclined position. 'There were four Families at the time of the truce. And for, maybe, fifty or a hundred years before that.'

'What about earlier than that?'

He squinted at her. 'What's brought on this thirst for history?'

Lydia outlined what had been going on, including Gale's department and the intense interest in the Families and the possibilities they represented. 'There's a new head of the department, Sinclair, and she seems to be following in his footsteps. Did you know about MI 13?'

Henry shrugged. 'I assumed the service were keeping an eye. Didn't know they had started a whole new department for us.' He sounded oddly pleased.

It wasn't strictly just for the Families, but Lydia knew what he meant. It was flattering in a way. She had to watch that. Crows did love to be talked about, loved the attention. Not as much as the Pearls, of course, but still. Weakness was weakness and the more you knew about your own, the better off you were.

'Your grandad talked about the early days.' Henry stared into the distance, remembering. 'He was fascinated, I think. Probably thought of them as the golden age.'

'When we first came to London?'

Henry smiled. 'Not quite that early. More like the stories he had heard from his grandfather. Stuff from when it was the wild west. Every sparrow with a little bit of shine and ha'penny in his pocket was on the make, looking to build a little nest in the big city. He said there were others, then. Otters and stoats, the brass lads, and the weavers.'

'Were there Families who didn't like the Crows?'

Henry tipped his head. 'Only all of them.'

'Okay. Fair point. Anyone in particular spring to mind?'

Henry was quiet for a moment. 'Why the sudden interest in ancient history?'

'There's something new happening. I'm wondering if it's actually something very old.'

'Something I need to be concerned about?'

Lydia weighed this up. Beckenham was far away from Camberwell and even further from Whitechapel. 'Not yet. I'll give you warning if that changes.'

He nodded. 'The Weavers were an interesting bunch. Always having spats with the Tailors. Your grandpa loved those stories. He loved a good skirmish. Said we could learn a lot from the way things used to be settled.'

'Tailors?' Lydia's mind flashed to the fancy shop on Saville Row. Paul in a suit of fine fabric and looking like an entirely different man.

'There are a few of the old guilds for clothing, all of them nice and official, but the Merchant Taylor's is one of the biggest. It's got guild status and fancy contacts, and bragging rights for being around so long. You know about the City of London livery companies?'

Lydia nodded. She kind of did. They had done a project in school and she knew that many of them dated back to medieval times and, although they still existed today, lots of them were essentially charities, rather than working their original trades. The Worshipful Company of Bowyers, for example. Which made sense, as the demand for long-bows wasn't exactly kicking in modern

London. 'They do ceremonial stuff, don't they?' Lydia's mind conjured men in gold-trimmed robes. And a guild crest picked out in a stained-glass window. And another vague memory from her lessons. 'Do they have something to do with the election of the mayor?'

'They have something to do with everything in the City,' Henry said. 'The livery companies are old establishment. North River stuff through and through.'

Lydia waited for Henry to get back to his original point. 'The Tailor Family might have shared blood with the founders of the Merchant Taylor's or maybe the Worshipful Company of Drapers, which was founded in the same century...'

'Drapers?'

'Woollen cloth,' Henry said, with a small shake of his head. 'But the Family went a different way to the guilds. Fitted suits in a more permanent way.'

It took Lydia a second to catch on. 'They were killers?'

'Assassins, yeah. Good at it, too, according to the stories. Had the ability to make themselves look like anybody they wanted. Disguises that got them all sorts of access, perfect for getting close to their targets. But they disbanded before I was born. You still have plenty of wet workers, of course, but there's no Tailor Family.'

Lydia sat back. Her whole body thrumming with electric energy. Sinclair's rumoured power might have some basis after all. 'Was that real? That they could change their appearance like that?'

'Your guess is as good as mine. You know what

stories are like. They do tend to grow a bit shinier in the telling.' Henry frowned. 'Why? What have you heard?'

'Sinclair is chasing rumours that sound a lot like the Tailor Family power. MI13 is hot under the collar for it.'

'Makes sense,' Henry said. 'Handy little trick. But she's bang out of luck.'

'You don't believe it exists?'

'I don't.' Henry shook his head, suddenly very serious. 'And I'll tell you why.'

FLEET MESSAGED HER TO SAY THAT HE WAS GOING TO the gym. Apparently he had slept for most of the day, catching up after the busy few days, and he needed to move. Lydia went up to bed, exhausted herself, but she was too keyed up to sleep. Her mind had been whirling with the possibilities since speaking to her father.

She listened to the front door open and Fleet's gym bag hit the hallway floor. A few minutes later, he appeared in the doorway, a glass of water in one hand.

'Hey,' he said softly, when he saw that she was awake.

His face was soft in the lamplight, his gaze warm. Lydia reached for him and held on. She didn't feel like crying, wasn't upset exactly, but she wasn't A-Okay, either. She felt like a baby bird that had been pushed from its cosy nest. Exposed. Raw. In danger.

'What is it?'

'Come to bed,' Lydia said, releasing him from her grip.

Fleet stripped off his clothes and got into bed. He

wrapped his arms around her and she tucked herself against his front. In the comfort of his embrace, she felt able to speak. 'There might be a fifth Family. I mean, there might have been. Once.' She took a breath, tried to order her thoughts. 'There isn't one now.'

'What?'

'Long before the truce. Long before the fighting that led to the truce. My dad told me that there used to be other Families. Some didn't have much power and what they did have faded through the generations. Some moved away from London, secured themselves a territory in Manchester or Birmingham or further north.' She took a breath. 'Some of them the Crows destroyed.'

'What do you mean destroyed?'

'Killed.' Lydia knew the proper word for what her ancestors had done when they had wiped out entire Families. 'Genocide.'

'Jesus,' Fleet breathed.

'I don't think the BBC is going to invite me on Who Do You Think You Are.' Lydia tried to force a laugh, but she couldn't. Her words came out as bleak as she felt. 'Wouldn't make a very heartwarming episode.'

Fleet hugged her tightly. 'I'm sorry.'

'I know it's history and it's not my fault or really anything to do with my family now, but...'

Fleet stayed silent while she gathered her thoughts. She tried again. 'I've always known we're not on the side of the angels. I've always known my family is filled with crooks and that the last few generations were pretty rough and ready. I've been trying to turn things around, move us onto the right side of the law. But this... this is inescapable. We're the bad guys. Killing off entire families. Cutting off bloodlines because they were a threat or because there was a bit of cash in it or to buff up our reputation. That's evil.'

There wasn't anything Fleet could say and Lydia was glad that he didn't try.

CHAPTER TWENTY-FIVE

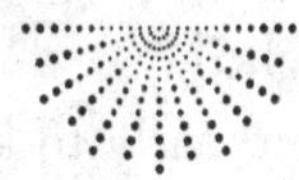

Jason was back in the house and back to studying Henriksen's phone. Lydia was trying not to hover around him. Knowing that she hadn't found the NewRipper or the cameo, knowing that ghosts were being pulled to weird rituals with the possibility of being controlled or exploded and knowing that she didn't know how to stop it made her extremely cranky. And gave her the urge to watch Jason like a mother hen.

Fleet had seemed distracted and had pulled on his running clothes before heading out to 'clear his head'. Ember had Lydia's laptop and was watching YouTube videos in the kitchen, laughing like a drain. It was good to hear.

Lydia was just thinking about going out for a run of her own, when Jason unfolded himself from his position on the sofa and punched the air in triumph. 'I've recovered his deleted messages.'

'Henriksen's?'

'Spectral85 suggested that they take their conversation off the forum, but there wasn't anything in his email or messaging apps. He was obviously getting worried and deleted the lot.'

'But you've found them?'

Jason held the phone out. 'Spectral85 requested a meeting IRL. They set it up for six o'clock. Fleet was scheduled for seven, right?'

'They got him there early to kill him.' It had been Lydia's suspicion and there was a flare of pleasure at being right, followed quickly by a stab of guilt. 'He really was set up.'

She scanned the message conversation. Henriksen was expressing concern that people on the forum were so invested in the existence of the cameo that they might do something illegal in order to find it. Spectral85 revealed that they were in possession of the cameo, having bought it on eBay and that they wanted to return it to the museum but feared repercussions from handling stolen goods. Henriksen agreed to act as the go-between to return the object, saying that it was the 'right thing to do'. He agreed to meet in a public place for the handover, probably thinking that he was taking reasonable precautions for his own safety.

Her phone buzzed with a message from Aiden. She hadn't been answering his queries and knew she wasn't being fair. He was fielding all the concerns from Family members about Scarlett, alongside all the usual day-to-day crap. Now that Ember was safe, she felt that she should focus on her own business, but whoever had set up Henriksen was still at large. And Sinclair had hinted that she knew more about Scarlett and that couldn't mean anything good.

Her mind whirled with all the competing questions and refused to stay on task. Instead of running down information on the head of the Pearl Family, she couldn't stop thinking about the families that her ancestors had eradicated. There would've been violence on all sides, she knew that, but there was something so calculatedly evil about killing off a whole bloodline. The bit of information that she was trying not to confront, but knew in her bones was this: to destroy a bloodline, they would have killed every member of that family. Men, women, children. Her nausea threatened and she took a few deep breaths until she no longer felt like she was going to eject her lunch.

WHETHER IT WAS READING UNTIL HER EYES WENT blurry or the summer heat or the lack of sleep over the previous few days, Lydia found her head nodding as she tried to focus on her screen. After jerking awake from a half-sleep a couple of times, she stretched out on the uncomfortable leather sofa and closed her eyes.

She hadn't dreamed of Maddie for a long time and the part of her that was still a little bit awake was surprised to see her. She was far ahead on a crowded London pavement, shiny hair in a ponytail that swung from side to side like a pendulum. A metronome ticking sound seemed to echo around the scene and Lydia's conscious mind shut off like a switch and she fell deeply asleep.

She was back in the garden at Charlie's house. The hornbeam tree was bare, just as before, but the moon was half-full now, not just a sliver. Pale clouds rode the sky and a few stars studded the black velvet of the sky. The air was very cold.

The twisted branches of the tree were creaking and the sound was like the cawing of a crow. She wanted to close her eyes. She wanted to wake up. She wanted to stretch out her wings and fly far away.

But Lydia was the head of the Crow Family and she knew she had to stand her ground. And, at least she was prepared this time.

The clouds crossed the moon and the monstrous crow stepped from the shadows. Its dusty grey feathers looking sleeker and blacker than before, as if it had sipped from a fountain of youth or had a really good spa day.

'Ungrateful child,' the crow said, its harsh voice scratching inside her mind like a creature scrabbling for escape.

She was just as terrified as before, but she was angry too. 'Why did you make us killers?' Lydia hadn't formed the question until it flew from her lips. She saw a crescent moon casting silver light on the Thames, she saw quiet quick figures in long black clothes, and the dark cobbled streets of old London running with the blood of the Families they had slaughtered. Men, women and children. Babes in arms. Had it all just been about power? Dominance? She hoped to feathers it hadn't been about pleasure.

The crow opened its beak and let out a caw that hurt

to hear. Lydia had her hands over her ears, but it didn't help. The sound was reverberating through her body, filling her head, pushing out every other thought. It was a sound filled with desolation and rage. And something else... Something haunted and lonely. Pain.

She woke up coughing. Feathers were so thick in her throat that she couldn't take a breath. Intense pressure in her head and a stabbing pain behind her eyes, her lungs burning with the need for oxygen. After what felt like an eternity, but must have been seconds, the feathers dissolved and she dragged in a breath.

Lydia was in no doubt that the original source of the Crow Family power had paid her a second visit. The question was: why?

Fleet had been gone for hours and his T-shirt was barely sweaty. Before she could ask him whether he had changed his mind about running, he confessed. 'Sinclair wanted to meet and I agreed. We had a conversation.'

Lydia's burns had healed quickly and were now just itchy. Fleet's skin seemed to be taking longer, but he was being typically stoic about it. She focused on one of the patches of red skin visible on his arms in order to calm the spurt of anger and hurt. Sinclair had kidnapped Ember. She had told the woman she wouldn't work with her, cooperate with her, spit on her if she was on fire. And Fleet had met her for a cosy little chat.

'I know you're upset,' he began.

Lydia held up a hand to stop him. 'I'm not upset. I'm furious.'

'You've hit a brick wall with your research into Scarlett,' Fleet continued, his tone annoyingly reasonable. 'Jason hasn't been able to find anything out about her past. Henriksen was a set-up and we still don't have a credible lead on the NewRipper. We need help. I don't think the Met are going to be much use, but MI13 have substantial resources and Sinclair is keen to make amends. I think we should use that.'

'She isn't keen to make amends,' Lydia bit out. 'She wants a new way to control me. A new way to find out more about my Family. All the Families. She's given up on going direct to me and is hoping to use you as a source instead.'

Fleet was shaking his head before she'd finished speaking. 'I've told her I won't give her any information on you or your Family. She knows I won't be used as a source.'

Lydia curbed the urge to laugh. Fleet thought he was helping. And Sinclair could be very persuasive. She took a deep breath before trying again. 'I know it seems logical,' she said. 'But you can't trust her. I thought I could use Gale in the same way—'

'She's offered me a job.' The words hung in the air.

'That's more soft-soap,' Lydia replied after a few seconds. 'She's flattering you, trying to make you feel important so that you start talking.'

'I don't think it is.'

The itchy patches of healing skin felt tight and she rubbed her arms to try to dissipate the sensation. She didn't want to fight with Fleet. But it wasn't just her skin that felt raw and tingling. She felt stretched thin, her emotions wrung out from the stress and worry. There was too much to handle and she didn't know which fire to fight first.

'She's offered an olive branch. A lead. She would have offered it to you, but you won't answer her calls. It's a way to make amends, but mainly she wants to flex. To show me the might of the secret service. Either way,' Fleet finished. 'I'm going to check it out.'

CHAPTER TWENTY-SIX

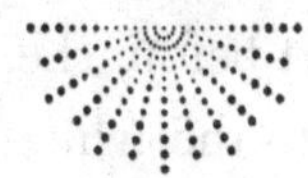

The nursing home was in a Victorian building surrounded by a large garden. There was a tall, well-kept hedge and a wide gravel driveway that curved through a tunnel of trees before reaching the house. Even this far out from the centre, it had to be worth a packet. Lydia had glanced at the rate sheet and knew that cash flow wasn't an issue, though. She made a mental note to mention luxury elder-care as a possible new business venture for the Family. It looked like a license to print money.

Sinclair had told Fleet that an ex-agent would be able to provide valuable insight into Scarlett. And that he would get to speak to someone who had enjoyed a successful career in the service which, she had been quite open about, she was hoping would help to persuade Fleet to join her team. She knew he was frustrated with his inability to get things done in the Met, the way he had been side-lined. Lydia was frustrated that Fleet was being manipulated, but she wasn't going to abandon him either.

The care assistant led them to an impressive living room with bay windows and a stone fireplace with an electric fire. There were chairs dotted around the room, most empty, but one or two with sleeping residents.

Lydia sensed Pearl before she saw their target. Her attention was pulled to the white-haired woman in the high-backed chair closest to the fireplace, before the care assistant had a chance to say 'this is Dorothy. Take as much time as you like. There's afternoon tea in half an hour and you're welcome to join.'

'Hello, Dorothy,' Fleet said, pulling a chair over for Lydia before sitting on the uncomfortable-looking footstool that was sitting unused nearby. Looking at the bulk of him next to the tiny figure in the chair, she realised he had chosen to be as low down as possible to make sure he wasn't towering over the elderly woman.

Dorothy's face was impressively smooth for a woman in her nineties and her crown of white curls stood out attractively against her dark skin. Lydia had braced herself for the Pearl effect, but she still found herself leaning more closely than was polite and she pulled herself back. Dorothy was beautiful. That would be evident, even if she hadn't been a Pearl. Impressive cheekbones, large eyes, arching brows... Lydia squeezed her coin in her palm, getting her brain back on track.

'We're here to talk to you about The Church of Lazarus.' Sinclair had given Fleet the name.

Dorothy blinked at him. 'You're very handsome.'

Fleet smiled. 'Thank you, Dorothy.'

Her gaze flicked to Lydia. 'You're scrawny.'

'It's not polite to comment on people's bodies,' Lydia said. 'Not these days.'

'Everyone is so sensitive now,' Dorothy said, her mouth turning down.

'Maybe we've developed higher standards for social behaviour.'

Dorothy's frown smoothed and she smiled. Radiant beauty shone from her face and Lydia leaned towards her.

'I like your spunk, young lady.'

Not a word Lydia would have chosen, but still. 'Church of Lazarus. We wanted to hear about your work with them.'

'Have you heard of the Official Secrets Act?' Dorothy asked mildly. 'I might be old and retired, but it still applies.'

'Sinclair sent us,' Fleet said. He produced a piece of paper from his pocket and passed it to Dorothy.

After a lot of business with her reading glasses, Dorothy glanced at the scant writing before glancing at the electric fire. Her sigh was barely audible before she began to tear the paper into tiny pieces. Her knuckles were swollen and it looked like hard work. 'Very well then,' Dorothy said, once she had destroyed the paper. 'They were a cult.'

'Officially defined as such?' Fleet asked.

Dorothy fixed him with a pursed-lip expression and raised a single eyebrow.

'They followed a charismatic leader?' Lydia guessed, after the silence threatened to thicken.

'All groups have a leader, but Lazarus was magnetic. And evil.' Dorothy removed her reading glasses and squeezed them so tightly in her hand that Lydia thought they would break. Her lap was covered in confetti-sized pieces of white paper. 'He talked a good game about disrupting the class system, redistribution of wealth, shattering the status quo so that the world could be rebuilt as a utopia, all the usual hits, but he wanted total control within his own little world.' She fixed her gaze onto Lydia. 'He was hell-bent on fathering as many children as possible, growing his own empire, created in his own image.'

'One of those,' Lydia said, trying not to sound horrified. 'That can't have been a fun assignment.'

'Having sex with a violent misogynist narcissist was just another day at the office, dear,' Dorothy said calmly. 'What got to me was the children. Lazarus's preferred method of recruitment was focused on lineage. He targeted a vulnerable young woman, always of legal age so that he stayed on the right side of the law. Then he impregnated her, making her even more vulnerable, more scared and dependent on him, and brought her into the cult. If they already had young children, all the better. More leverage for his mind games and swelling the numbers of his little empire.'

Lydia was almost speechless. 'Hell Hawk. How was this allowed to happen? Even back in the eighties?'

Fleet looked uncomfortable. 'Laws change. It hasn't been legal to force somebody into a cult for a long time, but our understanding of coercive control has developed significantly over the last twenty years.'

'Lazarus didn't just impregnate his followers as quickly as possible, he made us all believe in him, in his absolute power. For a while there, he truly was a god amongst men. If we stepped out of line, we had to atone. Atonement wasn't nice for any of us so we quickly stopped questioning his authority.'

Lydia wondered whether Dorothy realised that she had said 'us', how deeply the cult programming had taken root, despite her own training.

As if able to see inside Lydia's head, Dorothy gave them both a bright smile. 'It was a long time ago. And I would do it again, kids, don't you be feeling sorry for me.'

Before Lydia could respond, Dorothy continued: 'We got twelve people out. Twelve lives saved. More, if you count the unborn children who didn't grow up in the tender care of Lazarus. And that evil man went to jail, where he swiftly discovered his own kind of atonement.'

'That's a good result,' Fleet said. 'I've done some work on human trafficking and it's a difficult business.'

'Then you know,' Dorothy said approvingly.

'Lazarus died in prison?' Lydia guessed.

'Very quickly,' Dorothy said with no emotion.

By now, Lydia had a strong suspicion as to why Sinclair had sent Fleet to see Dorothy. 'One last thing,' she said, pulling her phone out of her pocket. She had snapped a picture of Scarlett using a covert camera during their less-than-cosy chat in Burgess Park. 'Do you recognise this woman?'

Dorothy put her glasses back on and studied the

screen for a long time. 'I can't be certain, she's much older here.' She peered closer.

Lydia dug her nails into her palm to keep quiet.

Finally, Dorothy passed the phone back. 'I believe that's Gabrielle. She was ten when we managed to close the cult and jail Lazarus.'

'Gabrielle?' Lydia tried not to be disappointed.

'That was her real name. Everybody got new ones in the cult, of course. I was Onyx.' She waved a hand to indicate herself. 'For obvious, if tiresome, reasons.'

'What was Gabrielle's new name?'

'Scarlett.'

Lydia and Fleet were quiet on their way back from the retirement home. Eventually, Fleet broke the silence. 'I've had some training on cults. A few years back, I was seconded to a human trafficking division.'

'I didn't know that.'

'You think of human trafficking as people being held against their will in some grimy basement flat. Chains and locked doors and violence.' Fleet glanced at Lydia. 'It's usually more subtle than that.'

'I think of women in Albania being told there's a lucrative house cleaning job waiting for them, that they will have money to send home to their impoverished family, then finding out they're being forced into sex work. Their handlers take their papers, bank all the money they make, scare them with stories of jail.'

'That's it,' Fleet nodded. 'So often that's it. But it's also coercive control. Whittling away at a person's confidence, isolating them, feeding them rhetoric, breaking down their sense of reality.'

'Which is where cults come in. I'm guessing they prey on the vulnerable?'

'People with abuse in their pasts, low self-esteem, poor mental health.' Fleet shook his head. 'It's hard to imagine, but I met people who didn't want to be saved. They defended their cult with every breath. Even when they were offered a way out, a new life, even in the face of every evidence that their beloved leader had been lying about the world.'

'Dorothy said the children didn't have a chance. They were born into it. Trained from the moment they were born.'

'Cult leaders are adept at offering rewards alongside punishments. People will do anything to keep the rewards coming and excuse any amount of behaviour if they believe it's for their own good, or the greater good, or whatever they've been indoctrinated to believe.'

'I've also thought of cults as religion on steroids.'

Fleet shook his head. 'They're abuse. Coercive control. Programming.'

'What's the end game? For the leader?'

'Sometimes it's fulfilment of their own delusional or extremist agenda, but sometimes there is no end game. It's a way of life that they control, in which they hold all the power. They get off on the subservience of their followers. There's a reason I didn't stay on the unit long term. I couldn't take it. Dealing with sexual predators day in day out,' Fleet shook his head. 'I wanted to help the victims, I always want to do that,

but I was finding it increasingly difficult to compart-
mentalise.'

'That's understandable.'

'Yeah, but it's vital work. Someone has to do it.'

Lydia wrapped her arms around him and hugged tightly. She knew the guilt of not doing enough, of not being strong enough. She was haunted by the victims she hadn't managed to help, the people she couldn't save.

CHAPTER TWENTY-SEVEN

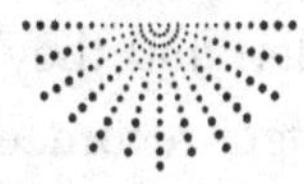

Fleet shared the information that he had been given by Sinclair on The Church of Lazarus. It was a small cult, active in the seventies and eighties, and centred around one man, who called himself Lazarus. He claimed that he had died for seven minutes and been brought back to life and given a divine purpose by God. He also said that the spirits of the dead were all around them and that he had the ability to control them. Any church member who stepped out of line was threatened by punishment from these unseen spirits, as well as subjected to very real physical punishment by Lazarus's own hand.

Despite knowing that all involved would be long gone, Lydia was unable to resist going to the last known address of the cult. When Dorothy's evidence had worked to bring charges against Lazarus and disband the cult, it had already dwindled to a smaller size than in its heyday. With age, Lazarus had begun to lose his power over the women. It was probably harder to convince people that you have power over life and death when your own body began to fail you.

After the cult was disbanded, and Lazarus jailed, the files documented Scarlett's journey into the foster system, as well as the addresses of the other victims. Two of the women, Maryam and Vanessa, had acted in a maternal way to Scarlett and they were closely bonded to each other. They were recorded as living together in sheltered housing, the social worker noting that they were unable to live entirely independently and would require ongoing support.

Lydia stood outside the old address of the cult. She wondered whether it was truly disbanded or whether they had learned the value of secrecy first-hand. Of course, without Lazarus, the cult had most likely dissolved. But Lydia knew that sometimes another person just stepped into the vacated role. She had her own case to follow, her own people to protect. But she knew she wouldn't be able to forget about them.

Fleet was shaken, too, she knew. He had gone to speak to the people at Hope, a local charity which provided support for the victims of cults and religious abuse. There was a chance they would be able to shed more light on Scarlett's upbringing or the time after, but Lydia got the sense that he needed to spend time with good people. People who were facing the horrors that humans could do and were trying to help.

She didn't know the area, but it had the suburban feel of Beckenham, but with more trees and greenery. Well-kept terraced houses with neat gardens stretched either side. She could imagine curtains twitching and wondered why nobody noticed that women were being held captive in this place. Did they not see people through the windows who never seemed to venture outside? How could something so evil have been happening over so many years and that evil not be palpable to those living either side?

She knew the answers to these questions, of course. It was partly the way London was, maybe any large city. Part of the way you coped with being squashed in with so many other people was by pretending a kind of blindness. It was politeness, in a way, giving each other the illusion of privacy, when proximity denied it. And then it became such a habit, such an entrenched mental framework, that you just stopped seeing people for real.

Lydia walked to the nearest shops, a small parade with a Tesco Metro, laundrette, and one of those cheap hypermarkets that sold everything from garden compost to fleece pyjama-sets. The man behind the counter was chatting on his mobile when she walked in. She estimated that he was in his fifties and his accent was Sri Lankan tinged with North London. It was a good bet that he'd been living in the area for a while. Selecting a pack of lighters that she didn't need and an out-of-date bar of chocolate, just to buy a little time with some purchases, Lydia went straight in with questions about the cult.

'No one speaks about those people,' he said. 'So don't ask.'

'They're not here anymore, though. Why are people scared?'

'Didn't say scared.'

'Okay. Do you know the house they used? Do you know who lives there now?'

He stared at her. 'Anything else? Buy seven get one packet free.' He indicated open cardboard boxes of single bagged crisps.

Knowing when she was on a hiding to nothing, Lydia paid for her purchases and left the dispiriting shop. An elderly woman was waiting, one hand on a shopping trolley and the other clutching a vape. The scent of fake-blueberry surrounded them. 'You won't get nothing from him,' she said, jerking her chin at the shop.

'Do you remember the family?'

'Cult you mean? Yeah, I remember them. Bunch of nutters. Used to hand out leaflets along the parade on a Sunday.'

'Did you speak to any of them?'

'Not him,' the woman said, shuddering a little. 'But I tried to speak to one of the girls once. She was a pretty little thing. Such a shame that she was kept inside so much. They all were.'

'She didn't go to school?'

The woman shrugged. 'Dunno about that.' She leaned in, blueberry vape breath wafting over Lydia's face. 'I do know she turned up back here after. Council must've fostered her or summat before, but once she turned eighteen, she moved right back in with them.'

'The cult?'

The woman shrugged. 'Some of the women. They stayed living together after it all kicked off. That's their culture, I suppose.'

Lydia didn't know if the woman meant 'south east

Asian' or 'cult' by this. She knew from Fleet's information that Maryam was originally from Malaysia and had met Lazarus while studying at the university.

'They lived on Clapton Road, number thirty-seven, and she came right back.' She tapped her head, 'Programmed, you see?'

The chances that Scarlett's cult-mates still lived on Clapton Road, if they ever had, weren't high, and Lydia tried to keep her expectations low. Still, she felt a rush of excitement when a soft voice spoke over the intercom for the multi-occupancy terraced house.

The woman who answered the door was in her seventies, had remarkably smooth light brown skin, and was dressed in a pink fluffy dressing gown and slippers. 'I'm sorry,' Lydia said. 'Did I wake you up?'

The woman shook her head. 'Did you bring my food?'

'No,' Lydia said. 'Are you Maryam Lim?'

She hesitated, as if taking a moment to be sure, and then bobbed with her whole body in what was halfway between a bow and a head nod. 'I'm expecting my meals,' she said. 'They usually come on a Tuesday. I put them in the freezer and they last me all week. That's one meal a day that I just put in the, ping ping thing.' She mimed hitting buttons. Presumably on a microwave.

Lydia wondered if the woman was cognitively all there. She had been through a lot in her life, so it wouldn't be a surprise if the strain was starting to show. Lydia made the decision not to lie to her. 'I'm a private investigator. I wanted to talk to you about Scarlett. Would it be okay if I came in for a little while? We could have a cup of tea and a chat.'

Maryam shook her head. 'I'm not supposed to talk about Scarlett.' She held her fingers to her lips. 'We don't talk to outsiders.'

'Is that what he used to say? Lazarus?'

The woman giggled, hiding her mouth with her hand. 'He did.' She laughed again, this time flashing teeth that were yellow and decayed.

'You're safe from him now, though. You can make your own decisions.' Lydia stepped over the threshold and Maryam obediently stepped back. 'Shall I put the kettle on?'

Lydia didn't like pushing her way into this woman's home. There was something vulnerable, almost childlike about Maryam, but she didn't feel she had a choice. Scarlett had wandered in as the new head of the Pearl Family and she was going to marry into the Fox Family.

The flat wasn't more than a bedsit with a bed, two straight-back chairs and kitchen area all in one room, and Lydia couldn't imagine where her fellow cult member had slept, let alone Scarlett. 'Is Vanessa home?' Maryam had bonded with another woman in the cult and the welfare reports had them listed as living together.

Maryam had retreated into the room to sit on the bed and folded her hands, as if waiting for further instruction. She shook her head and didn't answer.

'Would you like a tea?' Lydia turned to the kitchenette. There was a kettle and a mug filled with teaspoons, some of which might have been clean. The sink had clearly been used to wash clothes in the recent past, as a stray sock was blocking the plughole. There was a small undercounter fridge that was empty apart from a pack of chocolate mousses in individual pots and some medication.

'Citrine's gone,' Maryam said. 'She died.'

Lydia abandoned the idea of refreshments. 'I'm sorry. Was that the name that she was given? By Lazarus?'

'He said we couldn't survive without him,' Maryam said and giggled again. 'It's pretty funny the things he said. I know they're not true.' Her chin lifted at this. Defiant, like a toddler that didn't want to go for a nap.

Lydia found it difficult to hold her gaze. She was not a mental health professional, but her gut was telling her that there was something deeply damaged about Maryam. She hoped she was getting help, but the NHS wasn't exactly overburdened with resources. 'Do you have support?'

'I get my meals,' Maryam said proudly. 'And the girls from Hope take me to bingo. It's at the hall. I don't like to go out, but they say it's good. So I do that.'

Lydia didn't want to sit on the bed, so she moved a pile of clothes from one of the chairs and angled it to face Maryam. 'I don't want to upset you, but I wanted to ask about Scarlett. She was fostered after the Church of Lazarus was disbanded, but you stayed in touch?'

'Scarlett was our little girl,' Maryam said, smiling properly for the first time. 'We loved her. We raised her.'

'Where was her mum?'

Maryam shook her head. 'You can't ask about her.'

'Okay.' Lydia held up her hands. 'I won't. Is that why Scarlett came back to live with you here? After she turned eighteen? She missed you?'

Maryam looked confused. 'Scarlett was always here. She was only a little girl. Not safe on her own. We all looked after her.'

Lydia wondered if Maryam had blanked out the years that Scarlett was fostered. She would have been adjusting to life after the cult, herself. Fleet had explained that it wasn't as simple as being 'rescued'. Cult members often felt lost without the world they had known. 'But Scarlett came to stay here after she was fully grown? With you and Vanessa?'

'She looked after us. We had looked after her and then she looked after us. I told you, she was a good girl.'

'Did she work?'

Maryam's mouth pulled up a little at the corners. A secret sort of smile. 'She provided for us.'

No matter how else Lydia framed the question, she couldn't get any detail about what Scarlett did, how she provided, how the three women had managed. They would have had benefits, help from the charity and, Lydia suspected, Scarlett would have attracted support of a non-official kind. Even before the Pearl King had died and his power had flowed into the Family above, Scarlett was very attractive and had a magnetic quality.

She left Maryam a couple of twenty-pound notes. 'For your time,' she said, but the honest truth was that she felt sorry for the woman and didn't have anything else to offer.

Maryam nodded as if being left cash was a very

normal occurrence. She didn't get up from the bed when Lydia made to leave. Something else occurred to her. 'Do you know that Scarlett is getting married?'

Maryam's head jerked up. 'That's not right.'

'Yes, next week. That's why I wanted to know more about her. She's marrying a friend of mine.' Sort of the truth.

Maryam looked genuinely mystified. 'But she's already married.'

CHAPTER TWENTY-EIGHT

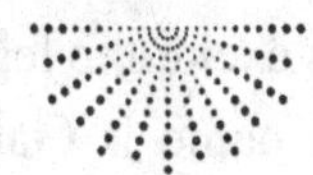

'It was her father,' Lydia said to Jason, still wanting to throw up as she said the words. 'She had been raised to believe that she was going to take over as leader one day, but that she was also promised to marry the current leader once she hit her teens. Who was her father. Maryam didn't see the distinction between being married and being promised to the great leader. Even though he's dead now. She said "marriage was forever and ever" and was getting upset, so I left.'

'Christ,' Jason said. 'That poor woman. Can you imagine what he did to them all?'

Lydia had been trying not to. 'What was wrong with that man? And how brain-washed were those women that they went along with it...I can't—'

Jason shook his head, his horror mirroring her own. 'Thank God they broke up the cult before...' He swallowed, shook his head again, as if trying to deny reality.

'I know.' Lydia could see Maryam's confused expression. The mix of knowing that something wasn't quite right in what she was saying, the little embarrassed smile that was like a very young child caught in a lie, but seeming to be unable to see just *how* wrong it all was. How did a person get to that state? Lydia's understanding of coercive control clearly needed work. But it wasn't an area she was excited to learn more about.

'So Scarlett's real name is Gabrielle. That's why I couldn't find anything about her background,' Jason said. 'I was looking for the wrong name.'

'Sinclair's obsessed with Scarlett's wedding. She thinks it's going to draw in the fifth Family with their special disguise power. It doesn't seem to matter how many times I tell her it doesn't exist...'

'Well, she really wants it to be true.'

'And she has very little reason to believe me. I know.'

'She might believe you, but think you're out of the loop. She's got tunnel vision.'

The light changed. Bright sunlight shifting to dark. Rain began to spatter on the windows. 'That's good,' Jason said, 'clear the air—' He disappeared. One moment he was there and the next he was gone.

'Jason?' She spoke his name, knowing that he had gone, but not quite willing to accept it. As if to underscore that this was bad news, there was the distant roll of thunder.

'Hello!' The front door opened and shut and Aiden's voice echoed through the house.

'Come through,' Lydia called back.

She stared at the place Jason had been standing a

moment earlier and willed him to reappear. Keep resisting, she willed him in her mind. *Come back.*

'Boss?' Aiden was in the doorway, watching her warily. 'If I ask you if you're feeling all right, will I get whacked?'

'I'm not Charlie,' Lydia said, for what felt like the thousandth time. She forced herself to look away from the Jason-free space and to uncurl her clenched fists. Her second-in-command was wearing a white T-shirt with a couple of gold chains, tracksuit bottoms and his beanie hat despite the heat.

'You're still pretty scary.'

Lydia couldn't help but be pleased about that. Especially since her future plans would leave her potentially exposed. Before Aiden could launch into whatever bit of Crow business had brought him to the house, she jumped in. 'I have an idea. About our future.'

'Our future?'

'In business terms. And as a Family.' Lydia knew that the Crow Family was a long way from the Church of Lazarus, or any cult, but she no longer felt she could change things for the good from within.

'Why am I getting a bad feeling?' Aiden looked like he was fighting the urge to flee.

'No clue. I'm offering you a promotion.'

He frowned. Took his hat off, as if it was somehow impeding his ability to hear properly.

'Well, more than that actually. I'm stepping down as head of the Family. I want you to take my place.'

Aiden opened his mouth to argue, but Lydia

barrelled on. 'You know my heart's not in it. And you're so much better at the business stuff.'

'Is this so you don't have to go to the wedding tomorrow, 'cause I think you'd still have to—'

'It's nothing to do with that,' Lydia said. 'You'll make a better head of the Family. You actually want to do it, for starters.'

'But you're the leader,' Aiden said, still sounding mystified.

'You're better at that side of things, too. People want to follow you.'

'I'm not Henry Crow's daughter.' He was twisting his hat now, his expression a pained mix of desire and despair.

'Maybe we shouldn't keep choosing our leaders based on blood.'

AFTER LYDIA HAD REITERATED HER SERIOUSNESS TO Aiden, and he had finally left, Lydia walked through the house, looking for Jason and hoping against hope that he would simply reappear. She called Fleet but it went to voicemail. Rain began to splatter the windows, going from light to storm-levels in a matter of minutes.

If Jason didn't reappear in the next five minutes, she would have to accept that he had been dragged away. Her whole soul rebelled against the possibility. Jason in pain. Jason being controlled, held against his will. Her fingers were bunched into fists and her coin was spinning wildly in front of her, so fast it was a blur. The door opened and she heard Fleet.

'I've got Maryam's address,' Fleet was saying as she met him in the hall. 'From the charity.'

'Jason's gone,' she said. 'And I've got a very bad feeling.'

'The cameo?'

Lydia was just about to fill Fleet in on her visit to Maryam, when he staggered to one side, his shoulders hunched. He made an involuntary noise of pain, and his face twisted. Before Lydia could react, his legs gave way and he folded to the floor.

'Fleet!' She rushed to him.

He was already coming round, pulling himself to a sitting position, and muttering a string of curses, almost chanting them.

She put her hands on either side of his face and looked into his eyes, willing him to come back. 'Fleet. It's okay. You're okay.'

His eyes focused on her and he stopped swearing. 'Lydia?' A moment later, his arms wrapped around her and she was hauled onto his lap. His face was buried in her neck and she felt him take a couple of deep shuddering breaths.

'You saw something?'

He lifted his head and nodded. His expression was bleak.

Lydia rubbed comforting circles on his back. 'Bad?'

It was a few seconds before he answered and he swallowed hard first. 'Have you seen pictures from chemical weapon attacks?'

She went cold, remembering horrific images in an old textbook. 'You saw something like that?'

'There were so many people,' he said quietly. 'Kids, too. Screaming. Skin peeling. Bodies piled up and people trying to climb over them to get out.'

'Get out from where?'

He blinked. 'I don't know. A big building.'

'Did you see anything else? Anything to locate it?'

Fleet closed his eyes, his forehead creased, and his body tense beneath her hands. 'Flashes of the city. A London bus. Busy streets. I could see the Gherkin in the mid-distance.'

FLEET TOOK A COUPLE OF PARACETAMOLS AND LAY down on the sofa 'just for a moment' to try and ease the pounding headache brought on from his violent vision.

Lydia sat on the carpet, her back against the sofa, and held his hand.

His phone buzzed and he let go of her hand to dig it out of his pocket.

This close, Lydia could hear Sinclair's voice. She couldn't quite make out all the words, though.

'I'll be there as soon as I can. Yes. I'll ask.' He finished the call.

She looked at Fleet questioningly after he had hung up. He was already siting up, holding his head as if it was still painful. 'MI13 have picked up a member of The Collective.'

Lydia was scrambling to her feet. 'And she told you?'

'You know we're speaking,' Fleet said quietly. 'She's invited me in to observe the interview process.'

'Where?' Lydia thought she already knew the answer and he confirmed it.

'SIS.'

The MI6 building by the Thames at Vauxhall.

'You should join us.'

'Us?'

'I'm going,' Fleet was pulling himself together in front of her eyes. The man who had been terrified and in pain minutes earlier was nowhere to be seen. 'Sinclair is information gathering. And you're the one she really wants there. Sinclair thought you'd be more likely to come in if the offer came from me, not her. But I don't think you want to miss this.'

Hell Hawk. He was right.

Damming her own curiosity, she pulled on her DMs and followed Fleet out to the car.

On the way, Sinclair messaged: 'I will meet you at the public entrance. The main door. Please be civil.'

'We need to tell Sinclair about your vision,' she began. 'You saw an attack on London, maybe this Collective guy knows something about it.'

Fleet nodded, his face tense. Before he could speak, Lydia's phone rang.

'They're all gone.'

It was Megan, and she sounded panicked. 'The ghosts?'

'All of them. I've been checking in, but there's nobody there. All the usual haunts are empty. Even Betty's not back and I thought she would never leave the river. I didn't think she could.' Megan was close to tears. 'Is your friend okay? Jason?'

'He's gone,' Lydia managed. Feathers were thick in her throat, but she wasn't going to break down. She might have abdicated as the leader, but she was still a Crow. 'We think there's going to be an attack. Central London. You should stay away.'

'I could,' Megan said, sounding a little steadier. 'Or I could help stop it.'

CHAPTER TWENTY-NINE

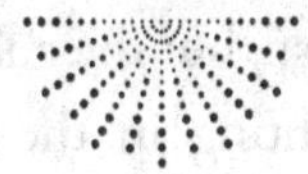

It wasn't Lydia's first time in the MI6 building. The last time she had been visiting her Uncle Charlie. Now the secret service had a different prisoner and she was cooperating with them. It was wrong in a whole new sense of the word, but turning away the resources of MI13 would be plain stupid. Fleet's vision put everything into stark perspective.

Sinclair led them to a nondescript room with comfortable office chairs and an abstract watercolour painting that appeared calculated to be calming. It made Lydia want to rip it off the wall and break the frame to make a sharp object. Fleet's presence didn't help much. She hated seeing him in this building, seeing him aligned with Sinclair's department. But he had just seen an attack on London, they needed to pull together.

Before Lydia could reveal Fleet's vision, Sinclair unfolded the case of a tablet and propped it up on the table. 'You see my actions as cruel and over-reaching, I wish you to see the kinds of threats I deal with on a daily basis.'

'You want my understanding?' Lydia guessed. 'You think that's going to stop me coming after you in retaliation?'

'Maybe,' Sinclair said, with disarming honesty.

The video was crisp, but the colours were muted and sickly. Either the lighting in the interview room was deliberately awful, or it was the best the camera had picked up. The man was in his fifties with a heavily lined face that betrayed years of scowling. He was leaning forward, agitated. 'You can't keep me here. I'm not saying a word until my lawyer gets here.'

'I've told you,' a smooth male voice said, coming from someone out of shot. 'We're not the police. We can keep you here for as long as we want. In fact,' the voice paused, 'there's a great deal we can do.'

'This is twenty hours after we brought him in,' Sinclair said. 'It takes less time than you might think for people to start talking.'

'Most people,' Lydia said, keeping her eyes on the screen. She was pretty sure Charlie hadn't told them a damn thing he hadn't wanted them to know.

'You're part of the problem,' the man in the video sneered. 'You're blindly following orders for a system that's corrupt. Toxic. It's broken and you can't even see it.'

'What's broken, Joshua? Apart from Carl. Were you the one who cut him?'

Lydia guessed that the interviewer was using the

agent's name to remind Joshua that he had been a human being.

'The poor stay poor and the rich get richer. Those in power are like toddlers with toys. They don't care about anything as long as they get to keep playing.'

The voice from the unseen man remained calm. 'You come up with these thoughts on your own?'

He twitched. 'I don't matter. It doesn't matter that I'm here. We are working for the greater good. Carl was an enemy and we don't let our enemies stand in our way.'

'You and your friends killed a man. This isn't a game. You were dropping leaflets, staging peaceful protests, all good stuff, and now this.' The unseen voice tutted. 'This isn't something you come back from. Murder. Torture.'

'We didn't torture anybody,' Joshua burst out, looking sick. 'That's not... that's not what she—' His mouth shut abruptly.

'What were you trying to hide? What did he know that was worth killing him? You building bombs, Joshua? How does that help the poor? Bombs hurt everyone. They hurt kids. You want to blow up children? I don't think you do.'

The man leaned back, his expression going blank.

Lydia could see that whatever the man had been about to say, he had locked it back down.

'Did you enjoy hurting him? Did you like the power? A group of you against one bound man. Not exactly a fair fight. Pretty sick, when you think about it.'

'I'm not saying anything. Thou shalt not speak to the unclean.'

'Who are the unclean? Everybody who isn't in your little club?'

The man shook his head. 'You can't keep me here forever.'

'We know all about your club,' the voice spoke again, dripping with condescension.

'The Collective. Are you a bunch of commies? Everybody is equal? Is that the shtick? I've got news for you, they tried that in Russia. And China. It doesn't work. Didn't you read Animal Farm at school?'

The man had tucked his head down, his chin on his chest. An arm became visible as one of the interrogators reached out to snap their fingers in front of his face. He jerked awake, making a small involuntary noise of distress.

Lydia hadn't seen a human being at that stage of exhaustion before. She couldn't help but feel bad for him.

'Let me try,' she said.

Sinclair slanted a look. 'You're not service.'

'I thought we were working together. Wasn't that the point of your little speech?' Lydia looked around. 'Besides, aren't you the boss?'

Before Sinclair could reply, Fleet stepped in. 'A little give and take would go a long way.'

'This isn't a small ask,' Sinclair said stiffly. 'It's against protocol.'

'Your pitch to me is all about the freedom to follow my gut. Less red tape. Less oversight from pencil-pushing management—'

'Fine,' Sinclair interrupted, not looking happy.

It gladdened Lydia's heart and she squeezed Fleet's hand surreptitiously.

'You go in with me,' Sinclair said.

'No,' Lydia corrected. 'I go in alone.'

Sinclair looked like she wanted to argue, but then she shrugged. 'You've got ten minutes, then I'll come in. Don't tell him you're not service, don't tell him your real name, don't promise anything.'

THE MAN DIDN'T GIVE OFF A FAMILY SIGNATURE AND Lydia felt a wash of relief. It was one less complication. Lydia had been fitted with a tiny earpiece, which meant she could hear Sinclair crystal clear and weirdly loud. She felt self-conscious as it was hard to believe that the man couldn't hear Sinclair's string of repeated instructions.

He had his eyes shut and Lydia wondered if he was just going to snooze through her interview, but when she sat down opposite her chair made a screeching noise on the bare concrete floor and the man twitched, opened his eyes.

'I don't care about The Collective,' Lydia said. 'Or Carl. If I found a spy in my Family I'd probably deal with it in the same way. Or something similar.'

The man blinked.

'I'm Lydia Crow. I'm head of the Crow Family.'

'This is not what we discussed,' Sinclair said in her earpiece. Lydia took it out and laid it on the table.

Joshua looked at the tiny device, frowning in confusion.

'You're being held by the secret service. I'm guessing you worked that out already, but I don't know how quick on the uptake you are, I mean you got caught, so I'm going with the basics. They can do whatever they want to you and you'll never see freedom again.'

'I will get my reward.'

'Is that what you were promised?'

His chin dipped and he didn't answer.

'By her, right? She promised you some great reward? Access to her, maybe? Or did she tell you it was love?'

No response.

'I promise stuff all the time. It's a great way to get people to do the dirty work.'

Lydia produced her coin and flipped it over the back of her knuckles. 'I also sacrifice people for the greater good. I think she sacrificed you. You strike me as disposable.'

A muscle twitched in his cheek.

'Or you're not disposable. Maybe I'm reading you wrong and you're a safe pair of hands. You're dependable. Maybe she trusts you to hold out under questioning.' Lydia paused, flipping her coin and letting it spin. 'But I bet she didn't imagine this. I bet she was thinking that you'd spend a few hours in a police holding cell, make a call to a lawyer, out after one night max. Not this,' Lydia nodded to the bare stone walls and floor. 'Underground in a secret department of the secret service. No rules. No phone calls. No escape. It's hard to believe she wanted you to go through this.'

'What do you want?'

'She's new, right? You've been in the group much

longer. I'm interested in what she wants. And why The Collective started following a leader.'

'Gabrielle's worthy,' Joshua said. Then pressed his lips together as if to stop himself from saying anything else. The name had slipped out, though. He couldn't take that back.

Lydia forced herself not to react to the name. Scarlett was the new leader of The Collective. The name Gabrielle couldn't possibly be a coincidence. Plus, she could feel his desperation. He wanted to talk about her. Anything that would manifest her here in this room, anything to make himself feel closer to Gabrielle. He hadn't been able to stop himself using her name. That sway made perfect sense if Gabrielle was Scarlett, with an abundance of Pearl mojo flowing through her veins.

'And Gabrielle asked you to collect his blood. Do you know why?'

Joshua shook his head before he could stop himself. Lydia felt a rush of triumph. He had been answering the last question, not denying the first.

'It's okay, Josh,' Lydia said. 'I know why Gabrielle wanted the blood. It's to make a ghost bomb. The blood activates it, makes it work. It pulls ghosts in and squashes them until they pop. Make one big enough and people die.'

Joshua's eyes were wide. 'I don't know anything about that.'

'But you see that I do, right? I've worked this much out and I'm going to find out the rest.' She flipped her coin into the air and made it spin slowly. 'So there's no harm in telling me the target. You can be the hero. You can save lives. Just give me the target.'

'Freedom,' Joshua mumbled. 'It's about freedom.' His voice had a strange tone. Lydia wasn't sure if she could detect Pearl or whether she could just tell he was repeating things he had been told and she was imagining the signature.

'You're not a killer,' Lydia pressed. She felt that she was battling Scarlett's hold over the man. Crow whammy hitting Pearl compulsion. Her fingers were tingling with pins and needles and she could taste feathers and blood in her mouth. 'You can tell me the target.'

A trickle of blood ran from the man's right nostril and onto his upper lip. His eyes rolled back into his head and he slumped forward. His head hit the table with a surprisingly loud bang. The door buzzed and the room filled up with people, one of them hustled Lydia outside.

Outside the interview room, Lydia confronted Sinclair. 'You sent Fleet to Dorothy. You knew that Scarlett had been born into the Church of Lazarus.'

'I did,' Sinclair said. 'You're welcome.'

For a moment, Lydia couldn't speak. She squeezed her coin to stop herself from taking a swing at the head of MI13. They might be a bunch of clowns, but she had no wish to be spirited away to a secret service dungeon. 'You knew this about the new head of the Pearl Family and didn't think I ought to know.'

Sinclair raised an eyebrow. 'I did try to warn you.'

'When?'

'I told you to watch out for newcomers.'

Lydia took a calming breath, squeezed her coin tightly. 'You could have actually told me.'

'Because you're always so open with information? Because we're such good pals?' Sinclair angled her head. 'You know as well as I do that information is power.'

Hell Hawk. Lydia stamped down on her righteous anger. She was the head of a criminal organisation and Sinclair was secret service. She was quite correct to withhold any and all information. 'Dorothy identified a picture of Scarlett as a woman called Gabrielle.'

Sinclair stared coolly back at Lydia, making her wonder if she had suddenly started speaking another language. She tried again. 'Scarlett. Who is the new head of the Pearl Family. She is also the leader of The Collective.'

Sinclair took another beat. Lydia had to hand it to the woman, she was calm under pressure and never rushed to fill a silence. 'I was not aware of that connection,' she said eventually.

Fleet spoke quietly. 'What was the blood question about?' He looked at Lydia and she knew he wasn't saying more in case she didn't want to share the details with Sinclair. They were past that now, though. Lydia might not trust the woman, but if Scarlett had collected human blood they had officially run out of time. 'We believe that Scarlett has obtained an object which attracts spectral energy and, with the application of blood to activate it, can force this energy into a critical mass. An explosion.'

'Why would Scarlett wish to create an explosion?'

'Why else would she have infiltrated The Collective? You heard him,' Lydia indicated the interview room. 'They are looking to disrupt the social order. She's grooming the group for action. Just as she was raised to do by dear old dad.'

'I suspected that Scarlett was marrying into the Fox Family as a way to build a larger, more powerful group, very much in line with her early programming,' Sinclair tipped a nod to Lydia, 'but perhaps she was spreading her bets. Also working The Collective as another possibility, in case things with her proposed marriage didn't work out.'

'You know The Collective are interested in causing chaos. And Scarlett has been busy creating an undetectable bomb. One she can detonate in the middle of Leicester Square if she chose.'

'You wanted me to see that I would have more freedom as part of your department,' Fleet tried.

'The intel we received was that The Collective were mostly harmless, pretty inept and ineffective, until Gabrielle, sorry, Scarlett, took over. She is focused on her wedding, on forming a power alliance. I don't see how blowing up a bit of London helps her with that.' Sinclair spoke directly to Fleet. 'I'm following my own remit. Something you would be at liberty to do if you join me. At the moment, you're an outsider and I will weigh your opinion accordingly.'

'I saw an explosion,' Fleet said. 'It was central London, just as Lydia says. The wedding shouldn't distract from that.'

Distraction. Lydia felt the truth of this thudding through her. Scarlett had dangled the fifth Family in front of Sinclair like a shiny toy. 'You need to bring Scarlett in for questioning,' Lydia broke in. 'At least delay the alliance and prevent her from using it as an alibi for her real plan.'

'No,' Sinclair said firmly. 'The wedding must go ahead.'

'Why?' Lydia knew that Sinclair wasn't really listening. 'We need more time to work out the target and how to stop it.'

'There is still a chance that the intel was correct. In which case, a big Family event is the best chance of bringing the fifth Family out of hiding. We will watch and wait and, if the fifth Family makes an appearance, we will have our best chance of intercepting them.'

'You going to kidnap someone new? See if they change appearance? That's your plan?' It was difficult for Lydia to get properly worked up, seeing as the fifth Family weren't going to be showing up anywhere. 'How are you going to tell they're Family?'

'You're going to tell us.'

'Done. It's none of them. Because the fifth Family doesn't exist.' She didn't add, 'because my ancestors murdered them all.'

'The more you say that, the less I believe you,' Sinclair replied.

Lydia squeezed her coin in frustration. 'You're focusing on the wrong thing. Scarlett is playing you. She fed this story to your agent deliberately, to keep you distracted. She knew it would be irresistible to the service. Can't you see that it's too good to be true?'

'You might be right, but I'm willing to take the chance. There's a possibility it's true and that's too great a prize to pass up. Imagine what a group like The Collective could do with the ability? If there is anything you know about the fifth Family, I strongly suggest you share.'

Lydia was holding onto her temper by the thinnest thread. 'Because the secret service would only use the power for good?'

Sinclair's lips thinned. 'Better us than them.'

'I'm not entirely convinced about that, but it doesn't matter. I told you, it doesn't exist. You are chasing a myth.'

'Since I'm talking to a myth right now, I'll reserve my right to keep looking.'

CHAPTER THIRTY

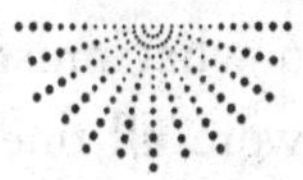

The sky had turned black and thunder rumbled in the distance. Despite the heavy rain, the air hadn't cleared. It was still dense and warm and now had the feel of electricity. Lydia thought that it was a good thing the Pearl-Fox wedding wasn't taking place in a wood. All those trees would have been dangerous when the lightning started.

She called Paul on the journey back to Denmark Hill, but he didn't answer. She left a short message. 'Call me. It's important.'

Back at the house, Lydia checked on Ember, forced Fleet to take some more painkillers and to rest on the sofa as he looked grey with fatigue, and then tried to work out what to do next. Jason wasn't back and Lydia was getting desperate. Whatever Scarlett was planning, she was going to explode a load of ghosts. And Lydia was damned if Jason was going to be one of them.

Paul returned her call and agreed to meet her. Fleet had fallen asleep on the sofa, his breathing deep and even. Lydia left him sleeping, and went to the edge of Paul's territory, near to Aldgate station. Aldgate was one of the 'old gates' to the city, back when Whitechapel was a village. Thanks to Megan she knew that one of the churches in Whitechapel had been used to bury plague victims and she imagined the old Londoners sending out their diseased dead to what must have felt like a safe distance. Now, they were all one seamless metropolis, people walking across boundaries, in and out of the old city, as if there were no division at all.

Lydia stood at the edge of Whitechapel and paid attention to her senses. She could feel the animal hum of Fox, faint but getting stronger. And there he was. The head of the Family. He stood just on the other side of the invisible line that demarcated Whitechapel and Fox territory. His eye was no longer swollen, but there was still a livid purple bruise across his cheekbone.

'Hello, Little Bird. Is this a last-ditch attempt to keep me on the market? Or did you want to join my stag party tonight? I'm sorry to disappoint, but—'

'I have to tell you something about Scarlett.'

'Fire away,' Paul said, spreading his arms wide as if offering an easy target.

Lydia spoke quickly, ripping off the plaster. 'She was raised in a cult until the age of ten. It was disbanded by MI5 and her father was jailed.'

'You think she hasn't told me? It's one of the things she likes about marrying into the Fox Family. A solid family unit feels familiar, but without the creepy cult vibes.'

'You already knew.'

'Of course.'

Lydia didn't have time to dwell on this. 'You told me that she believes in the superiority of the Families. Doesn't that bother you?'

'She has a point.'

Lydia stared at Paul in disbelief. 'You don't even believe in a hierarchy within the Foxes. What makes you okay about having one throughout London?'

'The Foxes are the best.' Paul shrugged. 'And I can't get that worked up about the rest of the city.'

'So you're on board with The Collective?'

Paul went still. 'The what?'

'Your fiancé's band of merry anarchists.'

'I know you don't want me to marry Scarlett, but this is just sad—'

'She's planning something big for tomorrow. The wedding provides an alibi for her and the main Family members. It's a cover.'

'Marrying me is a fucking prize,' Paul said. 'You're trying to tell me it's not the main event? Trying to hurt my feelings, Little Bird?'

'No. I'm trying to tell you that your blushing bride is planning an act of terrorism tomorrow. Central London. I don't know the target, yet, but it could be Whitechapel. That would work well as a misdirect away from herself. And you.'

Paul was no longer smiling. 'You have evidence?'

'Scarlett is the NewRipper. She can control ghosts and now she's worked out a way to make them explode. I ran into one of her experiments in a bunker. She's got an object that pulls ghosts to it and, kind of squeezes them until they implode. Or explode. Whichever, the energy gets converted into something seriously toxic. And if she's managed to boost the effects, feathers-knows how many people are in danger. Me and Fleet were badly hurt with a light splattering of the ghost-goop, and loads of ghosts have been going missing. Enough to power a much bigger explosion.'

'It's so hard to take ghost goop seriously,' Paul drawled sardonically, but his eyes were thoughtful.

'Scarlett has made an undetectable dirty bomb. She can walk right into any major attraction in the city with it. We need to work out the target and stop her.'

'I'm still not hearing evidence,' Paul said, with some regret. 'I can't accuse the head of the Pearl Family without causing a major diplomatic incident. And you have a solid motive to stop the wedding and prevent a Fox-Pearl alliance. Not to mention your obvious personal jealousy,' he added with a smile. 'You see my dilemma?'

'I'm not making it up.' Lydia looked Paul dead in the eye. 'You know me pretty well. Am I lying?'

ANOTHER HEAVY RAIN SHOWER PUMMELLED THE pavements on Lydia's way back to Camberwell. She felt like she had wasted valuable time in visiting Paul, but she had needed to warn him in person.

Back at the house, Lydia found Fleet awake and pacing the floor in the kitchen. The rain had been replaced with bright sunshine, as if the weather was having violent mood swings. Lydia knew how it felt. She shook her head in response to Fleet's question. 'He doesn't believe me. Thinks I just want to mess with his wedding.'

'Is he back?' Fleet asked.

Lydia walked through the house, checking, and out in the garden, walking across wet grass to the tree. The branches were filled with crows and she asked them if they'd seen Jason. They stared back. Lydia couldn't help but feel a little judged. 'It's not personal,' she said. 'I just don't want to be a leader.'

They stared at her. A row of black eyes and sharp beaks. 'Have you seen him today or not?'

With a harsh caw, each bird lifted into the air and flew away.

'Right, then. On my own. Got it.'

Next, she tried Maria. A man answered. Her personal assistant, as she was far too important to answer her own mobile phone. Or she hadn't given Lydia her personal number. That was Maria: all power games all of the time. 'Something bad's happening,' she said to the assistant. 'I need to speak to Maria now.'

'Ms Silver is unavailable, if you wish to leave your name and—'

'This is Lydia Crow. Put Maria on or I will fly over there and remove your liver.'

Diplomacy was important, but sometimes it was best to be direct.

The phone went silent for a moment before Maria

spoke. Her voice was unruffled. 'Always a pleasure, Ms Crow,' she said. 'What can I help you with?'

'The Fox wedding is a distraction.'

A slight pause. 'From what?'

'There's going to be an explosion in London. Tomorrow.'

'During the vows? Or after, instead of fireworks.'

'I'm being serious. Target is central, I think. In region of the Gherkin, probably a tourist spot.'

'You think? Probably? Lydia, Lydia, Lydia. This sounds very thin indee—'

'You'll be safe at the wedding,' Lydia ploughed on. 'That's to provide us all with alibis and to act as a distraction. You should evacuate your family, though.'

Maria paused. 'You're not trying to stop the wedding?'

'I don't care about the wedding,' Lydia said, and it was almost true. 'There will be an explosion. I don't know how near to Chancery Lane, but it could be close. I'm going to try to stop it, but I might not succeed. I've tried the secret service, but they need more evidence, so we're on our own. Get your Family out of central London.'

'This is real?' Maria asked after a moment of silence.

'It's real.'

'Okay.'

The relief flooded Lydia. She wasn't a fan of the Silver Family, but she didn't wish them to all be blown up. 'I don't have the target yet. I'll let you know when I find it, but I don't know how much time I'll be able to give you. You need to evacuate now. Just in case.'

'In case?'

'In case I fail to stop it.'

LATE INTO THE NIGHT, FLEET AND LYDIA WERE poring over the map of central London. They looked at landmarks and tourist attractions. There were so many possible targets it was impossible to know how to narrow them down.

'If she wants infamy, it's going to be somewhere well known.'

'And somewhere with a high concentration of people.' Fleet didn't have to remind Lydia that he had seen hundreds of people dead and dying. 'They were contained. I had the sense it was a big building, though. That should narrow it down.'

If only, Lydia thought. There were so many large buildings in central London.

Time ticked by. Fleet closed his eyes periodically and his face tensed. Lydia knew that he was willing another vision, or examining the memories of the one he'd already had.

She didn't want him to suffer, but it would be so useful if he could simply command his mind to show him the future.

In the early hours of the morning, she put on another lot of coffee to keep them awake. Ember walked into the kitchen, his face creased with sleep. He was wearing the dressing gown and pyjamas that Emma had sent as a gift and he looked adorable. Not that she was going to tell him.

'I'm sorry,' she said. 'Did we wake you up?'

'What's going on?'

Lydia hesitated. 'My friend Jason's missing.'

His eyes widened. 'Taken?'

'It's complicated,' Lydia said. Then she ran through the rest. Including the fact that Jason was a ghost.

Fleet looked worried, but Ember took it in his stride. 'Gran always said that there were spirits. She used to talk to her sister and she died, like, ages ago.'

'You don't need to be afraid, he's a friendly ghost,' Fleet said.

'But some bad guy has taken him? And they're gonna use a load of ghosts to blow up a building?'

Before Lydia could agree that he had summed it up perfectly, Ember's face twisted in distress and he suddenly looked much younger. 'Your friend is going to get exploded?'

'No!' Lydia said immediately. 'No. He's not. I'm going to stop it.'

'Okay,' Ember said, seeming to take this as fact. 'This woman is getting married tomorrow? Today, I mean.'

'Yes.'

'But you don't think she's doing the explosion at the wedding?'

'No. The wedding is her alibi. That means she'll have evidence that she wasn't involved, the police won't be able to place her at the scene—'

'I know what an alibi is,' Ember said witheringly.

'Right. And she's told a load of lies to the secret service, so they're going to be at the wedding too. She's got everyone distracted, looking at the wrong thing.'

'Except you.'

'Except me. But I don't have the exact target. That's what we're trying to figure out.'

'You could ask me,' Ember said. He opened the fridge and pulled out a block of cheese. 'Can I make a sandwich?'

'You don't have to ask,' Lydia said. 'Help yourself.'

Ember got a frying pan and put it on the stove. He began slicing cheese and buttering bread.

Lydia left him to it and spoke to Fleet privately. They came up with a system. Without knowing how many questions they could ask before Ember's ability switched off, or how exactly his ability worked, they decided to work in categories. Like the game twenty questions, you didn't go straight in with a specific guess.

Once they were ready, and Ember had finished his toasted cheese sandwich and a glass of milk, they met in the living room.

'You don't have to do this,' Fleet said. 'We're not asking you to—'

'We are asking,' Lydia cut in. 'But only because it's really important. But you don't have to say yes. It's completely your choice.'

'No pressure,' Fleet said. 'We mean that.'

Ember looked from Lydia to Fleet and then around the room, as if he was looking for someone. 'I offered, innit? You're not, like, pressurising me. He's not back, is he?'

Lydia frowned. 'Jason? No. Can you usually see him?'

'No,' Ember said. 'But it feels emptier in here than

usual.' He shrugged. 'I dunno whether I'm imagining things.'

'You're not. He spends a lot of time in here.' Lydia deliberately didn't look at the sofa. She knew that if she pictured Jason sitting cross-legged there, with his laptop open and fingers dancing over the keyboard, she would fall apart.

Ember nodded, thoughtful. After a moment, he spoke again. 'You really worried about him? Your ghost?'

'He's my friend,' Lydia said.

Ember looked at the floor.

Lydia couldn't tell what he was thinking by looking at the top of his head, but it didn't stop her trying.

After a few more seconds of silence, Ember looked up. 'Okay. I'm ready. But you can't get mad.'

'Of course not,' Fleet said immediately.

Lydia was slower to agree. 'What do you mean?'

Ember looked unhappy as he pulled the battered pack of playing cards out of his dressing gown pocket. 'People say they want answers, but then they don't like them. Gran warned me about that. People say they want the truth, but they're lying. They want to hear whatever they already think.'

'We're not going to be upset or angry with you,' Lydia said. 'Only grateful. I promise.'

Ember nodded. He sat in the middle of the floor and began shuffling his cards. 'What's your question?'

CHAPTER THIRTY-ONE

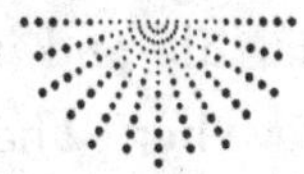

They started with the question, 'is the target within the City of London?'. It confirmed Lydia's suspicion and narrowed it down to the square mile of the old city.

That still encompassed a multitude of possibilities, including the Guildhall Art Gallery, the Barbican, the Bank of England and its museum, Leadenhall Market and The Gherkin. Not to mention Tower Bridge.

Fleet wrote down 'museum?' on a sheet of paper and tapped it, raising his eyebrows at Lydia. She nodded.

Ember was shuffling his cards again.

'Is the target a museum?'

Ember frowned, laying out cards and then pushing them back together. Eventually he looked up. 'No.'

'What if it is the wedding?' Fleet asked, not for the first time. 'You and all the rest of the Families will be there. And the secret service and maybe police, too. Who knows how many other dignitaries will turn out for a Family event like this?'

'We are being distracted,' Lydia said, desperate to make Fleet understand. 'It's perfect. We're all going to be there and MI13 are going to be watching us. It's a distraction and an alibi all rolled into one.'

'Are you sure?'

Lydia knew she was right. She had never been more sure of anything in her life and it was frustrating that people didn't just believe her. 'The Collective believe in disruption. They want to shake the establishment. We're not the establishment, the Families, we're the underground. Even if Scarlett wanted to blow us all up, I don't think she would be able to sell it to The Collective.'

'So we're looking at targets that hit at the conventional seats of power.'

Lydia thought about Scarlett's upbringing. She was raised to be the leader of a group, to exact obedience. Devotion. 'Or religious sites. What's more conventional than the Church of England?'

Ember was listening, wide-eyed.

'Is the target a church?' Lydia asked.

He dealt the cards and answered immediately. 'Yes.'

'We need a list of churches in that area,' Lydia said. 'Then we can go through them one-by-one...' She stopped speaking when she caught sight of Ember's expression. He looked like he was going to cry. 'What's wrong?'

'They've gone dead. I'm sorry.'

'Don't be sorry, you've helped so much. Thank you.' Fleet, as always, was quick with the right words. He patted Ember on the shoulder for good measure.

'Churches in the City,' Lydia said. 'Probably a big

one. Well known.' She remembered. 'I was outside St Mary-le-Bow when that ghost went for me. That's a famous one, right?'

Fleet opened his mouth to speak, maybe to agree, but Lydia didn't find out. His whole body tensed and his eyes glazed over.

It was over before Lydia had time to worry.

Fleet blinked, coming back to her.

She waited a moment, not wanting to speak too quickly and interrupt whatever vision he might be holding onto.

'What the hell was that?' Ember asked, staring at Fleet.

Lydia shushed him.

'Black and white floor.' Fleet said, his voice still a bit dreamy and his eyes unfocused. He closed his eyes for a moment, pulling himself together. 'Underneath all the bodies.' He blinked. 'Stone. Or marble, maybe? And I was right before, the space was really big. Hundreds of people there. Hurt.'

'Scarlett strikes me as showy. What if she's going for the biggest one?' Lydia had pulled up the website for St Paul's Cathedral, which sat on Ludgate Hill, the highest point in the City of London. She flicked through the gallery of images until she found one of the nave. The floor was tiled in black and white marble.

ONCE SHE HAD EXTRACTED A PROMISE FROM EMBER that he would stay south of the river, called Aiden to make sure there was a crew around the house that would follow Ember if he left and make sure he obeyed, she called Sinclair.

'We need to evacuate St Paul's.'

'I'm not going to do that,' Sinclair said. 'Not without solid intel.'

'I'm telling you there is going to be an attack. You've been after my help, after my information. This is it. This is how you stop an attack on central London, save the lives of thousands of visitors to one of the iconic attractions. This will make your career.'

'Or bury it,' Sinclair said drily. 'And I can think of several reasons why you might be after a little payback.'

Lydia squeezed her coin and put every bit of Crow behind her voice, willing Sinclair to believe her. 'Scarlett is the new head of the Pearl Family. She was raised in The Church of Lazarus and she believes in toppling the establishment. Hitting London in one of the symbols of the old order, in the heart of the legal and banking district, it's exactly what she was raised to do.'

A pause. 'I believe that you are sincere,' Sinclair said, 'but do you have evidence? What sort of device are we talking about? And where did it come from?'

Her hand was forced, so Lydia decided to lay out all her cards. 'A cameo was stolen from the British Museum last year. We think it has been activated with Pearl blood to attract ghosts. It pulls them in until the pressure builds to a point that the spirits explode.'

'Exploding ghosts.'

'I know how it sounds, but you remember the blood drained from your agent? I think that was taken in order to power up the cameo, to make it stronger. You've been looking for a new power, well this is what Gabrielle was trying to distract you from. She passed on the false information about the fifth Family and the disguise thing in order to distract you from the real goal. She's using this object to pull in ghosts and then force them out of existence. If there are enough of them, they produce a toxic substance. It burns, like chemical weapon burns.'

Sinclair didn't say anything, but Lydia could feel her incredulity through the line. 'You know about the Families, you know ghosts exist, why is this part so hard to believe?'

'I have a remit to find a valuable tool for the service. Instant and undetectable disguises. If I fail to fulfil that brief, I am not going to compound the error by crying wolf over exploding ghosts. However,' Sinclair continued, 'I will meet you. Bring everything you have put together on this incident and I will consider if there is enough to move forward.'

Lydia felt the seconds ticking away as she argued. There wasn't time to convince the secret service. 'I will meet you at five,' she said, ending the call. If she was wrong about this afternoon, she would show Sinclair everything. If she wasn't wrong, she might be dead. Along with a lot of other people.

Lydia stood in line inside the entrance of St Paul's to have her bag checked. You couldn't carry anything larger than a small backpack into the cathedral and every tourist and worshipper was checked for weapons. The illusion of safety in modern London.

Scarlett's anarchist group were going to tear that down, reveal it as a flimsy pretence. And what then? A reduction in tourism for the city? Fear spreading through the populous? Hadn't they learned anything from 7/7? Londoners were resilient.

Of course, Scarlett had been raised to think otherwise.

Visitors could attend the Eucharist services for free, but in between these the cathedral was open for sightseeing. There were organised tours and, according to the website, about five thousand people visited every day. Having never played tourist, Lydia's main images of the cathedral came from the media coverage of Margaret Thatcher's million-pound funeral. She knew the place was vast and could comfortably hold over three and a half thousand visitors at one time. Peak tourist season with bad weather threatening, Lydia guessed there would be close to this number packed inside.

There was a café in the crypt and stairs up to the dome, but the majority of those people would be crowded in the nave of the church, their necks developing cricks from gazing upward at the painted ceilings, intricate decorative metalwork, gilding, and grand carved arches in shining marble.

When Lydia got through the security-conscious entrance and entered the main part of the cathedral, she immediately went cold. Not just from the grand interior and the volume of people, or even from the realisation that she had been right, but from the chilled air created by a thousand or more ghosts.

Several people close by were pulling on layers or

rubbing their hands together, clearly also noticing the sub-zero temperature. Lydia assumed that they put it down to the chilly stonework and impossibly high ceiling of the massive space, but Lydia wondered how much colder the temperature would drop with this number of ghosts in one place.

And more seemed to be arriving, popping into existence as they were pulled in from around the city. Soon, it was hard to see where one spirit ended and another began. They were pressed in together, overlapping the live tourists in a way that created a disorientating tapestry of human features. Legs, arms and faces were multiplied in dizzying numbers, so that Lydia had to focus on the architectural features of the interior to rest her mind for a few seconds. She realised that she was holding her breath.

The living were moving around slowly, unconcerned, whispering to each other of the religious iconography or whatever it was that got cathedral-visitors hot under the collar.

'Where is it?' Fleet was saying. He was scanning the area with calm professionalism, but Lydia could detect the fear beneath his words. His breath fogged in the cold air.

'It's too big a space to search,' Lydia said, forcing air back into her lungs. 'The cameo is tiny.'

'I'm assuming you can see ghosts?' he asked quietly. 'It's freezing in here.'

'Uh-huh,' Lydia was trying not to freak out. She wanted to stretch her wings and fly far away. Two spirits close to them were taking an interest, stretching out their arms in supplication. One hand passed through Fleet's torso, and he gave an involuntary shudder. The spirits themselves looked terrified and the feeling was contagious.

'What do we do?' Fleet was looking to her for answers. And she had none.

The ghosts could explode at any moment and there were thousands of them. Twenty had created enough toxic goop to burn her and Fleet, she couldn't even begin to comprehend how much damage this many spirits would create. Would it be enough to kill? Unbidden, Lydia saw one of the images from a chemical weapon attack. Skin burned away, people screaming with lipless mouths, flesh that no longer looked human.

Pushing down her panic, Lydia flipped her coin into the air. She felt the spirits' attention snap to her. She had to trust that Megan was doing as she had promised, and was searching for Jason. If she happened to find the cameo, great, but her mission was to find Jason and get him to safety. That way, Lydia would be free to focus.

'We should evacuate,' Fleet said quietly. He spoke directly into her ear, so as not to cause a mass panic.

Lydia went on tiptoe to whisper back. 'We don't know how they will trigger it. If they're watching and they see lots of people leaving, it might make them do it.'

'But if they're going to anyway...'

'I'm going up there.' Lydia pointed to the gallery that ran around the inside of the dome. 'Vantage point.' Good position to view the crowd, but also an ideal place to stash the cameo.

There was a rope at the bottom of the steps with a

sign that told Lydia the whispering gallery was temporarily shut to visitors. Ignoring it, she took the stairs at a run. The spirits were being drawn to the cameo, and she hoped she would be able to identify its location by looking from above. A concentration of ghosts in one area that would be the X that marked the spot.

The spiral stone steps seemed to be going on forever and Lydia stopped for a brief break, her lungs burning from the effort. Looking up, she could see the spiral of steps and black ironwork banisters. It was pretty, sure, but she didn't feel as if she was significantly closer to the top than when she had started. That had to be the panic talking, so she told it to shut up and sprinted upward.

A narrow landing led to the gallery. It was a narrow walkway with a stone balustrade, more ironwork and some modern 'anti fall' netting. Peering over the edge at the black and white chequerboard floor thirty metres below, she could see why it had been installed. From this vertiginous viewpoint, she located Fleet. He was walking through ghosts, oblivious to them, but scanning the crowd of people.

She could also appreciate the sheer scale of the building. And the writhing mass of frightened spirits, most translucent, some more corporeal, and all moving in disjointed or shimmering ways, creating a heaving sea of faces, arms, legs, and torsos. Some were horror-show damaged, the spirit form holding onto their shape from when they died. Towards a black statue of a man on a horse, there was a clot of spirits. These were packed so tightly they were actually overlapping one another.

There were a few ghosts up here, too. A young man in a military uniform was shuddering near the middle of the walkway. He looked at Lydia with pleading eyes. 'I don't want to go down there.'

She heard his voice so clearly. His figure was vibrating with emotion, his edges blurring in a way that reminded her of Jason.

'You don't have to go anywhere,' she said. Hands raised, trying to be soothing.

His eyes made her realise he was even younger than she had first thought. He had a neat moustache and soulful brown eyes. She could see the colour as his form was solidifying as she watched.

'You see me?' He took a step in her direction, momentarily distracted from looking over the edge.

'I do,' Lydia said. 'I'm here to help.'

His face twisted abruptly. 'Nobody can help me.' His body turned back to the body of the cathedral and, with one movement, he leaned over the balustrade and toppled over the edge.

Lydia looked down to the floor of the cathedral. She couldn't see the spirit amongst the throng and when she turned back to the walkway, she saw he had reanimated there. Thinner and more translucent than he had been seconds earlier, but clearly the same man. He stared over the edge with the same intensity.

She wondered if the force of the object calling all these spirits would eventually break his loop, pull him close and then kill him for good. Would it be such a bad thing? This ghost was clearly reliving the end of his life over and over for eternity. If it wasn't going to result in an explosion that would harm hundreds of people, you could almost frame it as a kindness.

There were other spirits crammed along the passage-way. Women and men and, horribly, children. This gallery had seen a lot of death, unless they were all being dragged in from elsewhere. They all seemed to be drawn to the edge, to lean over the railing, to stare down. It gave Lydia a strange sense of being off balance, as if the whole walkway was tilting that way, tipping her toward the echoing space. She could jump into all that air, she thought. Maybe she would fly. Or maybe the moments before she hit the marble floor would be utter bliss. No more striving, no control over what came next, no more decisions or responsibility.

She shook her head to clear it. The spirit of a woman was uncomfortably close, her hand touching Lydia's upper arm. Pawing at it, really, as if trying to get purchase.

'There's something happening here,' she tried. 'Someone is pulling in all these spirits. Can you feel it?'

The woman nodded eagerly. She was translucent and vague, so the movement made Lydia want to hurl. She swallowed the nausea and soldiered on. 'Can you point to the source? Can you feel where the pull is strongest?'

Lydia's arm was cold where the woman's hand kept attempting to make contact. The ghost kept nodding as if she understood the question and was just about to answer. But then she didn't. Lydia waited for the spirit to speak, or to point a ghostly arm in the right direction. Instead, she just kept nodding and attempting to grasp

Lydia's sleeve. Lydia watched the ghost's hands pass through her own body over and over again and, suddenly, the nodding head was a warning. This ghost wasn't able to help, she realised. She would carry on these same movements for as long as Lydia stood there. 'Thank you,' she said, figuring there was no harm in being civil, and then moved along the walkway, trying not to walk through the ghosts.

There was no sign of Scarlett or anybody acting suspiciously with a cameo brooch. It was frustrating, but Lydia hadn't expected it to be that easy. Nothing ever was, in her experience.

Her phone rang and she answered it, keeping an eye on the spirits. 'I've found him,' Megan said. 'But he won't come with me. It's like he can't hear me.'

CHAPTER THIRTY-TWO

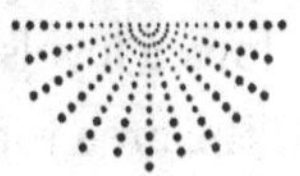

Lydia took the stairs down from the walkway, the phone pressed to her ear. 'Can you put him on? I'll speak to him.'

The ghosts that Lydia moved past were clearly frightened. She hated the thought that Jason was in the same state and her stomach churned with fury. How dare Scarlett do this to her friend? How dare anyone? These spirits had been through enough. They might not be most people's idea of 'alive' but it was still wrong to torture them.

Back on the ground floor, Lydia was instantly surrounded by ghosts. They pressed into Lydia as she moved through them, as if sensing her Crow power and wanting to get closer to it. 'Megan?' she tried. 'Are you still with Jason?'

Megan had clearly been speaking, her voice cutting in halfway through a sentence. Then she said: 'Jason's gone through the floor.'

'What?'

The ghost of man with a top hat was pressed against her and Lydia's left side was numb from the cold. 'He's—'

The reception was still patchy and Lydia was only getting every other word before the call cut out altogether. She had gathered that Megan was doing her best to follow Jason to the lower levels of the cathedral, and she frantically scanned the area for stairs.

The door to the crypt was closed with a sign 'closed for private function' on the outside. Lydia ignored it and slipped past, relieved that there wouldn't be members of the public down here at least.

The stone steps seemed to go on forever, Lydia's fear making time act strangely. She needed to get Jason to safety. She needed to stop the ghost bomb. Her mind kept short-circuiting at the thought of her friend exploding. And she had seen families inside the cathedral. Small children, even babies. What if she was too late? Inside the passage, her feet loud on the stone as she hurried down the steps, she could still feel the mass vibrating energy from the gathered spirits.

Enormous memorials lined the crypt, some tucked behind archways and in ornately carved nooks. She passed one for Florence Nightingale and another for Sir Christopher Wren. Either it had been used for a wedding in the recent past or was being set up for one in the future, as there were round tables with white cloths and strings of lights draping the vaulted ceiling.

There were fewer ghosts here than in the main part of the cathedral, but there were still a lot. It looked like the weirdest party with shades from every part of history, clumped in awkward groups. They all looked unhappy, and some were swaying slightly, as if stirred by a light breeze, but they weren't vibrating or screaming, so it counted as a win.

At the far end of the crypt, a position that would be roughly central to the entire building, there was a man crouched on the floor. He was hunched over an object and swearing to himself.

To her right, she caught sight of Megan's blonde hair. She saw Lydia and shook her head. No sign of Jason then.

'Having trouble getting it going?' Lydia said as she approached the crouched man. 'Don't worry, it happens to all guys at some point.'

The guy's head snapped up and he made a noise that was closer to a snarl than the English language. He was wearing a fresh shirt, but was sweating heavily, despite the frigid temperature created by the stonework and multiple ghosts.

Lydia guessed it wouldn't be long before he had pit-stains like the ones she had seen when she had collected Ember. 'Marty the Spook,' she said. 'You appear to have swapped sides.'

'Never,' Marty spat. 'I have only ever served one master. I was asleep before but now I'm awake.'

'Hell Hawk. I hate the true believers. So boring.' A young shade, probably the same age as Ember, had drifted close and was trying to put his hand into Lydia's, but it kept passing through. She forced herself not to look at the kid. Couldn't be distracted.

'I won't bore you for long,' Marty said with a horrible

smile. 'You will die with your godless brethren and the new order will rise for the good of all mankind.'

Lydia suppressed the urge to roll her eyes. Marty might have sounded like a brainwashed fool, but he was still in possession of the cameo and Lydia didn't know how long the ritual was going to keep the ghosts above bound to this earthly plane.

She curbed the urge to get closer to Marty and kick him in the face and, instead, produced her coin. In her peripheral vision, the ghost child moved closer, tilting his face to stare at the flashing gold.

'Do you know what will happen? If you get that thing activated?'

'Of course,' Marty said.

'So you know it's a suicide mission? Just checking.'

Marty didn't waver. 'Some things are worth dying for.'

Lydia swept her hand to indicate the ghosts in the crypt. 'I can see one or two people who would disagree with you.'

Marty glanced around. Then: 'It doesn't matter. I'm not listening to your lies.'

'I'm not a Silver,' Lydia said, irritation breaking through. 'I'm a Crow. And we're all about the harsh truth.' She flicked her coin into the air and made it spin slowly.

Marty stared determinedly down at the ground, refusing to look at it.

Lydia moved closer. She could get his attention, use her coin to mesmerise him into stopping whatever he was doing with the cameo, whatever was making it work.

An icy sensation swept through her hand and she glanced down. The kid was keeping pace, his hand still attempting to hold hers. He was translucent, but getting more solid with every second. She could see that his face was badly scarred, one eye closed with puckered skin. His mouth worked as if he was speaking, but she couldn't hear the words. 'It's all right,' she said automatically.

'Who are you talking to?'

Marty sounded spooked for the first time and Lydia realised the obvious. 'You can't see them, can you? The people you're about to kill.'

Marty looked up to the vaulted stone ceiling, as if he could see through to the cathedral above.

Lydia pictured the thousands of people walking around the cathedral, seeing the sights, reading the information plaques. 'Not just them,' she said. 'The ghosts.'

'They're just energy,' Marty said. 'Not people. They will be glad to be used as tools for the glorious mission.'

Lydia looked around at the unhappy ghosts. 'They really don't agree with you.'

In her periphery, she saw Megan moving slowly. She was surrounded by spirits, making it hard for Lydia to see her clearly. The group was so thick, it was impossible to see if Jason was there.

She focused on Marty. She needed to keep him occupied, to give herself time to work out what to do. Another step closer and she could see what he was hunched over. She had been expecting to see the cameo, but the chalk pentagram was new. Lydia had no idea if it was essential or just something the cult had seen on TV and assumed was necessary. There were some dried herbs scattered around, too, and something smeared on the white face of the cameo. Blood.

'It's not working, Marty,' Lydia said. 'Why don't you call it a day? You and I can go and get some fresh air.'

'It will work,' Marty said. Then he scowled. 'What did you do?'

'Me? Nothing. I'm just here to chat.' She willed him to look at the coin, but he stubbornly stared down at the cameo, seemingly unable to tear his gaze from its serene face.

The face was very beautiful. Even at this distance, Lydia could make out its fine nose and curved lips, the gentle expression in its unseeing eyes. She wanted to get closer, to trace its outline with her finger.

The ice-feeling in her left hand cut through her thoughts and brought her back to herself. The ghost kid was staring at her imploringly, shaking his head and holding her hand as best he could.

'Thank you,' she said to him and saw the relief in his one good eye.

Lydia looked back at Marty and around at the ghosts that were gathered around them. They were all watching the cameo. She avoided looking directly at the object, wary of its power, but studied the ghosts instead. None of them appeared to be looking at Marty. Only at the cameo. They were drawn to it, just as the professor's writing had suggested.

'You need to go,' she said, waving her hands to try to get their attention. 'This will hurt you. You'll explode if you stay here. You need to get far away.'

The ghosts ignored her.

Lydia tried with the kid. 'Can you talk to them? Tell them it's not safe here. They need to get away. Disperse.'

He cocked his head, listening. But then shook his head and resumed his attempts to grab her hand.

If the ghosts wouldn't leave the cameo, she would have to move it. Get somewhere remote and unpopulated so that as few people as possible would die. Ignoring the fact that she would be strapping the suicide vest onto her own body, she lunged forward. Her fingers brushed the cameo before something solid hit her from the side.

Marty was on top of her and she rolled. His hands were going for her neck, but she broke his grip with her wrists and bucked her body to dislodge him. For a moment, she thought she had succeeded in overbalancing him, but then he righted himself and bore down on her with his full weight. Sour body odour filled her nostrils, mixing with the tang of adrenaline.

Marty wasn't in the prime of life, but he was a trained spook and he knew how to fight. Plus, he had height and weight advantage. The next time he went to choke her, he succeeded in getting his hands around her neck, and Lydia knew with an awful certainty that she was going to lose.

Black spots were swimming at the edges of her vision, but she kept on twisting her body, bucking weakly in an attempt to dislodge Marty. She couldn't pull his hands away from her throat, his grip was too strong, so she stopped trying. She had seconds left before she blacked out, but her mind was suddenly crystal clear. She reached out her arms either side and rubbed at the floor. Lydia had no idea where they were lying, whether she was still in reach of the pentagram and the cameo but she was out of ideas and definitely out of time.

Her fingers brushed something solid and it skittered across the stone floor.

The pressure on her throat eased momentarily and Marty's attention shifted for a split second. Lydia used that moment to wedge her fingers between his hands and her neck and get a breath.

Marty was staring to the right, his eyes wide. Then his body arched in sudden pain. His hands flew from her neck and his whole body lifted. She rolled onto her side coughing and heaving in air.

Marty was screaming. She had never heard a sound like it coming from a human. Pure terror and pain in a raw animal sound that echoed around the stone arches. His body was suspended in mid-air and was jerking in every direction, sometimes spinning upside down and then pulling to the side. His arms flopped as if no longer under his control and then Lydia realised they were badly broken. His body was a chew toy, a rag doll, a child's lovey. But instead of being hugged, it was being thrown around. Marty wasn't screaming anymore and Lydia could see the ghosts that had amassed to play with Marty beginning to get restless and to look around.

Footsteps on the stone floor and Megan appeared in her field of vision. Before Lydia could say anything, Megan swept to the floor and grabbed the cameo. She pulled a lilac plastic bottle from her pocket and squeezed purple goo onto the pure and perfect face of the cameo, then rubbed it vigorously with her hands, before polishing it on the material of her pink T-shirt.

The scent of bubble-gum filled the air. 'That should do—' Megan began, but the rest of her words were drowned out in the sudden rush of air and wet thump of Marty's broken body hitting the stone floor.

Lydia sat up. Her throat burned and her body ached, but she didn't think anything was broken. The child spirit who had been trying to hold her hand floated up to Megan and reached out a finger to touch her.

Megan turned and smiled into his ruined face. 'Hi buddy. Lot of excitement today, huh?'

Lydia blinked back a sudden stinging in her eyes. It was nice not to be the only person who could see the spirits. Speaking of which. 'They're leaving.' The mass of ghosts that had killed Marty were dispersing, drifting upward to exit the building in the most direct route, or blinking out of existence in the way that Jason had done all the time when she had first known him.

She didn't want to look too closely at Marty's body but he had thankfully landed a few feet away from where she was sitting. There was chalk smeared on the ground and Lydia realised that she had managed to rub the chalk of the pentagram, messing with the symbols around the edge and breaking the image.

'I cleaned the blood off this,' Megan held up the cameo. 'I thought we might have to break it, but the blood thing seems to have worked.'

'Right.' Lydia still felt slightly dazed and emotional.

She wondered if it was the adrenaline or the near-death experience. 'Thank you for that.'

Megan looked uncharacteristically serious. 'I wish I'd done it quicker. Who knows how many ghosts were hurt.'

'They didn't explode,' Lydia said. She held out her arms. 'No goo.' Then a moment of terror. She would have thought she would have heard an explosion, but maybe the stone was so thick...

'No explosion,' Megan confirmed. 'No casualties. We did good.'

'Thank feathers.' Lydia closed her eyes.

'But they will be psychically damaged. They were dragged here against their will and some of them committed murder.' She lifted a chin to indicate Marty's corpse. 'That's damage.'

'You really care about the ghosts, don't you?'

Megan shrugged, still serious. 'I know them. They talk to me. It's hard not to.'

Lydia thought about Jason. He was as much a person to her as any breathing human.

The child with the damaged face was watching, listening. Lydia smiled at him in a way that she hoped was friendly. It was already easier to look at his injuries. You really could get used to anything.

Megan held out the cameo. 'You need this?'

'I don't—' Lydia realised that she probably ought to return it to the British Museum. But it had been stolen once... 'Thanks.' She took the cameo and shoved it into her pocket. That was a problem for another day.

A door banged and Fleet ran into the crypt. He

dropped to a walk when he spotted Lydia and Megan, relief plastered over his face. 'Are you—?'

'I'm all right,' Lydia broke in.

'I'm fine, too,' Megan added brightly.

'Thank you for your help.' Lydia realised she should have said it already.

'It's over?' Fleet had reached them.

'It's over,' Lydia said, rubbing her neck. She looked at Marty's broken body. 'I'd better call Sinclair.'

CHAPTER THIRTY-THREE

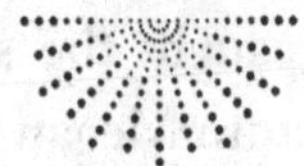

There had been no explosion, so there was no cause for alarm. Lydia knew that Megan had seen Jason at the cathedral, but he would be free to return home now. No blood-soaked cameo or weird ritual. No Marty. The ghosts had been unharmed. Jason was fine. Lydia told herself this repeatedly as she exited St Paul's. The hordes of visitors and Londoners were still walking around in the summer sunshine, taking selfies and slurping from water bottles, oblivious to the crisis that had just been averted.

Soon, there would be controlled chaos as the police and MI13 swooped in to deal with the dead agent in the crypt. Fleet had stayed with the body, guarding the crime scene until the rest of the constabulary arrived. When she had asked him what he was going to say to the authorities, he just shook his head.

If he went with the truth he would be put on sick leave before you could say 'sectioned under the Mental Health Act'.

Megan wished him luck before they left. 'Keep me out of it, yeah?'

'I'll do my best,' Fleet promised.

Now, Megan was slipping cat's eye sunglasses on and saying something about it being 'Cornetto time'.

Lydia realised that one of her necklaces had a tiny opal ghost charm. It caught the sun, turning different colours. She could picture Megan as a terrified six-year-old, suddenly able to see and hear the spectral world, and was filled with an awareness of how strong she had been forced to be. Despite it, she had made friends with the ghosts, made it her life's mission to look out for them. 'Thank you for your help.'

'Any time,' Megan said. 'What are you going to do with it?'

Lydia didn't need to ask what she meant. The cameo was a lump in her jeans pocket. It felt weightier than it should.

'You should chuck it in the river,' Megan said, uncharacteristically serious.

'Maybe,' Lydia replied. The sun was warming her through after being so thoroughly chilled.

'I've got a date with a burrito,' Megan said. 'Call me if you need anything. Or if you want to hang.'

'Will do,' Lydia surprised herself by saying. Had she made a new friend?

'Give Jason a kiss from me,' Megan added, walking backwards.

'Definitely not,' Lydia replied, but she could feel that she was smiling.

. . .

Lydia called Sinclair's number, but she didn't pick up. It was well past midday and the wedding was due to happen at three. She hailed a taxi for speed and called Paul from the car. He answered on the third ring, a smile in his voice. 'Little Bird.'

'I just stopped Scarlett from blowing up a load of ghosts in the crypt of St Paul's. She turned a secret service agent called Marty, so he was the one doing the ritual. It was her, though. Her plan.'

'I'm in Whitechapel,' Paul said. 'Meet me.'

'You're not at the Heath?'

'The place is crawling with secret service. Not my scene.'

Lydia wanted to say 'but it's your wedding day' but he had already hung up.

The entrance to the Fox's bar was through a barber shop. Usually, Lydia had to deal with some serious eyeballing from a pissed-off Fox, but the man with the sharp haircut and the body of a lumberjack opened the door for her. He raised his chin in a gesture which appeared to be a greeting. Or even an expression of gratitude.

Feeling discombobulated by the lack of hostility, Lydia made her way down the stairs and into the underground bar. The lights were low, reflecting warmth from the mirrors and making the coloured glass glow in the rows of bottles displayed behind the bar. There was music playing and, of all the places to be held captive, Scarlett could be doing a lot worse.

She was in a white bridal gown, but her hair was covered in a silk turban and her face looked a little unbalanced. It took Lydia a second to work out that it was because she had been interrupted half-way through doing her make-up.

She was behind a small table, her hands not visible and presumably tied. There was a lime green plastic cup on the table with a long bendy straw. 'Lydia! You've got to help me! He's gone mad!'

Lydia didn't reply. Paul was lounging against a wall. He was wearing jeans and a black T-shirt and his eyes were warm when he looked at her. 'Little Bird.'

In the shadows at the back of the bar, and flanking the entrance, were several Foxes. She recognised a couple of Paul's siblings, but there were more faces she didn't know. It occurred to her that she would never have walked into a situation like this before. Things really had changed between her and Paul. Hopefully it could mean a change in relations between the Crows and the Foxes, too, but that was no longer her concern.

'Everyone okay?' Paul asked.

'I stopped it in time. There are a lot of confused ghosts in London right now, but hopefully they'll be all right.'

Scarlett was clearly listening. Her face didn't betray any emotion, but the woman had had a great deal of practice.

'I'm sorry for what happened to you,' Lydia said.

Scarlett frowned, looking genuinely confused. 'What are you talking about?'

'You were abused, lied to, hurt.'

'The Collective loves me,' Scarlett said. 'They know the meaning of trust and loyalty.'

'I'm not talking about The Collective. They're your weapons. A bunch of idealists you radicalised to violent action. To murder.' Lydia took a couple of steps toward Scarlett, lowering her voice. 'I'm talking about Lazarus.'

Scarlett stared at her defiantly. 'You weren't raised right, so you will never understand. Without purity, there can be no true knowledge. With purity, there is control over life and death, there is ascendency.'

'How do you get purity, Gabrielle? I bet it hurts.'

Scarlett hadn't flinched when Lydia had used her name, but she thought she had seen a flicker in her facial muscles. 'That's not my name.'

'It was,' Lydia said. 'He took it away from you, along with your life, your freedom, your mother—'

'Don't speak of things you do not understand.'

'All right then,' Lydia said, even-toned. 'You're going to jail. You ordered the murder of five men, and conspired to kill hundreds of people using a supernatural bomb.'

The smile was back. 'Lydia Crow. I would have thought you would be smarter than this. You know I will not be convicted of these so-called crimes.'

'Maybe not. But you also murdered a secret service agent. You knew him as Carl.'

'You have no evidence of that,' Scarlett said. 'And I believe you already have the man responsible for Carl's accidental death in custody. I cannot be held responsible for the acts of another.'

'Have you heard of coercive control?' Lydia asked.

'You really should have. It's one of dear old dad's special-ities and is illegal these days. Plus, there are other forms of jail.'

The door to the bar opened and Maria stepped into the room, followed by two bodyguards. She was dressed for the wedding in a red form-fitting dress, silver Louboutins which had little shiny spikes all down the back of the heels, and a hat that sat at a sharp angle, defying gravity. She tested physics a little further by tilting her head at Lydia and Paul. 'This isn't quite what I was expecting to be doing today.'

Scarlett looked at them all with contempt. She might have been half-ready and tied up, but she managed to look regal. 'You think you can kill me? The master cannot be destroyed. I am immortal.'

'Is that what you were told growing up? I met Maryam,' Lydia said, 'that poor broken woman. What did she go through to protect you from your dad? I know you tried to look after her, in your own way. You did the best you could.'

'Stay away from Maryam,' Scarlett said. For the first time, Lydia detected a sliver of uncertainty.

'Where is the OG?' Paul said easily. 'Dear old dad?'

'He was judged unworthy,' Scarlett said stiffly.

'Died in prison within a few months,' Lydia translated.

'Well that's good,' Paul said. 'One less hit on the "to kill" list.' He stared directly into Scarlett's eyes. 'I've got a busy day as it is.'

Scarlett maintained eye contact, but Lydia could sense the tension. The Pearl was rolling from her, enticing as always, but there was something off about it. Curdled. 'I did this for us,' she tried. 'For all of us. The Families shouldn't be hiding in the shadows, we should be in charge of this city. The sheep sleepwalk and we walk among them as gods.'

Maria glanced at Scarlett. 'A terrorist act in St Paul's would've been very bad for business. *My* business.'

'I can usher in a new dawn.' There was a note of panic to Scarlett's voice now. 'No more government, no more police. We should be in charge.'

'A clean kill?' Paul asked, ignoring Scarlett to look at Lydia and Maria. 'We need to agree.'

'Sounds fine to me,' Maria said, examining her blood-red nails.

Lydia's stomach swooped. She couldn't have her last act as the head of the Crow Family be as executioner. Scarlett might deserve it, it might be the only way to exact justice for those she had murdered, but Lydia didn't feel that she had any right to carry out a death sentence. She shouldn't have that power. None of them should.

'Lydia?' Paul prompted when she hadn't spoken.

She swallowed, not looking at Scarlett. 'I vote for banishment. She leaves London. She doesn't come back.'

Maria made a quick gesture of irritation. 'What's to stop her coming after us?'

'I don't think she will,' Lydia said. She looked at Scarlett. 'Will you? You can start again somewhere else. Build a life. But if we get so much as a hint that you're a threat, we won't hesitate to eradicate you. You know we can. Working together, you know what the Families are capable of.' Lydia was banking on Scarlett's admiration for the Families to seal the deal.

Paul was looking at Scarlett with a blank expression, but Lydia could sense his anger. 'We need to agree,' he said.

'I'm happy for you and Maria to decide,' Lydia said. 'I've lost my appetite for blood, but I won't stand in your way.'

He glanced at Lydia before announcing. 'Banishment, then. She goes alone. She doesn't lead a group of any kind. We'll keep watch.'

That wasn't easily enforceable, Scarlett could disappear, but Lydia could see that Maria was fast losing patience with the debate.

'Fine,' she said. 'Banishment. But I want you two to remember that it wasn't my idea.'

Lydia hoped that the threat of the four Families, plus the attention of DCI Fleet in his new role at MI13, would be enough to discourage Scarlett from continuing her destructive activities. Or considering retaliation. She knew it wasn't ideal, but all she could feel was overwhelming relief that she wasn't going to be responsible for another death.

Once business was concluded, Maria nodded to Lydia and Paul and left. 'I'll walk you out,' Paul said.

Outside the barbershop, Lydia was letting her eyes adjust to daylight. 'Scarlett was raised to be the new master of the Church of Lazarus. Up to the age of ten, she was indoctrinated that she had a destiny, it's no wonder that screwed her up.'

Paul's expression was hard. 'We've all had shit to deal with.'

'Cult leaders lie about their power, they say that they are God, that they control the earth and everything that happens upon it, they say that they can read minds and see into souls, that they are the judge and executioner and the saviour. But it's lies. Brainwashing. A confidence trick essentially. Scarlett's different. When she said she could control ghosts, she was telling the truth. When she said she could influence people, make them desire her and listen to her and, through that, control what they did and felt and thought, she was telling the truth.'

'And she chose what to do with that,' Paul said. 'Not the first leader to go off the rails.'

'Are you going to escort her out of the city?'

'It's my job.'

Lydia wasn't about to argue. She could feel exhaustion lapping at the edges and wanted to go home for a long lie down.

'I'm sorry about ruining your wedding day.'

'Please.' Paul gave her a look that asked if she had lost her marbles. 'I was never going to marry Scarlett.'

Lydia thought about arguing that point. He had seemed pretty locked-in.

'A new head of the Pearls just wandering in? I had to get close to find out exactly what kind of threat she posed.'

'Scarlett wanted to punish me for destroying the Pearl Court. That's why she targeted my house with her ghost manipulator. When she got Mary, she must have realised she would make the perfect weapon for Tyler and his co-conspirators. I just don't understand why she wanted them dead.'

'It was a wedding gift,' Paul said. 'Killing the man who had hurt Aysha. She had done a lot of research on me before we met. Don't know how she found out about Aysha, but she did. First time we met, she let me know she'd been involved, hinted that she knew the #New-Ripper and had steered him toward the Cherish case and Tyler.'

Feathers. That had been a dangerous gambit. 'And that didn't make you suspicious?'

'I was already suspicious. A new Pearl just strolling in to lead a Family? New agenda, new ambitions, new faces. I didn't trust any of it.'

'You did an excellent impression otherwise.'

He smiled. 'Didn't anybody ever warn you? Foxes are tricky.'

'I thought you were sex-blinded. Good to know you kept your faculties.'

Paul flashed white teeth. For a second, they looked sharp. 'You've really got to get that jealousy under control, Little Bird. You know how much I like it.'

She took a deep breath to calm herself. The Fox would see any sign of emotion as proof that she was pining for him.

'She really was a true believer,' Paul said. 'That wasn't a lie.'

'All that stuff about our superiority. The Families.'

'And I'm not sure I disagree with her,' Paul said, with a disarming smile.

'Be serious. She was talking about anarchy.'

'Doesn't sound much worse than the current situation. Not that I can get all that bothered either way.' He made a dismissive sound. 'Politics. Gets in the way of a good time.'

'Total obedience and observance from the population,' Lydia pressed. 'One giant cult. With the Pearls as supreme leaders.'

'Sounds like a lot of work,' Paul said lazily. He stretched his arms above his head as he yawned, and Lydia tried to ignore the flex of his biceps, the sliver of skin that appeared between his T-shirt and jeans.

'Killing those who disobey,' Lydia continued, determined to stay on subject. 'Killing others just to show strength.'

'Doesn't sound doable with all of London.'

'It's not,' Lydia said. 'But that wasn't stopping her trying. She would have killed hundreds in the cathedral, injured many more.'

Paul stopped teasing. 'I know. You did good.'

Lydia didn't speak for a moment. The sudden sincerity in his words was like a gentle blow. 'Thank you.' She cleared her throat. 'I've got a bit of news.'

'What's that, Little Bird?'

'Aiden is the new head of the Crow Family.'

A pause in which Paul's gaze raked over her, inquiring. 'Is that a fact?'

'I'm moving out of Charlie's house.' Lydia didn't know she had decided until that moment.

'Can't say I'm sorry,' Paul said easily. 'What are you going to do?'

'Crow Investigations.' The words felt right. 'I'm staying in Camberwell and I'm still a member of my Family, I'm not turning my back on them entirely. But I never wanted to be their leader.'

'I can relate.' Paul flashed white teeth. 'I guess you're going to need a new door. Leave it with me.'

CHAPTER THIRTY-FOUR

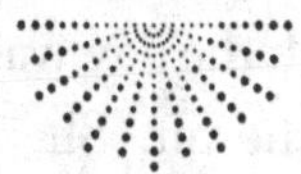

On the way home, Lydia felt her nerves increase. What if she had made another mistake? She had thought she had stopped it all when Mary moved on and she'd been wrong. What if Jason was still, somehow, being controlled? What if Scarlett hadn't been working alone?

When she crossed through the downstairs of the house to find Jason in the kitchen, her heart threatened to leap from her chest. He had his hands on hips as he surveyed the open cupboards. 'Sorry I didn't hang around,' he said. 'I had to leave.'

Lydia understood. He had been pulled to a place against his will. Of course he would have wanted to get as far away as possible the moment that control was released. 'We're not meant to spend too long north of the river,' Lydia said lightly. 'Camberwell rules.'

He smiled, grateful that she was keeping it light.

Then she ruined it by putting her arms around his cold form and giving him a quick squeeze.

Jason awkwardly hugged her back.

Lydia stepped away when the awkward got too intense.

The heatwave had broken after the spectacular thunderstorms and the air no longer felt heavy. The pressure that Lydia had been feeling behind her eyes had gone and, although the day was still warm, there was a little freshness to the air. She stepped out into the garden and down to the hornbeam tree.

There were two crows on the high branches, but they were soon joined by many more. Lydia greeted them politely and tried not to think about her dreams. The monstrous rotting crow with its deadly talons and beak, its unforgiving eyes. She put her hand on the tree and peered up through the branches. She couldn't see the moon at this time of day, but she knew it was always there.

Back in the kitchen, she spoke to Jason. 'I want to show you something.' The burst of inspiration had come the moment she had looked at the blazing sun burning through the glass doors and searing Charlie's pristine kitchen, making the metallic surface of the fridge into a blinding mirror. 'Fancy a trip?'

'Problem?' Jason immediately looked panicked and Lydia's heart squeezed.

She shook her head. 'Just a trip. A celebratory one.'

He brightened. 'Okay.'

The walk to the flat took twelve minutes. Lydia felt her heart lifting with every step away from Charlie's house. By the time she got to the blue door next to the falafel place, she felt like she was flying.

Jason hadn't said much on the way, but he gave her a questioning look as she unlocked the door. 'Don't judge it by the stairs. They're a bit grot.'

Lydia had the keys from the estate agent. She had been only too happy to give the head of the Crow Family free rein to inspect the property in her own time. There were perks to the job, but not enough to make her reconsider.

She held her breath as she opened the door and stepped inside. There was a chance that she had misremembered. That the tingling feeling of possibility she had felt had been a momentary madness.

Jason had moved ahead through the small entrance hall and into the main part of the flat. Lydia followed and immediately let out her breath. Her chest expanded and she felt her wings stretching in happiness. The view of buildings and rooftops through the large windows felt right. She was up high, surveying the world from a place of safety. The white walls were a little scuffed in places, but the room was well proportioned. It was spacious without feeling odd. Lydia could imagine her books on the built-in shelves framing the bay window, a desk in front.

The kitchen was a decent size, too. Not a dark little kitchenette, but with a window over the sink, and with everything Jason could desire.

She walked around, feeling her tension return. Jason hadn't said a word and she was trying not to watch him examining the place. If he didn't like it, she wasn't going to push. Jason had so little he had control over, both in his life and his death, she wasn't going to add to that list.

Lydia finished her tour of the flat, mentally imagining what she would do with each room, and trying very hard not to get her hopes up too high. She found Jason in the largest bedroom, which still had the collage on the wall. The police clearly hadn't got around to investigating Henriksen's death, just as Fleet had predicted.

'Not very subtle,' he said, indicating the wall. 'Doesn't it bother you?'

She considered the question, not wanting to be flippant. 'No. It was a ploy. Not real. And we won the game in the end.'

He smiled briefly, then turned serious. 'Why are we here?'

She took a deep breath. 'Okay. So. I really don't like living at Charlie's house. I hadn't really thought seriously about leaving, but then when I was here for the case. I don't know, I just got a feeling. It felt homely. I could imagine us here.'

'Us?' Jason brightened.

'Of course,' she nudged him with her hip and felt the cold spread over her skin. 'If you want to carry on living with me, of course.' It was polite to ask, but Lydia didn't actually know what would happen if they weren't together. She had been to Guillaume Chartes and had an object made with her Crow power in the hope that would act like a battery, keeping Jason powered up if something happened to her, but she didn't know how well it would work, or for how long.

'You would really move out of that house? It's so swanky.'

'I won't move if you want to stay there. This would be a joint decision. I won't force you into anything.' That had to be very clear. Jason had been through enough. 'I know Charlie's kitchen is really swish.'

'What about—' Jason stopped abruptly.

'What?'

He looked down, his mouth in an unhappy line. 'You're the head of the Crows. Don't you have to be in Charlie's house?'

'I forgot my big news,' Lydia said, trying to keep her tone casual even as her insides had started fizzing. 'As of yesterday, Aiden's the head of the Family. I've abdicated.'

He went still, looking at her with a mixture of confusion and hope. 'You can do that?'

'Last act as head of the Family. They're all pretty happy about it, actually. If I wasn't so relieved, I'd be offended—' Lydia had to stop speaking because suddenly she was surrounded by ice and her lungs had seized. Jason had wrapped his arms around her and was hugging tightly. She hugged him back and then stepped back.

He released her instantly. 'Sorry. Sorry.'

'It's all good,' Lydia managed, although she felt a bit odd from the sudden temperature drop. Another couple of seconds and her teeth would've been chattering.

'But... can Aiden be the leader? He doesn't have the Crow coin. He can't do that hypnotism thing you do.'

'He's still a Crow. And he's very good with people. They like him, and that seems to be almost as good.'

'But—'

'He reads people well, too. He's a quick thinker, but he hides his cleverness so people trust him. More than that, they want him to like them. With me, and Charlie,' Lydia forced herself to add, 'they're scared. Or they think we can do something for them. With Aiden, they actually want to make him proud. They want his approval. It works almost as well as having a Crow coin.'

Jason watched her for a few seconds. Then he said, 'You're really done, aren't you?'

Lydia tried to smile, tried to show that she was okay. 'I never wanted to be a leader. I didn't want to be the head of my Family, but I thought I could make a difference. And maybe I could, but every time I find something out about my Family and where we came from, it's something even worse than the terrible thing before.' She shook her head. 'I'm not convinced we should stay powerful.'

Jason didn't speak, sensing that she needed to get this off her chest.

'I don't even know that we deserve to survive.' She blew out a breath. 'And that makes me super-unsuitable to lead the Family.'

'I'm not sure that's true,' Jason said, 'but you should have a choice over what you do with your life. You have one and that's a precious thing.'

The conversation was dangerously sincere and Lydia wanted to puncture it with a sarcastic comment. She resisted the urge, though. She was definitely getting soft in her old age.

'What are you going to do?' Jason was gazing at her with something approaching wonder.

'Run Crow Investigations,' Lydia said. 'Be my own boss. Maybe take some time off. I don't know.' It occurred to her that she *really* didn't know. 'What do people do with time off?'

Jason shook his head, looking around the flat with shining eyes. 'Beats me. We could live here?'

'If you like it. There are loads of other options, but I just felt something...' She couldn't put it into words. Logically, she knew it made no sense. The hope that had been building started to falter. Was she being stupid?

'I like here,' Jason said. 'It reminds me of—'

'The Fork,' Lydia finished, relief flooding her system. 'If you'd asked me, I wouldn't have been sure that would be good, but I like it.'

'It feels like home.'

'Is that a yes?'

Jason smiled. 'It's fuckin-A, yes!'

Sinclair needed to be debriefed and Lydia knew she couldn't put it off for long. She was annoyed by MI13's refusal to help, but she also understood it. Maturity was irritating.

Lydia decided to embrace the inevitable and called the number from the fake-flyer. Sinclair herself answered, and she greeted Lydia by name. 'You left us with quite the cleanup.'

'You're welcome,' Lydia said. 'Were you close to Marty?'

'Not especially,' Sinclair said. 'His family has been informed.'

'With lies, I assume.'

'His cover is being maintained, naturally. And he will receive full honours from the service too. This stays within MI13.'

'How did this happen?' Lydia had many reservations about Sinclair, but her competence wasn't one of them. Still, she wasn't going to tell Sinclair that. 'Embarrassing for you, though. You were so concerned about a spy in the Families and you had a rando fanatic on your very own team.'

'It's beneath you to gloat,' Sinclair said. 'Marty wasn't born into it. The service screening would've caught it and he would never have been recruited.'

'So this was a recent conversion?'

'Scarlett was obviously very persuasive. Getting him on board in less than a year is impressive work really.'

'You sound like you want to recruit her.'

'Sadly, no. Too unstable. You can't recruit the zealots. They only pretend to change their ideology.'

'Speaking from experience?'

'It's a lot harder to change people's world view than you can possibly imagine. And a view that formed during childhood, I hate to say impossible, but...' Sinclair trailed off.

'Plus, with Scarlett you would never be sure she wasn't using her mojo on you.' This, in Lydia's opinion, was the vital point.

'I'm impervious,' Sinclair said robustly. 'Part of the training.'

Lydia thought about arguing, but then she remembered that she didn't care. Let Sinclair sink in blissful ignorance. 'We've had a word with Scarlett, she's moving on from London. Will you keep tabs on her?'

'As long as resources allow. Which leads me onto another matter. We should meet,' Sinclair said. 'I can come to you.'

'No need,' Lydia said. 'It's done. You owe me a favour. End of story.'

A long-suffering sigh. 'Very well, I shall speak to Fleet.'

'You shall not,' Lydia replied. 'He's not here right now, anyway, so you can't.'

'That's not an issue,' Sinclair said before hanging up.

Cryptic. Which was pretty much Sinclair's middle name, so nothing to get overly hot and bothered about.

Feeling that she owed her, and definitely for no other reason, Lydia called Megan.

'Lydia!' Megan practically sang. 'I am so happy to hear from you.'

Even her voice was blonde and bouncy. Lydia hit the reduce volume button a couple of times, then gave her the update on Scarlett. She felt a little bit proud of the truce and that the Families had come together to make a decision.

'I've been doing the rounds,' Megan said in return. 'Things look back to normal ghost-wise.'

'That's good,' Lydia said. She still had to work out what to do with the cameo, but she would do her best to ensure it wouldn't be a danger to the spirit population again.

'You think she'll go quietly?'

'Scarlett? She's a survivor,' Lydia answered. 'Maybe

this will be a new start for her.' It was a nice thought, but Lydia knew that Scarlett had been programmed from birth. She would need help, and need to be ready to accept that help.

'She'd better stay in new builds,' Megan observed. 'Not many can move around like your friend, but he's not the only one. And ghosts talk.'

'They'll watch her?'

Megan's voice turned uncharacteristically serious. 'If she's lucky, that's all they'll do.'

CHAPTER THIRTY-FIVE

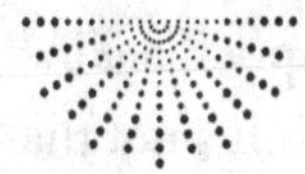

Now that Lydia had asked Jason, she needed to speak to Ember. She had the feeling that Fleet would be happy to live wherever she wanted, as long as they stayed on the right side of the river, of course, but Ember was a different matter.

She found him by the big pond in Ruskin Park. His shoulders were hunched inside the voluminous black hoodie. It made him look like prey, but she knew she couldn't tell him that. Or should she? Was it her duty now that it was on her to keep him safe? Her mind swam with the contradictory thoughts. She wasn't cut out for parenthood, of that she was certain.

'You okay?'

Ember glanced at her and lifted his shoulders in a shrug.

She told him about the new flat and her plan to move. 'I told you I hate the house. This place is much smaller, but there's a bedroom for you.'

Ember didn't answer, his gaze fixed on the pond.

'You unhappy about living with me? I told you I can find another home. You tell me what you want and I'll see what I can do.' Lydia knew she was babbling. She thought about Emma's advice. About how she had to be firm and in control and provide certainty. 'I can see you're not happy. Are you worried about the secret service? That won't happen again.'

He shook his head. 'It's not that.'

'I stopped the ghost explosion. You helped us work out the target. I haven't thanked you properly.'

Another shrug.

They stood in silence for a bit longer. Lydia was good at waiting. She had broken all kinds of people with a good long silence and maybe a flip of her coin. But this kid was the grandmaster. She tried to put herself in his shoes. He was a kid. What would be on his mind? 'You worried about school?'

Another shrug. Then, in a matter-of-fact tone, 'I hate it.'

'You'll be leaving soon. High school will be different.'

Ember gave her a long flat look. 'I know that. It'll be worse.'

'You don't know—'

'I do.'

A beat. 'You asked the cards?'

'Yeah.' Ember stared at the pond. 'I'm not going to go.'

'That something you saw in the cards or something you've decided?'

'Both.'

'Okay then.' There was a duck swimming next to a floating cigarette butt. Lydia hoped it didn't try to eat it.

They stood in companionable silence for a while, watching as another duck joined the first one and, across the other side of the pond, a man with patterns shaved into his hair surreptitiously dropped something into the water.

'Wonder what he's getting rid of,' Lydia mused. 'Could be drugs.'

'Why—' Ember started and then stopped. He answered his own question. 'If he's being followed by the cops.'

'Gotta love London,' Lydia said. And she really did.

When Fleet got in from work, Lydia was going to tell him about Sinclair mentioning his name, but he got in first.

'I just met with Sinclair.' He held up a hand. 'It was good. I'm happy about it and I want you to hear me out.'

Lydia put down her unopened bottle of beer. 'I don't understand.'

'You know she offered me a job?'

'Yeah,' Lydia was still trying to play catch-up. 'She wants you to run her department. Or that's what she said, I'm guessing it's a stitch-up of some kind. You can't trust anything that woman says.'

'It's a real offer,' Fleet said. 'I had an interview today.'

'An interview?'

He nodded. 'A real job interview for a real job. And I signed the Official Secrets Act.'

'So you can tell me about your interview but you'd have to kill me?' Lydia knew her tone was bordering on the petulant. 'You're seriously considering becoming a spook?'

He looked uncomfortable, but couldn't hide the sunshine glow that was flowing from his whole body. Happiness. Excitement.

'I won't take it if you don't want me to. You're more important to me.'

Lydia closed her eyes against his sunshine, needing a moment to think. The doors to the garden were open and she could hear the crows in the garden cawing. They didn't sound happy, but Fleet deserved freedom. If he wanted to work for MI13, he should be able to make that choice. She hated the way her Family restricted her, hated being forced into the leadership role, Charlie's house. She couldn't do the same to Fleet. She opened her eyes. His sunshine had dimmed and he was watching her from across the room. Wary.

'You really want to leave the police?'

'I really do,' Fleet said. 'Never thought I'd say that, but I'm done.'

Lydia nodded her understanding.

'When I joined, I was going to help people, make a real difference. And I was going to become a detective, work on big cases.'

'You did. You do.'

He nodded. 'But now I'm being shuffled from one meaningless project to another. I wouldn't even mind if I was just being given copper stuff, but I'm too expensive for traffic duty. I'll be sitting in meetings and on committees until I lose it over something and they can fire me, or I lose the will and resign.'

Lydia pushed down the guilt she felt. Fleet's career had been on the up before he met her. 'I'm not the head of the Family anymore, won't that make a difference?'

'It might,' Fleet said, 'but I actually don't care anymore. I always knew there were other things in this world, the Families and my own family's old ways. Stories from Auntie and just... a knowledge that myths weren't always dead things. But now I know the threats in London. And I know the Met can't deal with them, but I can. We can.'

'You *want* to work for MI13.' The truth hit Lydia like a physical blow.

'I'll be running MI13,' Fleet said. 'It's a tiny department, so that'll mean I'll pretty much have free rein.'

'You'll report to Sinclair?'

'She's my contact, yes. There are lots of senior management for MI5 and MI6 but MI13 is so small, there isn't a lot of oversight.'

That sounded good in theory, but it could backfire. 'What about support? What about when things go wrong?'

'I don't see how it will be any worse than my current position. At least I'm unlikely to be publicly crucified if an operation goes wrong.'

'You really are done with the police, aren't you?'

He nodded. 'They are blind to certain aspects and I want to fill that gap. Make sure that people who get hurt by a vengeful spirit get the same care and consideration as someone who gets knifed by an alive citizen. You can understand that, can't you?'

'Of course.' Lydia blew out a breath. 'I just thought that things were going to be easier for you now that I've abdicated—'

'That's not why, is it?' Fleet looked stricken. 'You didn't step down because of my job?'

'No,' she reassured him. 'It was a positive side benefit, but I wanted to leave. I don't want to be head of my Family, to deal with the businesses and all the politics. I want to run my agency and be my own boss. No one else's. Solve cases, help people.'

'And I can help you,' Fleet said eagerly. 'You have a very close contact within MI13. I have only been given an overview so far, but the data access is very exciting.'

'I'm not becoming a secret service asset,' Lydia warned him.

'I wouldn't expect that,' Fleet said. 'One-way street only.'

'I'm not saying we can't collaborate if it feels right,' Lydia amended. She was coming round to the idea.

'I'm going to work for both of you,' Jason said, popping up from behind the kitchen counter.

'Hell Hawk!' Lydia put a hand to her chest.

'What's wrong?'

'Jason just startled me, that's all.' To Jason she said, 'You nearly gave me a heart attack.'

'I was looking down here,' he indicated the cupboards, 'and you started getting into a serious conversation. I didn't want to eavesdrop but, in my defence, it was interesting. You're going to be dating a spook.'

'Apparently so,' Lydia said.

'What is it with you and the ghostly brethren?' Jason said, his shoulders shaking with laughter.

'You're not going to get tired of that joke anytime soon, are you?'

'I'm missing something,' Fleet said.

Lydia put her arms around him and reached up on her toes for a kiss.

'Never mind,' Fleet said, when they broke apart. His eyes were a little glazed and Lydia grabbed his hand to tow him upstairs. There were some things that required two fully alive human beings to do really well.

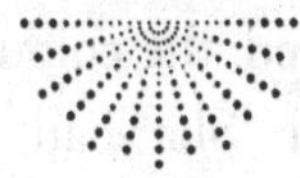

Moving day was joyous. Lydia had packed the kitchenware into cardboard boxes with Jason's help, but her own stuff fitted into a suitcase. She hadn't had that much in the way of possessions before The Fork was destroyed, but what she had owned, including her beloved book collection, had perished.

Fleet kept clothes and toiletries at Charlie's, but he still had his flat and hadn't ever properly moved in. This became apparent when his possessions also fitted into a suitcase. As Lydia had expected, Fleet was more than happy to leave Charlie Crow's house in his rear-view mirror.

The locks had been changed at the flat and security cameras installed. Lydia knew that, while in Camberwell, she was still going to be a known person. Besides, it meant she would be able to have a look at clients before they arrived.

Eating takeaway on the floor of the living room, as the sofa wasn't being delivered until the following day, Lydia felt a deep sense of contentment. The flat was a far cry from the grand house on Denmark Hill, but it was hers.

That evening, Lydia met Paul on Tower Bridge. He was a fast healer and his physical bruises had almost completely faded, the colours turning yellow and green as they healed. She had no idea whether he carried anything psychological from his almost-marriage to Scarlett. She knew he was never going to be honest about how close he had actually been to tying the knot.

The Fox hadn't volunteered any information about how he had got the injury and Lydia had gone past the point where she expected it, so it was a surprise when he gestured to his face and said, 'My brother.'

Paul had several siblings and Lydia wasn't a fan of any of them. She knew from books and TV that siblings often fought. She just didn't know if it was normal for it to be so physical or whether that was a Fox Family thing. 'Aren't you the boss? Seems a bit disrespectful.'

'He's been made aware of that fact,' Paul said.

Sharp teeth. Claws raking over skin. Hot blood splashing red. She shivered.

'He was expressing his dissatisfaction with my connections.'

Lydia frowned. 'I thought your family were okay with you marrying Scarlett? Did they suspect her early doors?'

'Okay is stretching it. And I think they were hoping my engagement would put a stop to this,' he gestured between them. 'When it didn't, they were less keen on the deal.'

She absorbed this for a moment. 'And he expressed his dissatisfaction by punching you?'

'Not initially,' Paul said, not meeting her eyes.

'Right, but I don't see—'

'He said things he shouldn't. I punched him. He punched me back. You get the idea, I'm sure.'

It hit Lydia what Paul wasn't saying explicitly: his brother had said something unacceptable about *her*. And Paul had responded with violence. She shouldn't be pleased about that. It probably said all kinds of bad things about her personality and lack of morality. And, as ever, the brush of fur across her skin. The soft earth of a den. 'I'm not here for this,' she said, trying to clear her head.

Paul's expression went hard. 'I know.'

She dug the cameo out of her pocket and held it out. 'I've told my family that I threw it in the Thames.'

Paul stared at her for several seconds before replying. 'You're giving it to me? Why?'

'Because I trust you to keep it safe.'

'Little Bird,' he said, and she felt his voice in every part of her body.

'You should know, it needs Pearl blood to activate it. Then it will pull ghosts in and force them to move on. It kills them, essentially. It's what Scarlett tried to use at St Paul's.'

'I won't tell anyone,' Paul said, taking the cameo. Electricity shot through her nerves as his fingers brushed hers. 'Not even my family. Don't want any temptation there.'

'Probably for the best,' Lydia said.

'Does this—?' Paul started to ask and there was a rawness to the question that meant Lydia couldn't let him finish it.

'I still love Fleet,' she blurted.

He went still. Then, 'I know.'

'I'm sorry,' Lydia whispered.

Paul didn't move. He was still looking at her with that unguarded expression. It tore at Lydia, pulling her apart from the inside. She had to be honest with him. She owed him that. 'I care about you. There is something between us, but I'm all in with Fleet. I can't offer you anything.'

'I know that.' Paul smiled. His Fox smile. The one that promised a good time. But it had a warmth to it, too. He shrugged. Packing his unguarded expression away, and glancing around as if readying for his exit.

Lydia thought he would leave without another word. She had just started to wonder if she had made a huge mistake, that hurting him when he was vulnerable would make him attack. Like an animal with its leg caught in a trap.

Then he spoke: 'You're not mine, I know that. But I'm yours.' Another crooked smile. 'And that's just the way it is.'

She watched him lope away, his stride easy and unhurried, until he merged with the other pedestrians and she could no longer see him.

. . .

Lydia had spoken to Ember about his heritage, his gift of future-telling, and given him a choice. Just like her own parents had done, back when Henry Crow abdicated from the Family business and moved to Beckenham. 'By raising me away from Camberwell, they made sure I could choose my own path. They bought me time, too, so that I didn't have to decide until I was an adult. I want you to have the same. And I know you're not happy right now.'

'I'd have to leave London?' Ember had asked and Lydia had heard the hope in his voice.

'Only if you want to, I'm offering you the option.'

The next day, he gave her his decision. It took over seven hours to drive to the causeway near the Scottish border. Lydia let Ember control the music choices and had stocked up on plenty of snacks. They stopped at the services for lunch and she bought him a round, squishy owl because she caught him looking at it in the shop. He had been forced to grow up far too quickly, but he was still just ten years old.

The island was just as Lydia remembered. Small, wild-looking, isolated. She was a city-girl through and through and the rolling sea and wide-open sky made her feel on edge. Still, it was quiet, if you liked that kind of thing. And there was help available for Ember.

Lydia had exchanged a favour with Bee in order to bargain help for Fleet. She was one of The Three Sisters and had the gift of foresight. She had helped Fleet when he was being driven out of his mind by uncontrolled visions. But Lydia wasn't here to beg a favour.

Strand House was the bed-and-breakfast place on

the edge of the tiny village. It was a pretty building, Lydia thought. Not her cup of tea, but very homely-looking. Esme Gray opened the door and a black cat stalked out from behind her, tail high in the air. She was a pretty woman with softly curling brown hair and kind eyes.

Ember dropped to a crouch immediately and held out his hand. The cat sniffed it experimentally before pushing its blunt head into Ember's palm to be stroked.

Lydia introduced herself. 'And this is Ember.'

Esme was staring down at the boy.

Lydia couldn't tell what she was thinking but, after a moment, Esme invited them in. 'Sorry,' she said. 'I just had the strongest sense of déjà vu.'

Ember looked up. 'I get that.'

Lydia was surprised the kid was speaking to her so quickly. It seemed like a good sign.

Inside, they were ushered through a compact hall-way, through a dining room that was clearly set up for guests, and into a warm kitchen.

The table was laden with home-baked biscuits and cake. There was an honest-to-hawk teapot with a milk jug and an assortment of mugs.

'I didn't know what you liked,' Esme said, going a little pink in her cheeks. 'I might have gone overboard.'

'It's great,' Ember said, his eyes huge.

'He has a big appetite,' Lydia said fondly. 'This ought to keep him going until dinner, as long as it's soon.'

Ember shot her a mock-annoyed look. 'I'm not that bad.'

'It's not bad,' Lydia said. 'It's bloody impressive.'

'Works out well,' Esme said. 'Luke says food is my love language.' Then she blushed even more.

Ember blinked.

After an awkward pause, Esme pushed a plate at Ember. 'Help yourself.'

He didn't need a second invitation. With a quickly loaded plate, Ember began the serious work of eating. Esme poured him a glass of milk and then sat at the table. The black cat stalked through the room like it owned the place and then jumped up onto the windowsill to survey them from above.

Lydia made small talk. Not her strong suit. And ate a really good coconut-tasting thing which, luckily enough, made talking a moot point.

The cat meowed loudly just before the outside door opened and a tall man walked in, stooping to take off his boots in an automatic movement.

'This is Luke,' Esme said, her gaze on Ember who had stopped chewing in order to size up the newcomer. 'My husband.'

'Hey,' Luke raised a hand in greeting. 'You must be Ember?'

He folded his tall frame into the spare seat at the table and reached for a plate. 'Have you tried the lemon cake, yet. It's so good.'

Esme smiled at him. 'You want tea?'

'Please.' To Ember he said, 'I brought you some books. Don't know if you're a reader, but...' He opened his rucksack and lifted out a small stack which included a graphic novel and a book with a very silly title and a cartoon cover.

Ember swallowed his mouthful before nodding. He wiped his hands on his hoodie before reaching for the books.

'Thank you,' Lydia said.

'Yeah, thanks.' Ember was already flipping to the first page of the graphic novel.

Luke had sandy-brown hair, wide shoulders and excellent bone structure. Like Esme, he also seemed like a proper grown-up, and she felt her nerves ease. Ember would be safe here, she knew that, but meeting Esme and Luke was starting to feel like he might be happy too.

'We've got his room ready,' Esme said. 'Do you want to check it out?'

It took Lydia a second to realise that Esme was asking her. 'No, it's fine. I trust you.'

'We can get most things from the mainland,' Luke said, 'so if there's stuff he needs.'

They chatted for a while about home-schooling and books, the island's weather and Bee, who would be spending time with Ember to help him with his gift.

When it was time for Lydia to leave and make the long drive back to London, Esme and Luke said goodbye and then found things to do elsewhere. Lydia was both grateful and frustrated. She didn't know what to say to the kid, how to be certain she was doing the right thing.

He put down the book, at least. Looked at her.

'I'll visit,' Lydia said. 'When I can. And you have my number.'

Ember had already made use of this with a string of cat GIFs. Crows weren't, generally speaking, cat people, but she appreciated the attempt to bond.

He stood up and Lydia wondered whether he was having second thoughts. She went to the back door of the kitchen, rather than through the house to the front, wanting to be out in the open as soon as possible. Emotion was clogging her throat and her chest felt suddenly tight. What if she was doing the wrong thing? What if he was unhappy here?

Late afternoon had become early evening and the air had cooled. There was a stiff breeze, too, which was a welcome change from the still stickiness of London. But the place smelled all wrong. Green stuff and sea salt and no hint of exhaust fumes. Wrong.

She turned back to the kid. 'You call me if you want to come back.'

He shook his head. 'I won't.'

'Okay.' Lydia tried to feel reassured. Was he just putting on a brave face? Did he feel secretly rejected? 'You asked the cards?'

'I don't need to.' Ember smiled at her, his sunshine glow pouring from his face and bathing them both in golden light. 'I'm home.'

Lydia wasn't a hugger and had no idea if Ember would welcome one either, but it felt strange to just wave and she couldn't shake the kid's hand. That felt ridiculous. She held up a hand, wondering whether a 'high five' was too lame, when he barrelled into her, thin arms wrapping around her waist and squeezing tightly. She hugged Ember back, feeling his small frame and thinking, fiercely, that if anybody hurt him, she would kill them. Maybe she was cut out for motherhood after all.

Ember stepped back, his smile still intact.

'Bye, then,' Lydia said, and moved down the garden path before she lost her mind and found herself promising to stay on the island to watch out for him.

Esme and Luke were good people and they would look after the kid. He would have guidance from Bee and the safety of the hidden island. Not to mention year-round beach access.

Before Lydia rounded the house and would be unable to see the door, she turned back for one last look.

Ember was in the doorway to the kitchen, watching her leave. His sunshine glow surrounded him in warm light, and the cat wound around his legs, purring loudly. He raised a hand in farewell and Lydia did the same.

BACK IN CAMBERWELL, LYDIA FOUND A JOINER fitting a handsome timber and glass front door, the twin of the one that Paul had fitted to her flat above The Fork. The gold lettering 'Crow Investigations' glowed in the afternoon sunlight and she found she couldn't even be irritated at his presumption.

As the joiner was finishing up, Aiden arrived. He gave the door a searching look, but didn't comment on it. 'Boss?'

'Not anymore,' Lydia said.

Aiden hovered in her new living room, looking uncertain.

'Come in,' Lydia said. 'You're making me nervous.' If Aiden had been having second thoughts about his new position, she didn't know what she was going to do. Now that she had made the decision, she knew she didn't want to go back.

Aiden slouched into the room and looked around. The room was a work-in-progress, but Lydia had her desk set up in the bay window and was in the process of cleaning the bookshelves before unpacking onto them. Her collection wasn't going to fill half of the available space and she relished the sense of possibility. The kitchen had been cleaned, and Jason was happily pottering about in there.

'This was downstairs,' Aiden held out a letter-sized envelope. 'It wasn't mailed.'

The outside of the white envelope had her name and address, but no postmark. She had set up her security cameras and would be able to see who had delivered it, if necessary, but she refused to panic. New start. No stress.

Aiden hadn't picked up on her new 'relax' mantra. He almost squeaked when she began ripping it open. 'It could be poisoned.'

As soon as her fingers touched the paper inside, she got a vague hit of 'Silver'. Sure enough, the note was from Maria. It was typed on thick white stock, with a fancy letterhead, and Maria's jagged signature at the bottom. She read it out for Aiden's benefit. 'Dear Ms Crow, The Silver Family wishes to express its gratitude for your recent actions. We appreciate the information that was provided and have included a gift which we believe to be commensurate. We look forward to our continued accord.'

He frowned. 'I can't tell if that's good or not. Why doesn't she speak normal?'

'Lawyer,' Lydia said. 'She's thanking me for warning her about the ghost bomb.'

There was a cheque for a large sum. Money was the Silver's love language, so this was a big concession. And much appreciated capital to help her cash flow while she built up her Crow Investigations client list.

'I don't know if I can do it,' Aiden finally said the words Lydia was dreading. 'I'm not ready.'

'Do you want to do it?'

'Yes,' he said immediately. 'I'm just worried—'

'You'll be great,' Lydia said. 'Far more organised than me, anyway. And not as psychotic as Charlie.'

He grinned. 'High praise. I'm blushing.'

'I trust you,' Lydia said, 'and you may have noticed I'm not big on that.'

Aiden hesitated, hope gleaming in his eyes. 'Can I come to you for help?'

'Of course,' Lydia said. 'I'm not far away. And not planning to leave this place anytime soon.'

'About that,' Aiden scrolled on his phone for a moment. 'Check your email.'

Lydia did so and discovered a forwarded set of documents, confirming that she was the new owner of the flat they were standing in. 'I was set up to rent it,' she said, which wasn't exactly the heartfelt gratitude that was undoubtedly more appropriate. But she was thrown.

Aiden shrugged. 'Severance package.'

'That's a generous package,' she managed.

'It'll make me feel better when I ask you loads of questions.'

Lydia accepted this but, secretly, she thought Aiden

was pandering to her ego. He wouldn't need to ask her stuff, Aiden fitted the job in a way she never had. Something else occurred to her. 'So you already knew you were taking the job when you came here?' He had to have had time to purchase the flat and get the documents.

Aiden smiled winningly. 'I just wanted to double-check you were good with it. Needed to know if you were going to be a problem.'

'You see?' Lydia said approvingly. 'You're perfect for the job.'

ONCE AIDEN HAD LEFT, LYDIA LEANED BACK IN HER chair and put her feet up onto her desk. She had a mug of coffee and the afternoon sunlight slanted through the bay windows, illuminating the large room. If she moved, she could see down the street and across to the top floors of the buildings opposite. She had never realised how important it was to her to be up high, but it felt right.

Jason was still in the kitchen. She could hear him humming and there was an enticing smell of something sweet baking. Emma had sent a message with lots of heart emojis in reply to her update about Ember. They were going to meet for dinner in a Beckenham pub that evening, and Lydia found that she was looking forward to it. Fleet was working late and was going to stay at his flat tonight, but they had weekend plans. Mainly involving the bedroom.

It was mid-afternoon, though. A couple of hours of the workday left and, as her own boss, she could choose exactly what she did with them. A crow landed on the sill of the bay window and she opened it to greet him with a couple of unsalted peanuts. There was a light summer breeze and it brought the scent of traffic fumes and spices from the falafel place. Lydia clicked into her Crow Investigations email and began scanning the inbox for cases. As she did, she realised that she was smiling.

THE END

THANK YOU FOR READING!

I hope you enjoyed reading about Lydia Crow and her family as much as I enjoyed writing about them!

I am busy working on my next book. If you would like to be notified when it's published (as well as take part in giveaways and receive exclusive free content), you can sign up for my FREE readers' club online:

geni.us/Thanks

If you could spare the time, I would really appreciate a review on the retailer of your choice.

Reviews make a huge difference to the visibility of the book, which make it more likely that I will reach more readers and be able to keep on writing. Thank you!

ACKNOWLEDGMENTS

Thank you for reading! Without your enthusiasm and support, I would not have been able to write ten books (ten!) in the Crow Investigations series and I am deeply grateful. I don't plan my books at all, which makes for an exciting, and often alarming, writing experience, but it also means that I can't answer questions about the future of the series or characters *absolutely* definitively. All I can say is that I *feel* like this book is the final chapter in Lydia Crow's story, but that I reserve the right to be wrong about that...

The Crow Moon was a tricky project. It's been a difficult year, personally, not least of which included a second frozen shoulder (my left side this time), but I am grateful to have creative work I care about deeply, and a job that involves staying in my PJs and typing. I am a fortunate woman and I never lose sight of that. Even when I have to pull apart the book for yet another round of rewrites at the eleventh hour...

To my writing coven, Hannah Ellis and Clodagh Murphy, and all my author friends – thank you for everything. This career would be so much harder, and less enjoyable, without you.

I have leaned on my friends and family a lot this year and want to say a special 'thank you' to Catherine Shellard, Rachel Bodey, and Emma Ward. As well as my lovely mother-in-law, Christine, and my dad, Michael Hughes.

Thank you to Stuart Bache for another brilliant cover, and to the team at Siskin Press. Many thanks to my wonderful ARC readers. In particular: David Wood, Lizzie Noblett, Kathryn Jamieson-Sinclair, Mel Horne, Karan Sebert, Faith Stevens, August Enger, Walt Wallmark, Caroline Nicklin, Catherine Evans, Carmel McMillan, Paula Searle, Eva Merrick, Julie Weaver, Sue Bruce, Liz Ottosson, Jacquie Thornber, Michelle Hunter-Gray, Sara Wolfe and Kristen O'Loughlin.

As always, my deepest love and gratitude to Holly and James, and my husband, Dave. He makes me tea every morning, is endlessly kind and patient, and talks through plot-holes while we walk in the woods. I don't know what I did to get this lucky, but I'm forever grateful.

ABOUT THE AUTHOR

Sarah is a bestselling author of contemporary fantasy. In addition to the Crow Investigations series, she has written the Unholy Island trilogy, which is set in the same universe.

Having always been a reader and a daydreamer, she now puts those skills to good use with a strict daily schedule of faffing, thinking, reading, napping and writing – as well as thanking her lucky stars for her good fortune.

Sarah lives in rural Scotland with her husband and extensive notebook collection.

Sign up to the Sarah Painter Books Readers' Club at the address below. It's absolutely free and you'll get book release news, giveaways and exclusive FREE stuff!

geni.us/Thanks

facebook.com/SarahPainterBooks

instagram.com/SarahPainterBooks